Cow on the Ice

ko på isen

THE AWEN CHRONICLES:
BOOK 2

J. A. GIBBENS

FriesenPress

One Printers Way
Altona, MB R0G 0B0
Canada

www.friesenpress.com

First Edition — 2022

ISBN
978-1-03-913267-2 (Hardcover)
978-1-03-913266-5 (Paperback)
978-1-03-913268-9 (eBook)

1. FICTION, THRILLERS, CRIME

Distributed to the trade by The Ingram Book Company

AUTHOR'S NOTE

I invite readers to visit with me at www.gibbensauthor.ca, also on Facebook as J. A. Gibbens (www.facebook.com/gibbensauthor), Linked-In (J. A. Gibbens), and Twitter (@gibbensauthor).

Readers are urged to refer to the Glossary at the end of the book for additional information.

Many thanks to Joyce McCombe for taking her time to read an early manuscript and provide me with feedback. Much appreciated. Thanks as well to Greg Gibbens, I.T. person extraordinaire!

The Awen Chronicles: Book 1 – L'Orté Point (2021)
The Awen Chronicles: Book 2 – Cow on the Ice: ko på isen (2022)
The Awen Chronicles: Book 3 – Epitaph: Full Circle (2023 est.)

DEDICATION

For my husband, Greg, with love.
Thanks for encouraging me to dream.

Come back.
Even as a shadow,
even as a dream.

~Euripides

TABLE OF CONTENTS

CHAPTER 1

"You're with Radio Sverige. Coming to you at 96.7 on the dial, this is 'News and Notes,' and I'm Lars Andersson.

"If you're just tuning in now, then you've missed an interesting discussion concerning the fine arts and the challenges faced by specialized branches of police across the continent in their efforts to eliminate fakes and forgeries from public acquisitions. That discussion will also be available on our podcast later today. And now we're going to bring this segment to a close with the help of Don McLean and his 1971 hit song, 'Vincent'."

"Starry, starry night . . ."

The topic had been interesting; however, Elsa Carlsson wasn't listening for the sake of entertainment but in order to catch her company's new advertisement, which was airing for the first time.

"Nanovo Group is researching Alzheimer's disease, bringing jobs and health to Sweden and across the EU. Don't forget: Nanovo."

The advertisement was brief and to the point, designed to keep Nanovo in the public consciousness. Lars Andersson had the ideal voice for it, giving the message gravitas while keeping it friendly, as was suitable for his morning show. It was a soft sell, unlike the stronger advertising campaigns run by similar companies in many other countries.

Elsa nearly turned off the radio after the advertising segment played but soon was glad she hadn't. She couldn't believe her good fortune when she heard Lars Andersson say:

"Perhaps we should invite someone from Nanovo Group to join us on the show and tell us about all the wonderful things the company is doing here in Sweden and around the world. If you're listening, Nanovo, give the station a call, and we'll set something up. We're here at 96.7 Radio Sverige."

Elsa decided to listen to the second topic on the show today to help her determine whether it would be advisable to have someone from Nanovo guest on "News and Notes" as the radio-show host had suggested. Lars Andersson announced that the next song would also be from 1971 and was by Carole King from the album "Tapestry."

"I feel the earth move . . ."

Apparently, the second topic would be "Earthquakes in Europe."

Elsa thought she should have one of Nanovo's clerical assistants collect the names of songs that might be appropriate to accompany someone from Nanovo, if they agreed to be with Lars on the show. Lars left on his own might select songs that dealt with drugs, but not in a manner that would be helpful in raising Nanovo's profile in a positive sense. The more she thought about it, the more concerned she became. It might become problematic—perhaps there was more of a downside to this idea than an upside.

"This is Radio Sverige at 96.7 on the dial. I'm Lars Andersson, and this is 'News and Notes.' Our second guest today is Dr. Ingrid Thorstenson from the Sverige Institute for Seismic Study, and she's here to talk with us about earthquakes in Europe, something many of us give little—if any—thought to. Welcome to 'News and Notes,' Ingrid. Let's start off with an easy question: When was the last time there was an earthquake in Europe?"

"Well, Lars, the most recent earthquake in Europe occurred last night actually."

"Really? It must have been so gentle that it rocked us to sleep, wouldn't you say?"

"Not really, Lars. Last night's earthquake was centred just off the coast of France, in the Mediterranean. It was a five-point-seven magnitude quake, but given the location and the depth, there has been no report of damage. And as you've indicated, you and most other people wouldn't have detected this quake or the hundreds of others that we experience each year."

"Other than your detection devices telling you that there's a quake, would there be any other visual evidence?" Without pausing for an answer, Lars continued. *"Well listeners, while Dr. Thorstenson gives some thought to my question, let's give a listen to Martha Reeves and the Vandellas, with their 2002 release of 'Earthquake'."*

A few minutes later, the song having come to an end, Lars repeated his question for the benefit of his audience and his guest was able to provide her answer, appropriately simplified for her audience–and Lars.

"Well, although there's been no damage reported, it's still possible that fissures in the surface might have opened—or closed—as a result of seismic activity, but have merely gone unnoticed. The recent activity occurred at the boundary between the Ligurian Basin and the southern subalpine thrust belt, also known as the Nice Arc. There is an eight-kilometre-long major fault for left-lateral strike slip movement called the Blausasc fault—"

"Yes, yes, Ingrid," Lars interrupted, *"but what does that actually mean?"*

You could hear the seismologist take in a deep breath then let it out slowly. *"In general, the fault lines extend from inland of France and toward the Greek island of Crete, so any topographical changes would be detected in that general area. And remember that, if those changes have occurred underwater, they're going to be even less apparent to casual observers . . ."*

And so, the radio show continued, with musical interludes occurring periodically to provide a welcome break. Scientists tend to drone on, assuming their audience is as enamoured of their field of study as they themselves are. That is not always the case, and Elsa thought the audience today might have tuned out completely if not for the music. The basic message was clear: earthquakes do occur across Europe, they are not always apparent to the general public. Fissures, cracks, and faults shifted, opened, and closed but remained unknown to most of us when earthquakes were centred beneath the Mediterranean. Elsa thought she would be pleased if something that basic about Nanovo were retained by listeners as a result of being featured on "News and Notes."

The voice of her car's navigation system interrupted her reverie, directing her to turn, so Elsa did as she was told and took the next right turn, steering her silver-grey Volvo sedan into the same parking spot she'd had for the past fifteen years. It used to give her such pleasure each morning when she arrived at the office, parking in the spot designated for President and CEO, Dr. E. Carlsson. More recently, her life had taken on a comforting monotony, and Elsa no longer felt the pleasure, or the pain.

A thought entered her mind and left her unsettled; she felt uncomfortable discussing such matters even with the closest members of her staff but knew that she must. Although she did not regularly listen to Lars Andersson's "News and Notes," she had done so sufficiently to state confidently that Lars Andersson doesn't do what he had just done: extend invitations to people or companies to become guests on his show while live, on-air. *Might Lars Andersson have heard something? Might he already know enough to create a problem?*

As had become their custom, Astrid was there to welcome Elsa and accompany her to the C.E.O./President's office, where they would discuss current concerns. Dr. Astrid von Euler was being groomed to take the reins at Nanovo. At the age of forty-six, Elsa had many more years of service to dedicate to Nanovo, but it was always a wise corporate decision to have contingencies addressed, and Astrid was key to the succession plan. While all the employees at Nanovo were important to Elsa, as they always had been since she founded the company twenty years earlier, both Astrid and Elsa's lawyer and personal assistant, Juji, were special to her within the Nanovo corporate family.

Elsa and Astrid found Juji waiting for them in Elsa's office. After Elsa took a moment to freshen up from her commute, the three of them joined the rest of the staff in the break room for the morning *fika*. Strong black coffee and an extensive selection of pastries awaited them. It was a difficult decision, but Elsa selected a chocolate biscuit and a cream bun. Astrid didn't copy her mentor, preferring a cardamom bun and a chocolate ball instead. Shortly thereafter, Juji joined them, having chosen *hallongrotta* and a vanilla heart.

Except for those who had been hired to fill vacancies left by retirees, and those who were hired to new positions created as the company had expanded, most of the staff had been employed at Nanovo for many years, and Elsa knew all their names. She made a point to share a few words with as many of the staff as was possible and spent some extra time with any who sought her out for a conversation. The half-hour quickly passed, and Astrid soon suggested that the three of them return to Elsa's office.

When they were back in Elsa's office and comfortably seated, Astrid began, "How did you find your drive from Hovås to the office today, Elsa?"

"Today was good. I find I can relax more with the information being provided by the car's navigation system. The drive takes about thirty minutes, assuming the traffic is light. It was today."

"It would be even more relaxing for you if you didn't drive at all. Why don't we arrange for a driver? Then you could just relax and read and think without having to watch the traffic as well. What do you say? It would make your drive here to Landvetter more pleasant, I think," Astrid opined. Landvetter lay to the east of Gothenburg and Hovås to the south-west. Travel from Elsa's home to the office necessitated encountering traffic around Gothenburg, or taking a more indirect back route, which presented its own challenges.

"After all these years, I'm used to the drive, so it presents no problem for me, but a driver might be a good idea anyway. I'd begun to consider that myself. Yes, please arrange that for me. I don't care if they drive my car or a company car or if we need to buy a more suitable vehicle; let's just get it done. Let me know what you've arranged once you've taken care of everything. Of course, security remains a concern."

"Consider it done," Juji said. "I'll send you a text with the details. Is there anything in particular that concerns you today?"

Elsa referred to her smartphone. Astrid and Juji waited and waited, then began to consider that perhaps Elsa had received a message requiring her immediate consideration. Just as Astrid considered interrupting Elsa's silence and inquiring, Elsa began to speak, "Lars Andersson on 'News and Notes' extended an on-air invitation for Nanovo to join him on one of his shows, and I wonder how we might safely do that. As our Canadian friends say, 'I wouldn't trust him as far as I could throw him'."

Astrid was the first to speak. "I was listening to today's broadcast as well and was quite surprised when I heard that. Leave it with me, and I'll arrange something suitable for us.

Without proper planning and the selection of the right person to represent us, we could be putting the company in a precarious position with someone like Lars Andersson. He might just be a cow on the ice."

"I thought our advertisement was appropriate," Juji interjected. "And regarding the other matter, my sister used to date Lars and says he'd sell his own mother to further his career."

"That's the sense of the man I was left with after listening to him this morning. Previously, it didn't matter to me, and I didn't listen to him regularly, but if we're to be talking about the company in a format over which we have very little control, then that sort of information is critical," Elsa said, nodding in agreement with Juji.

"I didn't see anything on your schedule today Elsa," Astrid said. "Shall we go down to my lab and take care of today's testing? If you've got the time, we could discuss the results more thoroughly than we've been able to do recently."

"I'm all yours, Doctor, but let us be efficient. I am looking forward to *fika*."

Juji and Astrid exchanged knowing glances with one another, but made no comment. Then Astrid and Elsa exited the office and headed to Astrid's lab. Juji was left to work on those tasks suggested by Astrid, as well as other matters they had discussed in texts sent surreptitiously during the meeting that had just occurred. She had one hour and forty-five minutes in which to make the arrangements before they would be meeting again, at lunch.

Juji made the required telephone calls and in short order her task was completed. She shared the information with Astrid via text, and as she concluded her work, her eye caught her reflection in the glass wall along the corridor. It was that of a slender, young-looking black woman with full lips and a high forehead, her hair worn super-short and natural. Juji Abebe was Elsa's lawyer. Not the usual Personal Assistant, she also had full authority to act on Elsa's behalf in matters of both personal care and property, including all matters concerning finance. It had taken years to make the arrangements, that were now being implemented in stages. Her motto, in all things: care, caution, consideration. Astrid did much the same on the corporate side, as she and Juji worked toward a unified goal, discussing each step thoroughly before implementation. Juji was also the firm's lawyer, and although she was officially named "Corporate Counsel," she had off-loaded the usual corporate work to her team of associates. However, she remained in charge—both in name and in deed. She liked Elsa Carlsson; she didn't like where Elsa was heading.

Astrid did the usual walk-through of her lab with Elsa, discussing the status of the current research being undertaken, just as they had each time the head of the company visited the head office. Astrid asked the usual questions and recorded Elsa's responses, as she always did. Elsa was a very impressive woman and possessed not only a very high IQ but also an eidetic memory, rare in high-functioning adults.

"Shall we use PEM?" Astrid asked.

"PEM?" Elsa replied, as she did each visit.

"Picture Elicitation Method. I'll show you a photograph on an easel, and I want you to look at it for thirty seconds. I will then remove the photograph from the easel when the time is up. Then you will continue to look at the empty easel while telling me what you remember seeing there. Describe the photograph in the greatest detail you can. Remember, no talking until I remove the photograph, at which time you will begin to describe it, okay?"

Elsa agreed, and Astrid led her through the test, recording the interaction so it could be studied later. At the conclusion of the test, and with Elsa's full cooperation, Astrid gave her an injection of a pale yellow and somewhat cloudy fluid, that she called Mnimi. For the next thirty minutes, they discussed a variety of non-work-related matters.

"How is your husband, Matthew?" Astrid asked.

"He is Matthew. He does much, but accomplishes little. I suspect there's something fishy going on. He is Matthew. Such is life!" It was clear that Elsa didn't want to talk at length about her husband. A short time later, Elsa added, "He is back and forth to Canada. I am thinking about visiting perhaps, but that may make things even worse. He is Matthew." She shrugged her narrow shoulders and heaved a sigh.

Astrid had known Matthew as long as she had known Elsa, so that was over fifteen years. He had been a moderately attractive man when he was younger, but he wasn't aging well. Matthew Gilbert Espie was a Canadian by birth, and the father of Elsa's two children. He was a residential architect but had never established himself or his vision with any clarity; his own business interests were not as successful as Elsa's. If Elsa suspected that something fishy was going on, she was most probably right. Matthew was always trying to impress young women, even if it meant employing those assets made available to him by Elsa. Astrid and Juji had enough on their plates. They had neither the time nor the inclination to help Matthew through his mid-life crisis as well.

The children appeared to take after their mother rather than their father. Both were in university: the eldest, their son, Lukas, was finishing his PhD while their daughter was close on his heels. Both had chosen pharmacology as their field of study. It was likely that Nanovo would be in their future. That was Juji's focus: securing a healthy company for the next generation.

When thirty minutes had passed, Astrid asked, yet again, "Shall we use PEM?"

"Certainly," Elsa replied.

As before, Astrid described the procedure in detail. Consistency was important if the data collected was to be of value in assessing the effectiveness of the Mnimi. Astrid could recite the instructions from memory, but it was clear that each time much was new information to Elsa. Astrid led Elsa through the test, recording the interaction so it could be studied later.

"Okay?" queried Elsa when the PEM test was concluded.

"Very good," replied Astrid, smiling warmly. "Let's meet Juji for lunch. I'm hungry."

CHAPTER 2

Elsa was thrilled; she had a boyfriend who drove a nice car and took very good care of her. Matthew would be jealous, so she decided not to tell him. She thought she might make him something special so he wouldn't be so jealous. She decided to call the girl who did errands for her; she would know how to contact Lukas. If only she could remember the girl's name.

Elsa's cellphone chimed and she answered, *"Hallå."*

"Good morning, Elsa. This is Juji. How are you today?"

"Oh good. Juji, I want you to call my boyfriend. Tell him I need him to take me some place in his fancy car."

"Where do you want to go, Elsa? Perhaps I can take you in my fancy car."

"To the kitchen; I need to do some cooking."

"What are you planning to cook?"

"It's not for you; it's for Matthew. He likes it in his brandy. I don't remember the name, just how to make it."

After a long pause, Juji asked, "What is the name of your boyfriend, Elsa?"

"Lukas. He has a nice car, and he takes me wherever I ask him."

"I'll phone Lukas, and he can bring you to Nanovo. Okay?"

"Okay. I can cook at Nanovo."

"If you get ready, he'll be there shortly and wait for you outside."

Elsa ended the call and went to get ready to meet her boyfriend.

"*Astrid, we've got a problem. Elsa is having a very bad day. I've arranged for her driver, Leo—who she is calling Lukas—to bring her to Nanovo. Call me as soon as you get this.*" Juji didn't like to leave such a text message, but she saw no alternative. She phoned again five minutes later and again five minutes after that, knowing how important it was to follow-up with Astrid and ensure that she had received the message.

It wasn't long before she heard the ringtone of her cellphone. It was Astrid.

"You seem really concerned, Juji. What's the situation?" Astrid asked, fearing the worst.

Juji described her most recent conversation with Elsa and confirmed that she had already phoned for Leo to pick up Elsa at home.

"Sounds as if she's crashing," Astrid replied. "I wanted to see how long the Mnimi would produce a positive outcome. Now I know. I'll be ready for her when she arrives."

Juji phoned Leo to confirm that he was at the pick-up location and requested that he send a quick text to her once Elsa was in the car. She had already confirmed with Leo that Elsa exhibited certain unique behaviours and might even call him Lukas. He was to ignore the error rather than attempt to correct her.

Juji was on the verge of phoning Leo a second time when she received a text from him notifying her that they were on their way. She gave the matter much consideration and decided that it might be best if she moved into Elsa's home, at least until Astrid achieved success in determining the dosing regimen for the Mnimi. It seemed the only option available. She planned to make a quick trip to her own apartment, which was nearby, in order to throw some clothes into a suitcase along with some personal-care items. The decision was hers alone to make and didn't require Astrid's input, though later they would discuss the findings and failings currently exhibited by Elsa.

"Welcome, Elsa; it's lovely to see you. I understand that you want to visit in my lab today, so I have made it ready for you," Astrid said, carefully guiding Elsa into Nanovo and ushering her directly into the lab. Fortunately, it was not yet time for the morning *fika,* so the employees were at their stations and not in the corridor where they might have encountered and further confused Elsa.

When they arrived at her lab, Astrid went through the usual routine with Elsa, culminating in the injection of Mnimi. Then for thirty minutes, she involved Elsa in inconsequential conversation to pass the time. Astrid hoped she would respond well to the Mnimi and that they would be able to join Juji in the break room for *fika*.

"What are you planning to do today, Elsa? Anything special?"

"I want to cook. Can I cook here?"

"Perhaps. What were you planning to cook?"

"Something special for Matthew. He is jealous . . . or . . . he was jealous. I don't remember. He likes something I cook for him. I remember that." The Mnimi was starting to work, and Astrid breathed a sigh of relief. She made a notation on her e-tablet to re-evaluate the treatment schedule and adjust the dosage upward.

"Your driver is very good, isn't he?"

"Yes, Leo is excellent. I like that he doesn't talk too much."

"Excuse me, please; I forgot to tell Juji that you're here." Astrid composed her message: *Mnimi working. Can meet for fika now. I told her I'd forgotten to tell you that she was here; might be good for you to say something similar. Since she's likely aware of having serious memory problems recently, it would be good for her to realize that others do as well. I think it will alleviate some concern and therefore reduce her stress level.*

They bumped into Juji in the corridor outside the break room, having arrived mid-*fika*. After selecting their pastries, they began to move toward the seating when Juji suddenly declared, "I have forgotten my coffee! Please excuse me." A short time later, upon returning with her coffee, she announced, "How silly of me; my mind must be on too many things today."

Elsa returned her own cup to its saucer, looked at Juji, and earnestly whispered, "Don't forget: Nanovo. Lars Andersson tells you that every morning on 'News and Notes.' How can we expect others to remember when we don't?" Then Elsa grinned. And so did Astrid and Juji.

The rest of the visit went well. Astrid completed her evaluation and advised Elsa that Juji would like to speak with her back in her office. When the lab's phone rang as they were about to leave, Astrid chose to answer it and watched as Elsa confidently made her way down the corridor and into her office without assistance.

When Elsa arrived back in her office, she discovered that Juji wasn't there to meet her. She waited, and in the silence of the room, she began to think. It was many years ago, but she remembered that she used to participate in a yoga class, held at lunchtime, several times a week and available to the entire staff. She had arranged for Nanovo to provide such benefits to its employees. Not only was there a generous *fika* and lunch but also the yoga class and, of course, the child care. She had brought her own children to work years before and had been pleased to be able to offer such a benefit to her employees.

Elsa rose from the sofa and made her way to the credenza behind her desk—a desk she didn't much use anymore as she didn't spend as much time as she used to on such matters. She slid open, then closed, the first couple of doors without finding what she was looking for, but on the third try, achieved success: her old gym bag.

Elsa emptied the bag of its contents and took it with her as she left the office.

It didn't taken Elsa long to find what she wanted. The store room was well-stocked. When she had trouble locating something, the employee on duty there had been eager to find it for her. The items were now contained within Elsa's gym bag. When she returned to the office, she shoved as much of the previous contents of the bag back into it as was possible. As she was finishing, Juji returned.

"Oh, you have your gym bag, I see."

"Yes, I had forgotten it was still here. I'm taking it home with me. I no longer do yoga class here."

"Elsa, I was wondering if I could please stay at your house for a few days. There is maintenance work to be done in my apartment and elsewhere in the building, so there is a disruption of utilities, noise, dirt, and unpleasant smells. I am not sleeping well; that is probably why I was so forgetful today. Would you mind if I visited with you? We could drive together, or you could drive with Leo and I could take my own car. Whichever you prefer."

Elsa appeared hesitant; however, she ultimately welcomed Juji to stay with her and seemed pleased with her final decision. "I prefer that you drive your own car and Leo remain available to me should I need to go somewhere. I think I'll go home now, unless you or Astrid need me."

"I'll contact Astrid and ask her for you," Juji said, then she sent the following message to Astrid: *I've managed to arrange to live at Elsa's in Hovås for a few days. I haven't figured out how to make this an indefinite arrangement. I think staying there would be a good idea. Unfortunately, she wants Leo to herself in case she 'needs' to go somewhere, so I'll need to drive as well. Elsa will leave shortly with Leo. I'll depart soon as well.*

With Leo driving, Elsa found the thirty-minute drive home particularly pleasant. Her mind drifted back to her youth, growing up on her family's estate. She had been a treasured child, a late-life surprise to her parents after many years of disappointment that they had been unable to conceive. She had been indulged, yet she had done all that she could in order to feel worthy of their adoration, for that's what it truly was: adoration.

She had been a diligent student and achieved outstanding academic results. And she had become a proficient pianist as well. There were no double majors available in the university course catalogue combining music and pharmacology, so she had abandoned the piano for test tubes and obtained an MD, as well as a PhD in pharmacology. She studied arrhythmias instead of arpeggios and chronic conditions instead of chromatic scales. It was a life filled with the study of stenoses rather than sonatas and of nocturia rather than nocturnes.

But it had been a good life, until recently. She had watched her parents slip away until, now deep into their eighties, virtually nothing but their bodies remained. They had left the family home in Hovås to receive professional care in an idyllic and safe setting elsewhere in the Gothenburg area. They were together, physically at least. Who knows? Perhaps their minds were together somewhere as well, since they were no longer within their bodies. She had witnessed their wretched decline and experienced the full-force of the responsibility for their care while she was yet a young adult trying to establish a life for herself.

And then Matthew had happened. She had found him charming and handsome, and he loved music. And he had said she was beautiful—no one had ever said that before. Others looked at her white-blonde hair and grey-blue eyes and declared her to be *icy.* Matthew had said she was *fire and ice.* She thought he had seen the fire in her soul, a fire that energized her and drove her to succeed and prove herself worthy—of what exactly, she'd never been certain.

She'd had no time to grow socially, to find her feet in society. Matthew had been the first man with whom she had been intimate— and the last. They married shortly after she discovered she was pregnant with Lukas. Nevertheless, she continued to work and founded Nanovo, expecting that Matthew would shoulder some of the responsibilities at home while he worked as an architect. She anticipated a future where they would live in a home he designed. That never happened.

She had urged him to design the Nanovo facility, but he never once put pen to paper or proposed any concept to her verbally. Instead, his interests took him to Paris, where he said there was work that he preferred. Nevertheless, she had made it happen for him. Her parents' estate was available to her, and she'd funded not only Nanovo, but also the Paris apartment, all the while ensuring that her parents' care remained secure. Unfortunately, Matthew's income barely covered his lifestyle in Paris and certainly not the mortgage on the apartment.

Leo turned the car off the main roadway and followed the winding drive through the private wooded acreage. It was still early in the season; the mixed forest of oak, birch, and aspen yet remained dormant. The only green in the landscape was from the abundant spruce trees dotting the land. The forested areas were broken into small patches by the craggy outcroppings, which became more numerous closer to the shoreline. Soon, the car crossed the short causeway to reach the old house on a small island.

Carlsson House was grand, built by Elsa's great-grandparents at the end of the nineteenth century. The family fortune had been founded in ship building, and then they had expanded into the importation of goods from around the world on those same ships. The architect for Carlsson House had been strongly influenced by Queen Anne Victorian styling, so the grand residence featured red brick with a steeply-pitched hip roof, a crow-stepped gable, and two turrets. Even the land immediately surrounding the manor had the feel of an English-style parkland, and the patches of exposed rock somehow melded into the landscaping. There were several outbuildings: a stable, cottage, equipment shed. They were all in need of repair, the horses long gone. This was home and she loved everything about it. Everything except the absence of Matthew. But he was Matthew, and she loved him. She planned to cook for Matthew. He'd like that.

CHAPTER 3

The days Juji spent at Carlsson House were uneventful, though there was some tension in the air. Juji advised Astrid that the tension likely was due to Elsa not being used to having someone else reside with her and that perhaps Elsa associated her more with her life at Nanovo than at home.

By phone, Juji outlined to Astrid a situation she was concerned about: "Lars Andersson has been phoning every couple of days, wanting to speak directly with Elsa and trying to arrange for our participation in a segment of 'News and Notes.' Sometimes he's demanding and at other times he's rather flirtatious. He's been both serious and cajoling. There's been a variety of approaches he's tried. Of course, he can't speak with Elsa, so that's a non-starter. But we'll need to answer him clearly about doing a segment, either scheduling it or passing on the opportunity. We're fielding calls from him regularly, and no one knows how best to respond. They certainly don't want to contradict themselves or each other."

"I've looked at her various test results," Astrid said, "both the performance testing and the blood and electro results, and I've reworked the treatment. I don't know why we get those crashes, but at least I've always been able to stabilize her again, and the improvement is prompt." Astrid's frustration was evident in the tone of her voice.

"Are you listening to me, Astrid? Lars Andersson. You've got to make a decision. Soon. Yesterday!" Under normal circumstances, Juji would not have been so truculent, but the time she'd spent with Elsa in Hovås was wearing on her nerves.

"I'm sorry. I understand. I'll take care of it and get back to you with a decision and plan," Astrid replied. "I promise. Sorry."

Despite the tension, Juji had decided to remain at Carlsson House to observe Elsa in her most familiar environment. Every day, she and Astrid had discussed the situation over the phone, since Juji had not been driving in to work at Nanovo. "Astrid, what do you think about having Leo move into the main house? He's been acting as a chauffeur, but he is a fully-trained psychiatric nurse with experience in the area. That's why I contracted him. And he's already signed a confidentiality agreement in addition to his professional responsibility to keep matters private. Elsa likes him—maybe a bit too much, actually—and I think a full-time companion might be good for her. What's your opinion?"

"You know more about him than I do. The decision is yours to make, of course. I just consider him a bit of an unknown. You and I have been doing well so far, but I can see that it may be getting more complicated unless there's some sort of breakthrough. If you've read him accurately, then I would agree with you about Leo becoming a live-in companion. However, I'm supporting your theory, not necessarily agreeing with your assessment of Leo. I just don't know him, but I'll trust your assessment. Now all you need to do is to suggest it to Elsa. Good luck with that."

"Okay, I'll set things up like that at this end and have a really long discussion with Leo. I'll let you know how it goes. We're going to see you tomorrow anyway, right?"

"Yes, for an evaluation and treatment, though the dose will be a bit different. It would be a good idea to arrive earlier than usual so the Mnimi will be in effect for *fika.*"

They chatted for a while, as friends do, then disconnected from the call. Juji sent Leo a quick text and arranged to meet with him in private.

Elsa had noticed a connection between Juji and Leo, and it annoyed her. Leo had nothing to do with the operation of Nanovo. He was all hers. She wished she could get rid of Juji, but she wasn't certain how to do that. Juji was her lawyer and a friend from Nanovo; she wasn't supposed to be a house guest.

When she saw Juji leave the house and meet Leo in the garden, she became fixated and determined. Elsa's gym bag remained in a cellar room where she had stashed it upon arriving home from Nanovo days earlier. She'd had no time to herself since Juji's arrival. Now she hurried down the steps into the cellar and her special room. She planned to cook there.

She began by cleaning the space, removing many years of dust and the grime, which accumulates seemingly out of thin air in rooms left untended for years. She looked forward to dealing with the gym bag, but first, the room needed a thorough cleaning. All too soon, she heard movement on the floor above; Juji, and perhaps Leo, had returned to the house. She was forced by circumstance to abandon the cleaning and mounted the stairs to check on them. Elsa had just closed the cellar door when they entered the room.

"Elsa, I have a few things to discuss with you, if you wouldn't mind, please. Shall we talk while we *fika?*" Juji made coffee while Leo found the various plates and utensils they would need.

Elsa retrieved a box of mixed biscuits from the cupboard, opened it, and placed it in the centre of the table. It irritated her to see Juji and Leo working so well together in the kitchen.

Juji brought the coffee to the table and began: "Tomorrow, there is an appointment for you at Nanovo at eight-thirty in the morning."

"I know that!" Elsa snapped, surprising both Leo and Juji with her tone.

For several very long moments, there was stunned silence, then Juji spoke again. "It's time for me to return to my apartment. The work there has been completed. I want to thank you very much for having me as your guest. I appreciate it very much." Juji was hesitant to say anything further, fearing that Elsa would take offence at whatever she had to say next.

Suddenly, Leo said, "Ms. Carlsson, now that Juji is leaving, I'm concerned for you. A woman such as yourself shouldn't be alone. You should have," he paused, "a gentleman." He paused again, then slowly and carefully continued, "To do things for you, which perhaps are uncomfortable, the necessary things. To help you and protect you. May I be that man?"

Juji was taken aback by Leo's choice of words, but a moment later, appreciated every one of them.

Elsa was thrilled; Juji was leaving and Leo would move in with her. "Yes, that sounds like a very good idea. Juji and Astrid will continue to take care of me at Nanovo, and Leo will take care of me outside of Nanovo. Leo, you may select any room you want as yours."

Astounded by this positive turn of events, Juji said nothing further.

The visit to Nanovo the next day went well. Elsa and Leo departed shortly after *fika,* leaving time for Juji and Astrid to bring each other up to date. They retired to Juji's office for their discussion.

"I couldn't believe it, Astrid. One minute she's clearly annoyed, nearly angry—so much so that I was hesitant to mention my idea regarding Leo—and the next, she's sweet and cooperative upon hearing Leo's suggestion that he move in with her."

"Something he said must have turned the tide. What did he say?"

"Initially, I thought he was going to blow it for us. I mean, he wasn't very clear in what he said, and some of the things could be taken in a couple of ways. I asked him about his approach, and he told me that, since it's impossible to predict what she will take from anything said to her anyway, there was no point in always being very specific about such things. He just let her fill in the details."

"But, you must, right? Isn't it better to simplify and clarify so there are fewer misunderstandings?" Astrid insisted.

"Remember, this is before her treatment. Leo says that it is impossible to know whether at that particular time she was fully aware that their relationship is purely professional and that he is her chauffeur, despite the fact that this was how he has been introduced. She has referred to him as her *boy-friend,* though he has done nothing to encourage that attitude. Whether that means she thinks of him as a young man, a boy, who is also her friend, or that she has a romantic interest in him, especially since Matthew isn't around, well . . . that's hard to say. What Leo said encompassed all of those possibilities.

It was so general that she could interpret it as she wanted and it didn't matter because all roads would lead to Leo taking up residence at Carlsson House."

"I guess that, ultimately, the only important outcome is that it worked, so we now have someone wonderfully capable taking care of her. Good."

"How did things go in the laboratory today?" Juji asked.

"Elsa was clearly better than the last time when we had that crash. I have increased the concentration of the Mnimi; however, I'm wondering if there isn't something that periodically interferes with it, as if there's an interaction of some type. I've examined a list of the few medications she's taking for other rather minor problems, and there's nothing there. I've considered herbal sources and other OTCs, but nothing appears problematic. If she were a drug addict, I'd be inclined to think that whatever drug she's taking to affect her brain is having an interaction, either directly or through a metabolite. But she's not a drug addict. Is she?" Astrid asked, exasperated.

"Not that I'm aware. Are you suggesting that some psychoactive drug, other than the Mnimi, is modifying the effect of the Mnimi?"

"Yes, precisely. Some of the data actually reminds me of the consequences of GBH. Perhaps I should test for it."

"The date-rape drug? I can see why you're puzzled. How strange. Do you think it is increasing the effectiveness of the Mnimi, or decreasing it?"

"I hadn't really considered the possibility that this unknown drug might be improving her response to the Mnimi. One always thinks that such a thing is hindering the functionality of the treatment. Interesting."

"Interesting, but not particularly helpful to you, is it? What sorts of psychoactive drugs—illicit drugs—might she be taking unknown to us? And how would she be getting them?"

"Well, the variations in response to the treatments began before Leo, so we know he's not the conduit for them. Before that, I can't say, but I can't think of anyone who might have assisted her in obtaining such a thing. It's not even obvious to me what drug or drugs she might be using. Nothing has ever shown up on her blood tests, though we haven't specifically tested for such chemicals."

"I don't envy you the challenge. Might it be connected to her genetic heart condition?"

"I seriously doubt it; her Romano-Ward Syndrome is thoroughly addressed each time she visits. I administer an EKG to monitor her for long QT and talk to her about taking her potassium regularly and avoiding stress and exertion. Her blood tests always show a good level of potassium, and the EKG has always been fine. She didn't even faint when she became angry with you, so that's good. She's never complained about feeling light-headed or having palpitations, so I think the Romano-Ward is being well-handled." Clearly, Astrid was puzzled.

"Do you have the older blood samples that you could test now for such drugs?"

"Some. I'll begin to evaluate them immediately, and I'll test for certain metabolites too. See if I can narrow this down."

"Leo will report to me each day, so if you have any questions you need answered, just let me know. And now, I've got to spend some time selecting songs for 'News and Notes.' I never thought that, as a lawyer, I'd be organizing the corporation's playlist," Juji said, chuckling. "Then again, I've already compiled all those photo albums in electronic form for her, though I'm hoping we never need to use them."

"For all the problems at my end, I don't envy you that mind-numbing task. My guess would be that most of the songs about drugs aren't celebrating the benefits of acetylsalicylic acid, let alone anything we produce. Perhaps you could find songs that address the issues we treat with drugs instead of the drugs themselves," Astrid suggested.

"Now there's a thought! And you're right. So far, I've found no song that I can use, and Lars Andersson usually makes use of several for a single topic on his show. Perhaps I'll just scream in frustration and set that to music," Juji said, ushering Astrid from her office.

Elsa was feeling well and confidant by the time Leo returned her to Carlsson House. When he asked her how she was planning to spend her day at home, she said she wanted to sort through some old keepsakes in the cellar. He accompanied her to the cellar to take a look and decided that the boxes filled with mementos of generations of Carlssons constituted an appropriate task for her and might reinforce her memories. Since she declined his assistance, he spent his time in the study, reading. He had already secured the doors and windows, and his position in the study gave him a good view of the entrance to the cellar. He'd made certain of that.

With Leo out of her way, Elsa pushed aside an old carpet hanging on a portion of the stone wall, thereby revealing a latched but unlocked door previously hidden behind it. The room beyond was her father's old laboratory. She had already spent some time cleaning the room. She quickly assessed the space and its contents, seeing it more clearly now than she had the previous day. The lights still functioned, and there was benefit of natural light through the cellar window, its glass panes washed a milky white. She removed the various chemical reagents; they would be deteriorated and possibly unstable after so many years. Then she examined the electrical devices, removing any that were no longer useful. Fortunately, the items that she herself had added when she updated the small laboratory years before were still functional. She had a temperature-controlled magnetic stirrer and a balance, which she had already recalibrated. And there was plenty of glassware: flasks and funnels of various types, a Liebig condenser, watch glasses, and clean jars with lids. She even managed to locate filter paper for the vacuum filter, both items in good condition.

When the laboratory was emptied of old junk, cleaned, and organized in the manner she required, she set about assembling the apparatus she planned to use. She brought the gym bag into the room and removed the reagents she had obtained at Nanovo. Some of the chemicals were her second or third choice, but she could work with them. Industrial production was quite different from what one could do in a small laboratory with more limited resources.

The reactions were straightforward. She would be combining chlorine and ethanol in an acidic solution. If the pH of the solution rose, turning from acidic to basic, she would end up with her product decomposed by hydrolysis and forming chloroform instead.

First, she weighed out the trichloroisocyanuric acid, a white powder. She would have preferred a better chlorine source, but could generate free chlorine successfully from the acid. Then she remembered that her ethanol needed to be dry, so she added calcium oxide to the ethanol. Shortly thereafter, Elsa recalled that chlorine reactions should be performed under a fume hood, so she moved her apparatus to the fume hood and tested the fan. It worked, but rather noisily. She also located her safety glasses and gas mask, just in case there was an accident. She was very familiar with this sort of procedure. Not only had it been a large part of her academic training and resulting professional training, but as a young child she had learned the basics while working alongside her father in this very laboratory.

As she puttered about in the laboratory, preparing to perform the synthesis, it occurred to her that the reaction might best be initiated in an ice bath. However, she was concerned that, if she went into the kitchen to obtain the ice, Leo would be alerted to the fact that she was engaged in something in the cellar. That would undoubtedly complicate things for her.

Instead, she finalized the apparatus, made certain she had all the necessary reagents, and did what little she could before needing the ice bath or starting the reaction to which she would be committed for a much longer time. Then she left the laboratory, securing the door behind herself and covering it with the old carpet as before. She moved all the past-date reagents and the old laboratory equipment that was no longer useful, placing them on a table at the far side of the outer room. After a final look at the space and with regret that she couldn't complete her task, she climbed the stairs to look for Leo.

"Leo, I would appreciate your assistance," Elsa called out. "I have some things that require disposal. I was surprised to come across them in the cellar. They must have been there for a very long time," Elsa informed him.

Leo was surprised at what she had found in the cellar and visibly relieved that she had asked him to dispose of the old chemical reagents and laboratory equipment. He was pleased to carry the items outside to one of the old sheds and made plans to see to their disposal as soon as possible.

Meanwhile, Elsa was determining what she might do to camouflage the sound of the fume hood's fan, since she would be using it for the duration of her cooking. She decided on music. Classical. And loud enough to drive Leo to wear headphones or earplugs, or work in an out-building for a while. She was pleased that such an idea had occurred to her. Tomorrow, she would cook.

CHAPTER 4

Taking the old chemical reagents and laboratory equipment into the shed for later disposal had given Leo the opportunity to phone Juji.

"She seems to be doing very well since the treatment. I must say that I am concerned about what other chemical surprises might be hidden here. The house is far too large for me to search; it's unlikely I'd find something if it's hidden. With the Romano-Ward, I need to be especially careful not to upset her for fear of triggering syncope," Leo reported, keeping an eye on the house through the shed window.

"Quite right, Leo. Just keep your eyes open and take advantage of every opportunity to search. The kitchen should be easy. Aren't men always hungry? You could search in the kitchen and claim you were either looking for a snack or a particular dish."

"So far, the only thing I was wondering about—and perhaps you could ask Dr. von Euler—are bottles of Benedictine and Chartreuse Jaune I noticed. They've been opened, but they're still three-quarters full. Are alcoholic beverages permitted?" Leo asked.

"For you or her?" Juji replied, in jest.

"No, I don't drink alcoholic beverages at all. I usually drink a lot of coffee, but it seems that Elsa prefers Robusta beans over Arabica, and their intense bitterness is a bit much for me. Personal preference, I guess. But please, ask Dr. von Euler about any alcohol restrictions for Elsa."

"I will do that, Leo. We'll see you in a few days when you bring her to Nanovo for her next treatment. Thank you for calling me with this update. Please, don't hesitate to call if there's anything else that occurs to you. Our aim is to keep Elsa safe and get her as healthy as possible. Hopefully, the three of us can make some headway toward both of those goals," Juji summarized before they concluded the call.

The days passed without incident, though Leo found himself somewhat frustrated by the quality of coffee and the selection of classical music Elsa would play at full volume while she continued her work in the cellar. She seemed to be a fan of Tchaikovsky, Ligeti, Mahler, Shostakovich, and Prokofiev, or at least of their loudest works. Holst's "Mars, the Bringer of War" ultimately drove him to wear earplugs. He remained unaware that Elsa had positioned her sound equipment directly beneath where he sat in the study.

Elsa's mood appeared to lighten and brighten, and eventually the volume of the music diminished as it too became lighter in style and emotion. Leo had ventured into the cellar the day before their trip to Nanovo and was pleased to see her busily sorting through her boxes. He noticed that sometimes she would get side-tracked from her task, taking time to study the photos and relive the memories generated by the contents of the boxes. Each day there had been a few containers of refuse he would be asked to carry out for disposal, but there had been no additional laboratory equipment.

"I want to go to Paris. After we make our visit to Nanovo, I want to go to Paris. I have an apartment in Paris," Elsa announced as Leo drove to Nanovo the next morning.

"When would you like to go, Ms. Carlsson?" Leo cautiously inquired.

"Please, Leo, call me Elsa. In public, you may call me Dr. Carlsson if you insist, but when it is just the two of us—or in the presence of Juji and Astrid—then please, use 'Elsa.' Now, Paris . . ."

Elsa appeared to drift away, and it was unclear whether she was having an episode or merely thinking of an answer to Leo's question.

"As soon as possible," she finally said. "I would like to leave today, of course, but we're not packed and don't have tickets. I know that there is a direct flight from Gothenburg to Charles De Gaulle airport with Air France, but it is not every day, so that will be a factor. Once you take a connecting flight, it takes much longer, and I'd rather not do that. Two hours travelling is preferable to ten hours. And the train takes even longer. So, we fly!"

Elsa's treatment at Nanovo went smoothly, and their Air France flight to Paris was arranged for early the next morning. Both Astrid and Juji had expressed their approval for such a trip, especially with Leo to accompany Elsa. They had been unable to get Matthew to visit in Gothenburg and thought that it would be good for Elsa to see her husband. He had claimed that the house he was working on in Canada was taking all his time. He also habitually claimed he was either just recently returned for a too-brief period of time, or was currently in Canada, supervising the project. It was impossible to determine how Elsa viewed his absence, just that she missed him. Among overcoming the challenges of her own health issues, providing care for her parents, being available to her fledgling children, and the demands of Nanovo, there had been little time to take care of Matthew, save for paying his bills.

Elsa and Leo brought only carryon luggage, so it was but a short time after deplaning that they were in the hired car and on their way into Paris. The traffic was particularly heavy, and over thirty minutes passed before they turned westward on Boulevard Périphérique, marking their arrival in the city proper. The apartment was located on the far side of the city, in the sixteenth *arrondissement*, on Boulevard Murat. They might have taken the train and metro from the airport, but Leo had been left to make the arrangements, and he determined that he was less likely to lose Elsa in a private car than in switching between trains.

Their destination was a Haussmann building with a stone façade facing the street. There appeared to be six floors: the ground floor with shops, the next being a mezzanine floor containing storage space and some apartments, then the noble floor with balconies and richly designed window frames. Above that were two floors of smaller apartments, with only Juliette balconies. The fifth floor sported a running balcony, and while it rather looked as if that were the uppermost floor, there was yet another atop it, containing the attic rooms.

The building and its immediate neighbours were all Haussmann buildings and bordered the periphery of the block, surrounded by streets on each side. In what would have been a common yard, central to all these buildings, subterranean parking had been constructed in recent years and at great cost, its roof providing a common courtyard for the residents.

Their car pulled into a parking spot on Boulevard Murat, and they exited, walking toward a pâtisserie, Le Petit Prince, on the ground floor. The large door that provided entrance to the apartment building was located in the wall to the right of the pâtisserie. The old door was painted a deep burgundy and bore elaborate mouldings. Elsa had the security code, but such things were changed periodically and Leo was visibly concerned that Elsa's would not be current.

But there was no need for Leo to be concerned. A moment later, a slender young woman with alabaster skin and long black hair exited, and he was able to catch the door open with his foot. She turned and flashed Leo an appreciative smile, indicating she was clearly available should he be interested. He watched her depart, a stunning figure in grey and blue.

Inside the door was a small lobby with mailboxes lining the wall on one side. On the other side there were two doors—one was marked "Concierge" and the other, "Stationnement," indicating access to the subterranean parking. A graceful marble staircase with ornate carving reached toward the upper floors, encircling a classic personal elevator with an ornate open brass cage.

Elsa immediately began to climb the stairs. Leo followed. It had been unlikely that the two of them would have fit into the elevator, even without the carryon. While his size was advantageous most of the time, providing him with physical strength and an imposing presence, there were times such as now that it might have been a hindrance.

After climbing two flights, Elsa stopped at a door. On this floor, the Carlsson apartment was the sole residence. Matthew promptly answered the door in response to Elsa's knock.

"Did you forget—" he began, then took notice of Elsa. And Leo.

After a bit of confusion concerning Elsa's presence and discomfort over the presence of the imposing Swede introduced only as Leo, Matthew welcomed them to enter the apartment. Elsa then explained to Matthew that Leo was her friend who kept her safe.

Objectively, Matthew looked as if he once might have been considered physically attractive. Now in middle-age, his dark hair was beginning to grey at the temples, and while he appeared to be of average height and build, his posture was somewhat poor. Although Matthew wasn't over-weight, his muscle tone was soft, and he was developing a paunch. He didn't seem to be relaxed, but wary instead. Finally, Matthew offered them coffee and left for the kitchen.

The apartment had undergone a major renovation and was totally modernized, though the furnishings featured many antiques from the Belle Epoque era, and the artwork favoured Picasso. There were closets on either side of the foyer, and a corridor ran from one end of the apartment to the other. The two principal rooms were the parlour and dining room with high and gracefully decorated windows looking out over the boulevard, the drapery puddling on the floor on either side of the windows. The patterned parquet flooring gleamed, and fine carpets were placed to define the conversation areas. A bedroom with bathroom was located at each end of the apartment. The kitchen was modern with Euro galley-styling and located on the courtyard side of the corridor with access to the courtyard several storeys below. On the other side of the entrance, a similar space housed a small study, across the corridor from the living room.

By the time Matthew had returned, Elsa had already informed Leo that his room would be at the study side of the apartment. The main bedroom—hers and Matthew's—was located at the far end. Matthew caught merely the tail-end of the conversation.

"It is such a shame that you didn't tell me you were coming, Elsa. I must leave first thing in the morning to return to Canada. The house is nearly finished, and I want it to be perfect for when you see it for the first time. I have an early flight and planned to take a room at an airport hotel tonight." He held up his plane ticket for them to see, then dropped it into a zippered folder, which lay on the table. "To tell you the truth, I made the reservation just before you arrived and was planning to pack up and make my way out to CDG by subway and train as soon as I got everything squared away here. That's why the bedroom is such a mess—last-minute laundry."

Elsa looked disappointed. Leo excused himself and offered to leave them alone while he went to visit the little park on the corner, or perhaps the Bois de Boulogne for a longer walk. "I might find something interesting at the pâtisserie," he said as he departed.

As soon as the door closed behind Leo, Elsa rose from her chair and fell into Matthew's arms. His embrace brought a smile to her lips and her eyes. "I have something for you," she whispered.

Matthew peered inside the small gift box she presented to him. His eyes widened. "You've been cooking! Thank you." He took the package to the bedroom. "I just need to figure out how to pack it," he said matter-of-factly upon his return.

Since very early in their relationship, Elsa had used her pharmacological skills to manufacture a modern Morpheus for Matthew. Initially, she too had sometimes used the hypnotic, but it was a rare occurrence, and then she'd just stopped altogether. It was how they had met. A friend of his was a mycologist who needed Melzer's reagent, necessary for the correct identification of some mushrooms and had sought out Elsa to manufacture a small quantity for his use.

The reagent employed chloral hydrate, the hypnotic sometimes called the modern Morpheus—opium being the original Morpheus. Over time, chloral hydrate became increasingly difficult to find due to the development of more helpful anaesthetics and sedatives.

Eventually, Elsa had become distracted by corporate and familial concerns, so Matthew did without. He had tried cocaine but didn't like it. He preferred a hypnotic but worried about getting into trouble with the law as a result of trying to locate a new source. He couldn't trust that Elsa would be cooperative and manufacture other substances for him; each time he broached the topic, she'd deflected. She could make anything, but she wouldn't. Increasingly, she had surrounded herself with the people from work: Juji, Astrid, and now Leo.

"Look, my dear Elsa . . . I must prepare to leave. I have no choice. You should have contacted me about your visit. Unfortunately, I have arranged for an exchange of residences. Kent and Lucy, the couple in whose home I've been staying in Canada, have been travelling the world, which is why their home was available. They are spending April here in Paris, so I suggested they reside here in the apartment for the month. They arrive sometime tomorrow; the housekeepers must have time to prepare the apartment. I am so very sorry."

"But Matthew, just the one night—" Elsa cut herself off. She could tell from the stiffness of his body that there was nothing she could say that would change his mind. Matthew could be stubborn. She was heart-broken but would soldier-on, as always.

Matthew took her hands in his and kissed her fingers. He gazed into her eyes and smiled. "Why don't I write down the address in Canada for you? And perhaps you can cook again before you visit, so you can bring some with you."

Eager to please Matthew, Elsa smiled and nodded.

"So, temporarily, I'm at this address just west of Toronto. It is the Gillespie estate. Remember that friend I told you about who was looking to sell his business? Well, this is the home of that friend: Kent Gillespie. The house I'm building for you and me is located just up the street from their residence." He drew a little map to show the relative locations. "These are the addresses. Just use my cellphone number to contact me when you can see your way clear to come over. I'll make all the arrangements for your arrival."

Elsa couldn't help herself. She sobbed uncontrollably. Her body quaked and shook, and she saturated her sleeve with her tears, which left their mark on her cheeks. Matthew had kissed her and smiled, thanked her for the gift, and even started to make plans for her visit to Canada. What more could she want? But he hadn't asked about the children, and he hadn't asked how she was feeling, or what she had been doing. She thought she must be selfish. Poor Matthew was working so hard for them; she must show appreciation.

"I understand. It is just that I love you, and I miss you when you are away from Gothenburg so long at a time. But I will do as you have suggested," Elsa said, adding, "Perhaps you have some time that we could spend walking in Parc Monceau? Or perhaps Parc de Bagatelle in the Bois de Boulogne?"

She had barely uttered the suggestions when she knew she had committed an error. Matthew shut down. She knew she had offended him. She hadn't meant to, but clearly, she had done so.

"I'm so sorry, Matthew. Leo and I shall return to Gothenburg immediately. I was wrong to have come here, especially unplanned. I apologize for having upset you—for causing all this trouble."

Elsa used her cellphone and called for Leo to return. It didn't take him long to arrive. After his departure from the apartment, he merely had purchased an almond croissant at the *pâtisserie* and perched on a bench in the little park at the corner, with a good view of the building's entrance through which he had only recently exited.

As soon as it became apparent that they weren't going to remain in Paris even for the day, Leo recalled the hired car. He waited outside the building for the car to arrive, giving Elsa time alone with her husband before their return to Gothenburg.

"Now, Elsa," Matthew began, "I'll contact you when I'm ready to reveal the new house to you but not until then. You can see that surprise visits just don't work, can't you? They are very disruptive."

"Here, I will give you one of my new business cards," Elsa replied, handing Matthew a card, that bore her name but Juji's contact information.

He thanked her and tucked the card—unexamined—into his wallet while she watched. When Leo phoned to say that the car had arrived, Matthew escorted Elsa downstairs to join him. They used the little elevator, and Elsa pressed against him for the duration of the trip to the ground floor.

The entire matter was sad, especially when Matthew chose merely to wave from the doorway rather than kissing her goodbye before she climbed into the car.

As their vehicle entered the flow of traffic on the Boulevard Périphérique and headed back to the airport, Leo asked Elsa if there perhaps was some place in Paris she would like to visit, now that she was here. Elsa couldn't bear to make eye contact with him and just shook her head like a heartbroken child. Leo rifled through his bag and found the potassium supplements and water he carried. He handed one tablet to Elsa, making certain that she swallowed the rather large tablet with sufficient water. Romano-Ward syndrome could be triggered by strong emotions like excitation, anger, or fear, and Leo couldn't be certain what Elsa was experiencing. "How do you feel, Elsa?

Are you light-headed or feeling faint at all? How about heart palpitations. Anything? Your vision, is it blurred?" These were all symptoms of a heart problem called a long QT.

"No, I am fine. Thank you, Leo. I am upset, but I'll be fine. I'm just sad. That's all, just sad," she said in a quiet voice. With that, she buried her head in his shoulder and softly cried.

Although he had spent only a brief time with him, Leo now held a strong opinion of Matthew Gilbert Espie, and it wasn't at all positive. Leo busied himself on the phone in order to arrange their return flight to Gothenburg. With a bit of luck, they could just make their flight. In the unlikely case they were unsuccessful, he was told that there were many seats available on the evening flight. This at least was good news. Next, he sent a text to Juji, outlining the events of the day with a suggestion that the information be shared with the doctor. In so many ways, this had become a very long trip, but with a little luck, they would be home for dinner.

CHAPTER 5

"I've found something, Juji," Astrid said, arriving in Juji's office directly behind her and speaking even before Juji had reached her own desk.

"Huh? Ah, what? What are you referring to, Astrid? I'm not really with you," Juji said, scrambling to set down the items she held in her hands and then take her seat. "I haven't had time for my coffee this morning.

"But before we get into anything further, I have something I really must say: Astrid, I need you to make a clear decision about 'News and Notes.' Lars Andersson accosted me in the grocery store yesterday. Can you believe that! We can't continue like this. I know that you're concerned there's been a leak at our end somehow, but if that should be the case, we'll need to address it. Time to face whatever is out there. Either Lars has something up his sleeve, or he's just very interested in the public good, which would be enhanced by an effective Alzheimer's medication. Whatever it is, we can no longer avoid facing it."

"You're right, of course. I have been procrastinating . . . but in all fairness, these crashes with Elsa have concerned me. Yes, we will do a segment on 'News and Notes' with Lars Andersson. I have already decided on the spokesperson; I just hadn't told anyone."

"Good. Sorry to have come on so strong. I guess we're both frustrated and concerned. Now, what was it you wanted to tell me? I'm all ears."

"I was doing a broader range of tests on Elsa's blood samples, and I found something rather interesting. There is a cow on the ice, Juji, and I'm not referring to Lars Andersson. Somehow, Elsa has been poisoned, but insufficiently to have harmed her fatally. I need to do two things: first, a combination of haemodialysis and intravenous magnesium sulphate to treat her, and then I need to locate the source of the poison. It involves a search of Carlsson House, and I'm not sure how a search will go down with Elsa."

"I'm shocked, Astrid. What poison are you talking about?" Juji said, slumping in her chair in disbelief.

"I found a metabolite, trichloroethanol, in some samples."

"So, we'd be looking for a source of trichloroethanol?"

"No, a chemical called chloral hydrate. Once it's in the body, it begins to breakdown into trichloroethanol, which we can test for," Astrid explained.

"What does it do?"

"Well, in Elsa's case, since she has Romano-Ward Syndrome, which results in a long QT—"

"I don't know what that is, doctor," Juji interrupted.

"It's something we can pickup on an EKG and refers to a characteristic of the heart beat. A long QT is a disruptive beat. In Elsa's case, chloral hydrate could cause *torsades de pointes,* which you're probably going to ask me about. That's a form of polymorphic ventricular tachycardia."

"Sure it is," Juji said wryly. "Ah, lawyer here, not physician, not researcher. Lawyer."

"Okay, let me describe it like this: Elsa has a genetic condition, that has resulted in her heart problem. Her heart's wiring is faulty, but she is tolerating it well, as many do. She inherited it from at least one of her parents. This becomes problematic under certain stressful conditions, which are more prevalent now than they were when she was younger. She was also better able to deal with stress when she was younger, which is why we try to minimize that now. Anyway, chloral hydrate is particularly problematic for someone with her condition. Either she is ingesting it on purpose or by accident, and she's either obtaining it herself, or someone has spiked a food source."

"What sorts of foods could you put chloral hydrate into so that it has a good chance of going undetected?" Juji asked, intrigued by the puzzle, which had presented itself.

"Apparently, chloral hydrate tastes rather bitter, so you'd put it in something already fairly bitter, but that the individual enjoys."

"How do Benedictine and Chartreuse Jaune taste? I've never had either," Juji said.

"Why have you zeroed in on those two? Either one could camouflage the bitterness effectively."

"Before they left for Paris, Leo told me he found opened yet three-quarter-full bottles of each of those. I meant to tell you, but our default was that Elsa shouldn't be drinking, so I had him remove both from the premises."

"It's called a Mickey Finn," Astrid informed her.

"What is?"

"Chloral hydrate in an alcoholic beverage is a Mickey Finn. It'll knock you out within an hour, depending upon the dose. It was actually used to combat insomnia in the late nineteenth century. Overdosing, or even using low doses regularly but for too long, can both cause serious medical problems. Let's find out if Leo still has the Benedictine and Chartreuse Jaune bottles. I'd like to test the contents."

Fortunately, Leo had not disposed of either the Benedictine or the Chartreuse Jaune. Rather than waiting until Elsa was due for her next treatment, Astrid requested that he bring Elsa to Nanovo the next day. She required intravenous treatment with magnesium sulphate. Astrid would decide later if there remained a necessity for haemodialysis.

The visit went smoothly; Elsa appeared to be responding well to the Mnimi treatments. Fortunately, she was also cooperative with today's intravenous treatment and had slept through much of it. While Elsa slept and Leo and Juji enjoyed *fika*, Astrid completed the analysis of the Benedictine and Chartreuse Jaune. She detected a moderate quantity of chloral hydrate in each.

"Elsa, do you ever use the Benedictine or Chartreuse Jaune that you have at home?" Astrid inquired.

"Sometimes—though rarely—I like a bit of Benedictine in my coffee. I try not to use too much. It is Matthew who particularly likes both of those to drink. I would sometimes join him for the Chartreuse Jaune. He bought those bottles just before he left for Paris last time. He said I could use them. However, I try not to use too much, so it will be there when he returns. Now Leo tells me I shouldn't have any alcohol at all, so I won't. That should help with your testing, right?"

"Yes, Elsa, it will help. And yes, is not good for you to have alcohol. I was also wondering about something else. Whereas most people prefer the Arabica bean coffee, you buy the cheaper Robusta coffee. Why?" Astrid asked. "Don't you find it bitter?"

"A bit. Again, that originated with Matthew and has now become the kind of coffee I drink out of habit. It's not bad for me, is it?"

"No, I just wondered. And since Matthew currently isn't at Carlsson House, but Leo is, perhaps you could switch to the Arabica or at least a blend. Just keep the Robusta for Matthew, and buy something for yourself that you and Leo can enjoy," Astrid suggested.

By the time she had completed all the testing and treatments for Elsa, it was lunchtime, and Astrid, Juji, Leo, and Elsa enjoyed their meal together with the rest of the Nanovo employees. Astrid had recorded her findings and considerations on her e-tablet, including her decision not to share news of the chloral hydrate poisoning with Elsa at this time. It would only distress her, and that wasn't advisable.

"I'm considering travelling to Canada to visit Matthew," Elsa announced to the trio during lunch.

"Is he expecting you?" asked Juji, fully aware of the situation as it had unfolded in Paris.

"No, you're right," Elsa said reluctantly. "I mustn't surprise him. I'll wait until he has finished the house." Elsa was quiet for a moment before asking, "Have you made any decision about Lars Andersson's invitation regarding 'News and Notes'?"

"I think we might focus specifically on our development of a treatment for Alzheimer's and other forms of dementia," Juji said. "I've got a list of acceptable songs he can use. Enough of them that he can choose among them and not feel that I'm dictating his playlist, which of course I am. I was actually quite surprised that so very many songs have been written about these topics."

"Astrid, who will be the Nanovo representative who makes the presentation during 'News and Notes'?" Elsa inquired. "I'm no longer the right person, so perhaps you are—unless you think this matter is best presented by someone who hasn't quite got the benefit of all the details as you do. It needs to be presented in a simple manner for the general public, and you might find yourself drawn into presenting far more detail than is actually appropriate."

"She's got a good point, Astrid," Juji opined. "I can think of a time rather recently when your explanation required an explanation."

Elsa's treatments with Mnimi appeared to have achieved consistency and demonstrated significant benefits in the management of her diagnosed dementia. Astrid regularly tested her for the presence of trichloroethanol but found none. While Astrid expressed her optimism to Juji, she was also cautious. Nevertheless, she finally reported to Elsa the presence of chloral hydrate in both the Benedictine and Chartreuse Jaune. Elsa had appeared perplexed by the news and could offer no explanation for the presence of chloral hydrate in either beverage. However, Astrid received enthusiastic agreement from her that she would never again consume any alcoholic beverage. Elsa was focused on stemming the progress of her dementia and lived with the hope of its reversal. She was focused on getting better—for herself, her family, and Nanovo.

Elsa had been an unusual test subject. While there were benefits to that, there were also changes noted in the functioning of her atypical brain. One day, subsequent to the departure of Elsa and Leo from Nanovo, Astrid explained to Juji that she had noticed the development of patterns previously associated with savant syndrome. While there as yet had been no indication of what skill might be demonstrated at such a level, Astrid had focused her testing in this area. Savant syndrome was associated, though rarely, with those demonstrating severe mental disability in other areas. It was not diagnosed in the absence of severe mental disability. Elsa appeared to be developing savant syndrome, yet she seemed to be functioning at a very high level intellectually and, more recently, had given the impression of being her old self. Even her eidetic memory skills were returning, something very rare in mature humans. Was she nevertheless undergoing a form of neural disintegration that had evaded detection? Mnimi was a test drug, and there was no way to know for certain how the treatment had been impacted as a result of the chloral hydrate interference.

Juji had just reached her car when her cellphone rang. *"Hallå,"* she answered.

"Juji, Leo here."

"Yes, what's wrong?" she answered, always fearing the worst when it came to Elsa.

"Not wrong, just different. And perhaps this should be shared with Dr. von Euler. I think it's important."

"What is it you think Astrid needs to know?"

"Remember when you and I attended a screening of 'Ziegfeld Girl' at the Gothenburg library during their 'Films of the Forties' series?"

"Vaguely. That was a very long time ago, Leo."

"Do you remember the song that Judy Garland sings, 'I'm Always Chasing Rainbows'? Well, I was dealing with some of the boxes Ms. Carlsson wanted removed from the house for disposal. As I was returning to the house, I heard a piano being played. It was Ms. Carlsson. I didn't know she could play. Anyway, the music sounded to me like that song Judy Garland sings, specifically the part where she sings the title phrase. That part seems rather simple, so I just thought it was nice that perhaps she was remembering something from her past. All of a sudden, the tempo of the music changed, and it became this very involved piece of classical music. And she played it so beautifully! I asked her about it, and she called it 'Chopin's Fantaisie Impromptu, Opus sixty-six.' It was incredible, Juji. Her fingers flying over the keys, the modulation, the emotion . . . simply beautiful."

"I understand that she was quite accomplished as a pianist in her younger years. I'll definitely share that information with Astrid, Leo. As a matter of fact, I'll do that right now. That certainly does seem to be significant. Thanks for letting me know right away and not waiting until later in the week when you bring her here for the treatment."

"Now she's switched composers. She's into George Gershwin; I think I can hear 'Rhapsody in Blue.' Let me get closer so you can hear."

They were both silent while Leo stood outside the music room so Juji could get a better sense of Elsa's playing. It was truly inspired. Moreover, Elsa's expression was one of peace and contentment. Serenity.

CHAPTER 6

Can you honestly say you're sharing a meal with someone when they're six-thousand kilometres away? Lucy wondered as she prepared lunch in their borrowed Paris apartment.

That morning, she'd visited the open-air market, which was held Tuesdays and Thursdays and lined the walkways and the periphery of the small park near the apartment. She had purchased rather too much produce and cheese there, but it all looked so wonderful! Additionally, she had popped into a few *boulangeries* on the way home—just to look—but hadn't left empty-handed. The visit to what was rapidly becoming her favourite *pâtisserie* had certainly come at a cost, measured in calories. And then she'd discovered a luxury *traiteur,* where she had selected her lunch for today. She had selected something she thought Kent would enjoy for his lunch—or perhaps dinner, if he planned to stop elsewhere for a noon meal while he was out.

As she gazed at the abundance of food she had brought back to the apartment, she wished Kent were home to enjoy it with her. She wasn't certain what he was doing, but he had left mid-morning, saying he needed to "check on something." There were only two occasions when Kent would become cryptic: when the idea he was entertaining was still in its infancy and when he had a special surprise for her. She wondered which this might be.

Lunch was scheduled for one in the afternoon, Paris time, planned to coincide with Yoichi's breakfast at seven in the morning in Toronto. It had been a compromise.

She set her computer on the dining table and laid out her meal, trying to select a reasonable quantity of the items she'd selected. In the end, she relied upon the well-apportioned lunch chosen from the offerings of the *traiteur* and carefully stowed away the remaining foodstuffs, leaving them in their wrappings.

At the appointed time, Lucy connected with a somewhat sleepy-headed Yoichi. "*Bon matin*, Yoichi!" Lucy chirped when she appeared.

"Yeah, you're too cheery," Yoichi said, in an exaggerated grumble. "I haven't had my coffee yet this morning. I guess it's 'good afternoon' to you, right?" She sipped her coffee and planned to indulge in a breakfast of cream cheese on a bagel. A small fruit salad with strawberries, blueberries, and bananas was visible on the screen, flanked by a small container of plain Greek yoghurt and a ramekin of muesli.

"Yeah, I just got back from a bit of grocery shopping."

"How are you doing with the language? And what are you having for lunch? I can't quite tell."

"Language-wise, I'm doing very well. It's not as difficult as I thought. All the high school French came back to me and provided a foundation I've been building on. I'm doing better every time I go out!"

"Good to hear. So, what have you got for lunch?"

"Well, I picked up a three-course meal from a fancy *traiteur*—that's like a caterer, I guess. I've got an appetizer of salmon in gravlax with fresh vegetables, then a main of cod with pan-fried gnocchi and chanterelle mushrooms with apricot. And for dessert . . . well, I'll describe it when I get to it. It looks simply divine."

Not only was Yoichi Lucy's long-time friend—they had known each other since they were room-mates at Queen's University in Ontario—she was Lucy's agent and also the owner of the Song Gallery in Toronto. Lucy painted under the name "Awen" and had achieved considerable international success as an artist specializing in flatwork, working in both oils and acrylics. When Lucy had selected Awen as the signature on her paintings back at the start of her career, she couldn't have known the significance it would hold for her. That had only been revealed to her four years ago, during their L'Orté ordeal. The realization had further inspired and motivated her artistic endeavours, and Yoichi had been thrilled with the results.

Once they were caught up on each other's news, Yoichi introduced the subject of business. "So far, I've not got any significant product for you, Yoichi. Sorry," Lucy said. "I've spent a lot of time taking photos, doing sketches, planning . . . but nothing saleable from France so far. This apartment doesn't really have the space for a studio. I mean, it's big and has good light at certain times of the day, but I'm afraid I'll damage something by getting paint on it. I guess I could paint outside, but the courtyard isn't very inspiring and I'm not really fond of painting *en plein air* anyway."

"Are you certain you're not just afraid that you'll end up producing another sleep painting?"

A few years earlier, while under extreme stress, Lucy had produced two large paintings during her sleep. But the stress was now gone from her life, having disappeared upon the resolution of the matters concerning L'Orté Point.

"No, actually that doesn't even enter my mind, Yoichi. Truly, that's all well-behind me. I'm certainly not experiencing any stress here. The greatest challenges have been what to eat and what to see. There's just so much! I'll discuss it with Kent; perhaps he can inquire about studio space in Antibes. We're travelling to the south, to the Côte d'Azur, after we leave Paris. I expect we'll be there until the end of the summer. Picasso spent time in Antibes, remember? Perhaps my style or subject matter will evolve and you'll detect influences from Monet, Munch, Matisse, or Renoir."

"I rather hope not, Lucy. I quite like your style. I think you'll just absorb all there is to offer as you travel and then express it as Awen. I've never been able to place you within any group, except in the most general sense, and I like that."

Yoichi disappeared for a moment to get a refill of her coffee, leaving Lucy to prepare an espresso for herself, clear her table setting, and position her dessert for Yoichi to enjoy vicariously.

"Okay, what is that?" Yoichi queried, clearly intrigued.

"As most desserts here appear to be, this is both complex and delicious. It's a fig mousse, and there's a biscuit with the texture of shortbread, except that it's been soaked in an alcoholic beverage I can't identify . . . and there's whipped cream. It's simply dreamy." Lucy closed her eyes, smiled, and sighed as she indulged herself, clearly exaggerating for effect.

"Hmm-mm, I bet that, back when we shared a room together during our first year at Queen's, you never expected to be collecting all these experiences, eh?" Yoichi said.

"No, you're right about that. I don't think I had much in the way of a plan, you know. Things just fell together. Heck, the first time I was in a plane was that class trip to New York City. I remember we barely had time to finish our drinks and were already landing."

"That was your first time?" Yoichi said, her surprise apparent.

"Yup. Don't you recall? I had to rush to get proper identification for the trip."

"Yeah, I vaguely remember that." She paused, obviously remembering their NY trip with fondness. "Good times." She sighed and then leaned in a bit toward her computer. "While that dessert lulls you into blissful surrender, I actually have a favour to ask of you." Lucy had just taken a spoonful of the fig mousse so Yoichi continued without waiting for a response. "The summer after that trip to New York, I travelled throughout the eastern Mediterranean on my own, but . . . not really on my own."

"Okay, now you've got me confused."

"My parents thought I was on my own, but I was kinda travelling with a guy I'd met in one of our classes. Do you remember Nate Bellamy?

Lucy scrunched up her face, trying to force a memory. "Nope, nothing."

"Really good-looking guy, a bit cocky, anti-establishment—really a bad-boy type. I can tell that's not ringing any bells for you. You were probably already too into Kent by then to notice. Anyway, I took off on my trip with a list of contacts, people my parents knew in the places I was planning to visit. I was welcome to stay with them or just look them up for assistance. I thought Nate and I would be travelling together, but he kinda did his own thing so much that you couldn't really say we were *together*. At the time, it was a bit disappointing for me, thinking this hot guy and I were thousands of kilometres from home . . . Yeah, I know, kid's stuff."

"What happened?"

"So, we're in Cyprus and planning to go to Turkey from there. I looked up a friend of my mom's. She and I had breakfast together, and on her way to work, she dropped me off at some archeological ruins, Paphos, where I was supposed to meet up with Nate."

"Did he show up?"

"He did. By this time, I was starting to find him rather obnoxious. All those personality traits I'd thought were so appealing—probably because they wouldn't have been acceptable to my parents—well, they were starting to get to me. Mind you, he was still killer-cute."

"So, what happened?"

"After we saw what there was to see at the site, I told him that I'd been advised that the best way to return to the town of Larnaca was to catch a shared taxi or taxibus. In Israel, they called them *sheruts,* but I don't know if they have a specific name in Cyprus. These minibuses, or *sheruts*, run along a route without a schedule and pick-up passengers whom they then deposit along the way. We get to the roadway, I'm thinking to wait for a *sherut* to drive by, when he decides to hitch-hike! Of course, I don't want to do that, and I wouldn't have if it had been you and me alone, but I figured this could be okay. A car stops. There's the driver and a passenger in the front seat. Nate and I get in the back. So far so good. As we're driving, we chat a bit with the guys in the front seat, just some simple exchanges, since neither of us spoke either Turkish or Greek, but the driver and his passenger seemed to understand English. Then Nate gets it into his head to claim that his father's some big-shot diplomat. He creates this elaborate fiction to impress these guys. To show off. All I'm thinking is: now they think it's worthwhile to kidnap us! I just remember feeling so scared. It just wasn't a smart thing to do."

"What happened?"

"Nothing. We got to Larnaca safely, but I think that was merely by luck. Nate attached himself to some Americans who liked to party hearty, and I lost interest in the bad boy and everything he represented. The next night, all of us ended up on the same overnight ferry to Mersin in Turkey. I kept remembering passages from the book, 'Midnight Express', so I isolated myself from that group and did the rest of my travelling on my lonesome. I haven't seen Nate since we graduated."

"So, why are you talking about some guy you last saw over fifteen years ago, Yoichi?"

"He recently contacted me. He's got a gallery in Paris and suggested we do some work together—him in Paris and me in Toronto, blending our offerings to the two markets. I'm always interested in a business opportunity, but then I remember Nate and that car ride . . ."

"Does he paint?"

"He did. I recall that he was actually very skilled, flawless technique. That's what came to mind when you mentioned absorbing the techniques and styles of various artists who had been on the Riviera. I know that, for you, it's inspirational and that your work will be truly Awen and not derivative. When Nate painted, it's as if he'd become Munch or Picasso, or Renoir . . . There was no Nate-style. His paintings were as genuine as the hotshot diplomat story he'd fed to the guys in Cyprus.

"Of course," she continued, "I don't paint much either; I prefer the business side of things. I'm uncertain about Nate, and I'm not prepared to fly to Paris and have him dazzle me with lies. You'll see through that, or perhaps he won't even try to deceive you, since it's me he wants to do business with. I trust your gut. I trust mine too, but I'm not hauling it there on a plane for six hours to test my theory."

"What is it I can do for you then?"

"I'd appreciate if you could just visit his studio and speak with him. Have him show you around and spend time, so you get a feel for him as a person. And get a feel for his business, if you can. I'm not asking you to vet him for me . . . well, perhaps I am, just a bit. If, in your opinion, there are no red flags, then I'll look into things more myself. However, if you think there are, then I won't follow up with him. My default position on this is to *not* go into business with him. No matter how attractive he is physically—assuming he's aged well." Yoichi sighed audibly.

"Doesn't Donald's work bring him to Paris at all?"

"Yes, and I've considered asking him, but I think with your professional background you're better able to make a determination. Besides, I think it's perverse to have your current boyfriend assess a former boyfriend. Perhaps, if you don't see any red flags, then I'll ask Donald to drop by when he's in town–perhaps."

"So, he's really good-looking, eh?"

"Dangerously so."

CHAPTER 7

"You know, songs have been written about being in Paris during the month of April," Lucy said as she and Kent wandered along the streets of the sixteenth *arrondissement* after visiting the Marmottan Museum.

"You want me to sing?" asked Kent.

"Oh, heavens no! However, I do appreciate your offer," Lucy replied, playfully hip-checking him as they walked toward the Jardin du Ranelagh.

"I know that you really like Monet's waterlily paintings, but you know what appeals to me? This statue," Kent declared, walking toward a statue honouring Jean de La Fontaine. "I like the fox and the crow, but I really don't recall who La Fontaine is. Do you?"

Lucy shrugged. Instead, the answer came from an elderly man standing nearby. "La Fontaine is a much-loved seventeenth-century French poet and fabulist. This statue commemorates 'Le Corbeau et le Renard,' the crow and the fox, which provides a lesson about flattery."

The gentleman was well-dressed, with a hat, cravat, cape, and cane, though his finery was as well-worn as he was. His features were strong and classic, his bone structure was good, and despite his advanced age, he exuded vitality. His face lit up as he provided additional examples of La Fontaine's fables and the lessons they imparted. This was his territory, and he was justifiably proud of his heritage. His English was as good as was Kent's French, and the two men took up a conversation, each stumbling happily along in their attempt to use the other's native tongue.

Lucy wandered off, snapping a few photos of things that gave her ideas for paintings, though nothing was approaching a distinct theme or concept for a series. It was apparent that her muse was taking a break. Eventually, she rejoined the men.

Speaking in French, the gentleman introduced himself to her as Serge Proulx. Kent had mentioned to him that Lucy was a professional artist, and Serge seemed particularly interested. Kent listened as Serge and Lucy touched on a variety of art-related topics. Lucy didn't struggle as he had when he tried to work on his French, and he envied her facility for learning new languages. It appeared to be a genetic trait she shared with her late paternal grandfather.

"*Excusez-moi*," Kent interjected, suddenly realizing with whom they were speaking. "Do we have the pleasure of speaking with *the* Serge Proulx of Proulx-Allard?"

The gentleman broke into a smile, somewhat embarrassed, yet pleased to have been recognized. "*Oui, monsieur*, my partner, Jean-Pierre Allard, is no longer with us, so I am all that remains of Proulx-Allard. I am flattered that you recognize the name. As you probably know, Proulx-Allard is no longer an active participant in such construction projects. I have been retired. Put on a shelf. Forgotten."

The conversation continued for a short time until Serge announced: "I am sorry to leave you, but I am on my way to visit Jean-Pierre at Cimetière du Père Lachaise, where he now rests near Haussmann and our friend, La Fontaine."

He took a few steps to continue his journey, paused, then turned to face them once again. "Would you mind if I gave you a telephone call to arrange something further? When I was younger, I would have thought such behaviour forward and unseemly, but I am now old and have no desire to waste time worrying about such things. I have enjoyed our conversation too much." They exchanged business cards and went their separate ways.

Over the coming days, Kent and Serge arranged to meet at various locations throughout the city. For many years, the firm of Proulx-Allard had been the foremost in France in the area of restoration and revitalization of historically significant properties. Kent enjoyed the conversations immensely, and both he and Serge benefitted from the exchange.

"So, what's on your agenda today?" Kent asked Lucy during breakfast.

"I've got a brunch call scheduled with Yoichi at one, so I may pop out earlier to buy something special for lunch. And I've got a ton of photos to evaluate; I've got to sort them and get rid of the garbage and the duplicates. What about you?"

"When you told me that this was an at-home day for you, I made arrangements to meet Serge. We're visiting the Louvre today, but not for the artwork. Today I learn about what all went into the renovation and modernization of the entrance between 1981 and 1989."

"I'm sure you'll find it fascinating," Lucy said, rolling her eyes for exaggerated effect. "The sky's been rather grey recently, but as soon as we get a nice, bright and sunny day, I'd like to visit Sainte Chapelle on Île-de-la-Cité . . . and perhaps we should just brave the line at Nôtre Dame while we're there. Ever since I first heard the term 'flying buttresses' in my high-school French class, I've wanted to see Nôtre Dame de Paris. Apparently there are buskers on Pont Saint-Louis . . . just to let you know, so you don't make conflicting plans with Serge."

"Message received and understood," Kent replied, offering a smile. Lucy accepted.

During breakfast the next day, Kent announced, "We've been invited to dine with Serge at his home Wednesday night. Shall I accept?"

"A party, or just the three of us?" Lucy pressed.

"As I understand, just the three of us. I have a feeling he'd like to discuss art with you."

Serge's penthouse was a thirty-minute walk from the apartment on Murat. Kent took one look at Lucy's footwear for the evening and called a cab. Lucy wore her auburn hair up, clearing her neck to accommodate the ruffled neckline of her black cocktail dress. The sleeves were long and sheer, French-seamed and accented with ruffled cuffs. The dress was more fanciful than her usual choices; she had purchased it in Toronto with gentle but relentless urging by Yoichi. Hearing in her head the admonitions she had received from Yoichi over the years, Lucy had arranged to receive a manicure as well. *Yoichi will be pleased,* she decided.

Both dinner and sunset were at eight in the evening, and since they'd been invited to arrive at seven, there was plenty of time to enjoy the view. To the west, the Bois du Boulogne could be seen from the luxury apartment's large terrace; and to the east, beyond the Jardin du Ranelagh and the Tour Eiffel, the rest of Paris was on display, increasingly in lights. The principal rooms with marble floors, high ceilings, and elaborate gilt trim overlooked the city. The light display at the Tour Eiffel twinkled as the sunset drew to a close, and the stars competed for attention with the city lights.

Serge excused himself, leaving them to examine his art collection, and returned shortly thereafter with Baccarat crystal flutes of champagne, and a small plate of *hors d'oeuvres*. They raised their sparkling glasses in a toast to new friendships.

Lucy was impressed by the sheer abundance of art on display. "Your collection is significant, Serge. How did you come about selecting these particular pieces?"

"For the most part, I didn't. This was the collection assembled by my partner, Jean-Pierre. We used to have a small château in the country as well as this apartment in Paris, and after his death—when I sold the country-house—I discovered that I couldn't bear to part with any of the art, so I found space for it here—though I think the quantity detracts from the quality."

"Perhaps," Lucy answered, cautiously. Despite being a large apartment and expensively decorated—grand in both styling and furnishings—it was cluttered, the result of having merged the contents of a fully-decorated country-house with a fully-decorated Parisian apartment. It was obvious that the pieces were well-loved. It was equally obvious why Serge found it difficult to consider parting with any of them.

"I know it isn't presented well, and though I am ashamed, I cannot seem to favour one over the other. I have begun to look into having some of these auctioned off, but I find it's quite different being on the other side of a sale. It is so much easier to make a purchase than it is to part with a work of art."

"There must be many reputable auction houses for art in Paris."

"Yes, I'm sure there are, but I haven't been able to attain a level of comfort in dealing with any of them. Perhaps I am too emotionally involved, too close to the collection."

"It reminds you of Jean-Pierre, doesn't it? Was this solely his purview, or did you actively participate in their acquisition?"

"The finishing details, decoration . . . those were always Jean-Pierre's responsibility, and he relished his role, as you can see. I've always been focused on the basics, the bones of a project. Jean-Pierre began by purchasing only those items he thought would be useful to future clients, and then there was a metamorphosis, and he purchased because he loved the work and wouldn't sell it to a client even if it was perfect for them. So, I think I now have a greater density of paintings than the Louvre. Do you agree, Kent?" Serge chuckled.

Kent nodded, as Lucy spoke again, "Have you not been able to find someone who is well-connected within the art scene here to assist you in identifying those pieces you definitely want to retain and those you actually wouldn't miss from the collection? There'd still be a lot in the middle group, the undecideds, but at least you'd have made a start to the task."

"I have. Unfortunately, it has been a matter of *omnis homo mendax,* which means—"

"Every man is a liar," offered Kent. Serge solemnly nodded.

"What happened?" asked Lucy.

"Nothing serious. I just wasted a lot of time dealing with people I ultimately didn't feel I could trust, and then someone I thought I could trust . . . well, I discovered that he lied to me and had not taken any of the steps he'd claimed he had toward preparing the paintings for sale. Let's just say, he was not a *bel ami*. Therefore, I am currently locked into inaction."

"If what you want to do is to sell them, then I'd just interview representatives from the most high-profile art-auction houses. Even if you can't feel a connection with the rep, at least you know that they likely won't do anything to harm their firm's reputation. But that's just my personal opinion."

"Here's one I wouldn't mind selling; it's very unsettling to me," Serge said, drawing Lucy's attention to a large canvas with a powerful and dark scene depicting a peasant woman screaming while holding a wounded and bleeding child in her arms as she runs from flames against an apocalyptic background. "This is the 'Siege of Sevastopol' by Dzhon Portnoy. I feel that I can hear the sound of her screaming each time I pass in the hallway."

"Portnoy's technique was unique," Lucy said, examining the work in detail, "but it never became popular, never developed into a trend like impressionism or pointillism, which followed it, though some consider it the foundation of mixed-media flatwork. They are very rare, and I've never had the opportunity to view an original up close. This is quite a treat for me."

"Why are they so rare?" asked Kent.

"I was just going to ask the same question," added Serge, perplexed.

"The story is that Portnoy would complete a themed series and put them up for sale. After a respectable period of time—determined solely by Portnoy—he'd destroy all those that hadn't sold. Then he would begin another themed series, concluding that with a destructive phase as well. That's why Portnoys are rare, but it's also a contributing factor to why his technique never really grew to become an art movement. Ultimately, Portnoy let the salability of his work to the general public override their artistic value.

The *entrée* was Languedoc oysters, served raw and accompanied by Chablis, a Valmur Grand Cru. The plump and briny shellfish were fresh from Brittany and served with a wedge of lemon. Although initially hesitant, Lucy feigned confidence in tasting the first one and was surprised to discover that she enjoyed it.

The following course, salmon with asparagus in puff pastry with Hollandaise sauce, was served without a new wine. Instead, there was a palate cleanser serving of citrus sorbet.

Conversation flowed easily, and the time between courses, though considerable, passed quickly. An elegant and well-aged Margaux was served with a main course of duck breast in a burgundy-based sauce, accompanied by a small plate of tiny new carrots and snow peas. And, of course, there was impressively artistic bread from Poilâne. The salad course followed: avocado and romaine lettuce with balsamic vinegar and olive oil.

Eventually, Serge presented the cheese board with a variety of cheeses and yet another wine, a Vin Jaune possessing characteristics similar to a sherry. Lucy noticed that the wine went particularly well with the semi-firm Comté cheese she had selected, both the wine and cheese having originated in the same region in the east of the country.

Dessert was predictably small in size but big on style and flavour. "The dessert is the *Puit d'Amour*, or 'Well of Love.' I hope you enjoy it; it is very old-fashioned, as am I. It is from the oldest bakery here in Paris, Nicolas Stohrer, which opened in 1730. Nicolas Stohrer was pastry chef to Louis XV." Then he added, "Like me, Nicolas has since retired."

Lucy looked down upon the serving of puff pastry filled with a pastry cream and glaze. *Where to start?* she wondered.

The cream was a Bourbon vanilla, and the glaze was caramel. A smile spread across her face; she took her spoon in hand and indulged herself.

By the time Serge served the espresso at the end of the meal, Lucy felt light-headed—from both the alcoholic beverages and the exquisitely intoxicating flavours she had enjoyed throughout the meal.

Conversation continued along in a friendly and often jovial vein. "I shall arrange for a special tour of Nôtre Dame for you!" Serge declared. "Restoration work is being done, so we must schedule a time when our presence will not disrupt too much. I think you would both find it interesting to see the process of bringing about the restoration of such a significant building. I shall make some calls, and when I have scheduled a day and time, I'll let you know."

"That sounds wonderful, Serge. I look forward to it," Kent replied. "Whenever we've walked nearby, it seems that the line-up at the entrance is very long and slow-moving. We've always just ended up having ice cream some place nearby instead."

Serge's laugh was warm and hearty, the kind of laugh which only happens in the presence of friends. "It is always this way. However, we shall not be among them!" he proclaimed.

Although they had known each other a relatively short time, they recognized that they had established and now shared a well-founded friendship. Eventually and somewhat regretfully, the evening drew to a close, leaving the threesome to look forward to their upcoming visit behind the scenes at Nôtre Dame de Paris.

"Serge sent me a text," Kent said, then read it aloud: *"Private Nôtre Dame de Paris tour Monday, April the fifteenth. Meet at five-thirty in the afternoon Fontaine de la Vierge in Square Jean-XXIII."*

"Seems pretty late in the day, doesn't it?" Lucy commented.

"He said that there'll be fewer workers on the site at that hour, so we won't be in the way and can get into places otherwise inaccessible to us. But if you'd rather postpone to another day, apparently eight in the morning on Tuesday, the sixteenth of April is possible as well, though accessibility is generally more reduced than it is on Monday, depending upon what work is being done. Your choice."

It seemed to Lucy that Kent was keen to accept the earlier invitation, so she agreed to the meeting on Monday. There didn't seem to be any reason to prefer one over the other. No matter when they went, there would be workers about.

CHAPTER 8

It was already Friday; they'd been in Paris for nearly two weeks. "What are you, or we, doing this morning?" Kent asked.

"I've got an errand to run for Yoichi. Let me grab a map and see where I need to go. What about you?"

"I've got to pick up a pair of shoes and pants I ordered. Any chance we're headed in the same direction?"

"Unlikely. Seems I'll be heading toward Sacré Coeur. The gallery is in Montmartre, right there," she said, pointing to a spot on the tourist map. And you?"

"Hey, I'm headed into the same area. Great. When we're both done, we can wander over to a park, perhaps La Villette or Buttes-Chaumont, or we can look for Jean-Pierre at Père Lachaise. I feel like wandering."

It hadn't taken Lucy and Kent very long to navigate the Paris Metro with confidence. They walked from the apartment on Murat to the Molitor station and caught the tenth line in the direction of Gare d'Austerlitz.

The train wasn't crowded. They took their seats in the car and people-watched. Lucy's attention was drawn to an interaction between a man and a child, likely father and son. The young man was fit and well-groomed, and wore dress jeans, a medium-grey cashmere pullover, and a fine black leather jacket. At his neck, he sported a textured scarf, patterned in subtle complementary colours and tied in a fashionable manner. The young boy, who appeared to be about seven years of age, was also well-attired in a manner suitable for his age. He wore a plaid shirt, which peeked out from beneath a tan-coloured pullover. His jacket was softly tailored and appeared to be a tweed. At his throat was a bow tie and on his head a newsboy-styled cap in a darker shade of brown. The boy wore large glasses. Lucy was impressed by his sense of style.

She watched their interaction, managing to overhear some of their conversation. The boy asked questions of the man, inquiring about the function of the subway train. The man provided answers when he could and admitted to the boy that he did not have all of the information. They agreed that they would work together at home to research the subject more completely. They were still chatting as equals when the train reached the Sèvre-Babylone station, where Lucy and Kent exited in order to change trains.

They made their way through the crush of the crowd at the station and waited on the platform to catch the twelfth line in the direction of Front Populaire. Lucy noticed a small group of teens who were dressed somewhat scruffily. They were loud and attracted attention from other passengers waiting on the platform. It seemed intentional.

Soon their train arrived. It was crowded, and the addition of the new passengers made it even more so. Lucy and Kent pressed together, standing near a mature woman and her young-adult daughter, who wore a small backpack and held tightly to one of the support poles. They spoke German, a language Lucy neither spoke nor understood. Behind the girl stood one of the teens, a boy from the rowdy group on the platform. Another stood nearer the doors while the balance of the group remained on the platform.

The event unfolded very quickly. The teen deftly unzipped the young tourist's backpack. She was oblivious to what was going on behind her. The teen's fingers gently and purposefully touched the open zipper of the outer pocket on the backpack as he began to reach for his prize. At that moment, both Kent and another adult male passenger standing nearby grabbed the teen and pushed both him and the second teen, standing nearer the door, out of the car just as the doors began closing. With their plan thwarted, one of the teens attempted to spit at the men but only succeeded in dribbling spittle onto his own chin. The door closed, and the train left the station.

During the ride, Lucy, Kent, and the man—who identified himself to Kent as an off-duty police officer—attempted to advise the young woman against carrying her valuables in such a manner. The police officer explained that the teens were part of a gang of pickpockets. Their raucous behaviour in the station had been a diversion, permitting those who eventually entered the train car to identify their target and position themselves appropriately. One would remove the wallet from the backpack, then pass it rapidly to the second teen at the door, who would have tossed it to a receiver on the platform just as the train's doors were closing and it was preparing to leave the station. They would then depart at another station and regroup, all before the tourist had any inkling of having been robbed.

It was unclear whether or not the women understood any of the information being thrust upon them. Unlike other passengers who had witnessed the episode, they remained totally oblivious to the situation and thus remained the least affected by it. *Perhaps they need to suffer an actual loss before realizing the dangers inherent in inattention,* Lucy concluded.

Lucy and Kent exited at Abbesses. This put them equidistant from their two destinations. They made plans to meet at the base station for the funicular at Square Louise Michel, downhill from Sacré Coeur, and Kent went off in search of the store where his order awaited.

It wasn't long before Lucy came upon Galerie Bellamy, an unpretentious art gallery featuring some contemporary art work, none of which impressed Lucy. She studied the paintings through the gallery windows for a time, then entered, uncertain how she was going to investigate things for Yoichi.

Nathan Bellamy did not appear to be present in the gallery. There was no one in the showroom, but Lucy thought she heard someone moving about in a back room. She decided to open the door to the room and take a peek. She only had a moment before the man himself stood in front of her, blocking her view of the interior of the room. She had managed only a fleeting glance at the contents of the room, but something about it bothered her. She couldn't quite put her finger on it.

As Nathan introduced himself to her as the gallery owner, he simultaneously and rather unceremoniously ushered her out of the back room, returning her to the showroom. Yoichi's description had been accurate. Although no longer the young man Yoichi remembered, he was instead a devastatingly good-looking mature male. And he knew it, as well as the effect he could have on women. Lucy could understand Yoichi being taken in by him in their younger days. He used his tone of voice and his gaze as bait to lure the unsuspecting. But Lucy wouldn't be taken in; she already suspected.

"I'm sorry. I was on my way elsewhere and thought I'd just take a quick look at what you are showing. I didn't mean to intrude." *Yes, I damn well did,* she thought.

"Is there anything out here that calls to you?"

"Unfortunately, no. I'm looking for emerging artists with good technique who have something to say. And I'm always on the lookout for less well-known older works, the kind that show up in estate sales." Lucy thought that either of these might be the key to gaining re-entry to the back room.

"Well, I just might have something for you. I've only just recently taken a shipment of a small quantity of works from a country estate near Lyon. I am currently in the process of authentication, but I don't think there's any reason not to show them to you."

"Ooh, sounds exciting," Lucy exclaimed. "Who is the artist?"

"Portnoy, Dzhon Portnoy, mid-nineteenth century. I have the first, which is fully authenticated—'Siege of Sevastopol'."

Lucy was stunned. "I . . . I'd love to examine it," she managed to stammer. "I'm unfamiliar with Portnoy. I think I've come across his name but only in a general sense. The impressionists and pointillists over-shadowed him, if I recall correctly."

"Yes, indeed— that's what makes this so very collectable. Give me a moment to fetch it. The light is better out here."

While Nathan Bellamy was out of the show room, Lucy did some quick thinking and soon knew what she had to do next. "Nathan," she called after him, edging toward the door through which she had been ushered just a short time before, "I really want to see what you have; I'm very interested. But like I said, I merely dropped by on my way to a scheduled appointment. Time has gotten away from me and I've got to run off now, but I'll be back later. How late will you be open?"

Suddenly Nathan was back at the doorway, and Lucy was being ushered out once again. "Oh, I'll stay open for you, my dear. When I meet someone such as yourself, with a keen eye and a love of quality art, I will do all in my power to bring the two together—the art and that special someone."

"I don't know how long my appointment will take, but I shall return later today. I promise."

Lucy smiled at Nathan as she exited the gallery. *What's good for the goose is good for the gander*, she thought, giving him a little finger flutter wave.

Kent found Lucy bouncing with excitement near the funicular. "What's up?"

After she finished telling her tale, he frowned. "Shouldn't you just notify the authorities?"

"I have no evidence to share with them, and they aren't likely to give credence to what I have to say, unlike you."

"Okay, what do you want to do?"

Lucy outlined the plan she had devised while waiting for Kent. They had time to think it through and refine it, if needed, since she wasn't expected back at Galerie Bellamy until later.

"What about you, Kent? Were you able to pick up what you'd ordered?"

"Yes, indeed. I'll show you when we get back to the apartment. What would you like to do now?"

Lucy and Kent spent the time as they had originally planned, walking through the various parks in the area and people-watching. Lucy took a few photos, but her mind was focused on what she had learned at the gallery and what she was now planning. Eventually they returned to Montmartre and Galerie Bellamy. Lucy entered first, as planned.

"Hellooo? Monsieur Bellamy? I'm back! Just like I said."

Nathan emerged from the back room, affecting a smile when he saw her. "Why don't I bring them out here for you?" he proposed, his tone indicating it was much more than a mere suggestion.

Moments before Nathan re-entered the showroom, Kent arrived and made his presence known, assuming the identity of a commanding and rather obnoxious, though likely well-heeled, tourist. Apparently, Nathan wasn't in a sufficiently strong financial position to ignore either potential customer, so he tried to satisfy each of them at the same time. As per their plan, Kent made the entire affair confusing. Both he and Lucy took photos of whatever artwork they could, unbeknownst to Nathan. Kent kept Nathan busy and with his back to Lucy as she photographed 'Siege of Sevastopol.'

She'd barely pocketed her phone when Nathan was again by her elbow, this time with another offering: an Artemisia Gentileschi. In order to provide Lucy with an opportunity to photograph the Gentileschi, Kent demanded Nathan's presence regarding one of the works in the showroom. Lucy needed to get into the back room, but Nathan was too quick. Reading the situation, Kent announced that he was prepared to purchase one of the paintings on display. Nathan increased his attention in favour of Kent, and Lucy slipped into the back room, photographing every piece of artwork available to her. As she approached the door to return to the showroom, she could hear Kent pontificating about some nonsense.

When Kent had verified that Lucy was out of the back room, he suddenly announced, "Oh, my . . . my wallet's gone! I've been robbed!" Kent rushed from the showroom, supposedly on the hunt for either the wallet or the culprit who had stolen it. Nathan was left holding a painting, which was partially wrapped and completely unpaid for. Nathan wouldn't see this customer again.

In a display of confidence that the loud customer would indeed return, Nathan put aside the mediocre painting he thought he'd nearly sold and returned to assist Lucy.

"I find both of these very interesting," she said. "I'm at an impasse, since at that price, I can only get one of them. Not to suggest you've priced them inappropriately, Monsieur Bellamy, not at all. It's just that I've done far too much buying on this trip already, according to my husband, so it'll need to be one or the other, not both unfortunately. I think I need my husband to help me make the final decision, if you don't mind. What time do you open on Saturday?"

It was agreed that Lucy and her spouse would return to Galerie Bellamy the next day, at ten. It was a promise Lucy had no intention of keeping. As she moved to leave the gallery, a slender young woman with alabaster skin, piercing blue eyes, and black hair entered. She wore a blue dress beneath her grey coat and carried herself with the assurance of a model.

It was only a short walk to Square Louise Michel, where Lucy found Kent sitting on a park bench. "I was just thinking I might need to go rescue you," he said, only half-joking.

"If I could please have your phone, Kent. I'm going to put all the photos into a Dropbox for Yoichi to examine." After sending the photos she and Kent had taken of the artwork at Galerie Bellamy, Lucy placed a phone call to Yoichi.

"Hi, Lucy. I didn't expect to hear from you. What's up?" Yoichi asked.

"I've got big news for you, Yoichi. I strongly—make that very strongly—advise you to avoid any dealings whatsoever with Nathan Bellamy."

"Well, that's certainly clear enough. Explain."

"I've sent a mess of photos to our joint Dropbox. Many will be useless, but you'll also find some very interesting ones. In particular, I want to draw your attention to the Portnoy, specifically 'Siege of Sevastopol' and the Gentileschi. I know for a fact that the Portnoy is a fake, and there may be others in the photographs. I've not gone through them myself."

"Why are you so certain about the Portnoy of all things?"

"Because I saw the original in a private collection on Wednesday and was able to examine it thoroughly. I also know for a fact that the owner at one point considered using Bellamy as his agent for the sale of his Portnoy, but something happened to scare him off, something that just gave him a bad feeling about Nathan. Granted, he didn't use Nathan's name; he merely referred to him as a 'bel ami,' or 'nice friend', but I'm absolutely confident—especially since the 'Siege of Sevastopol' is involved."

Lucy described to Yoichi how the visit to Galerie Bellamy had played out. Yoichi was most impressed by Kent's involvement.

"Kent's probably met that type for real, so he could mimic the character convincingly. He's all back to normal now, right?" Yoichi asked in jest.

"Yes, no problem there. I strongly suspect the Gentileschi is a fake as well. The room smelled of oil paint and turpentine, so it's likely that he's painting back there as well as storing stuff. The paintings on display in the showroom are all quite poor, probably desperate artists displaying their wares on consignment and hoping to sell to tourists."

"Wow, this sure isn't the report I was expecting. I guess I won't be doing business with Nate after all. I'm so happy I asked you to visit and check him out for me."

"I'm leaving this with you now, Yoichi. What I discovered clarifies things for you, but perhaps it should be taken even further. I think Nathan is a danger to the art world. Do whatever you want; I'm not going near him again. Oh, by the way, 'devastatingly handsome' in his youth doesn't exactly translate to having the same devastating impact now that he's mature. There's no soul to the man; he's just a veneer marked by affectations."

"Bonsoir!" Chloë called out in greeting to Nathan as she entered Galerie Bellamy.

"Bonsoir!" Nathan replied, then locked the door to the gallery behind her. "How are things with Chernyye Volosy?"

She followed him to the back room. *"Bof-bof,"* was her non-committal reply. "I am leaving Paris."

"Sit and tell me. Where are you going? Not back to Lyon surely. London perhaps?"

"No, to Canada apparently," Chloë replied, draping her grey coat across a wooden chair and taking a seat on a small settee. She kicked off her grey stilettos.

"The obvious question is: 'why'?"

"Gil is in Canada. He is building a new house there and buying a business. It will give me . . . *us* . . . easy access to all of America. I think it will be good."

"But I thought things were good already. The local market is good, and you're making good use of your situation in Antibes as Chernyye Volosy, so why leave?"

"I've just returned from Antibes," Chloë explained. "The recent court ruling out of Monaco may have sensitized the Russians. Even as Chernyye Volosy, I don't seem to have the access I used to have. I'm tired of working on a project and then having it snatched from under me—under *us*—just when it should be passing from me to you for execution. I think they're holding more in gems and cryptocurrency now, but we're not active in those areas." Chloë was visibly annoyed. "I've got to consider my future."

"And you see Matthew Gilbert Espie in that future, do you?" Nathan asked, his expression and intonation indicating an intention to demean Gil.

"More than here with you, Nate. We've had a great run, but I think the time has come for me to call it a day." Chloë paused. "Tell me, how did you come to blow the last Antibes deal? The Gentileschi?"

"I didn't *blow* it, Chloë," Nathan said, irritated. "I've merely lost control of the original. As long as Witherspoon doesn't arrange to auction it, I can still sell the copy. You know, I invested a lot of time and effort into this as well; it's not just you. I have a series of new Gentileschi sketches ready to complete. I thought we could work on a few more this evening. All you need to do is stand or sit or lie down . . . is that asking too much?"

"What about the Portnoy?" she said. "I still think you're better placed to deal with the old man than I am. I keep telling you that he's not interested in me. He might find you more to his taste. Mind you, I think he's got someone else in mind now. I checked on him since returning from Antibes, and he seems to have found himself a good-looking and considerably younger friend."

"The old man just dithers. I've got my Portnoy ready to go, actually might have it sold already. But I'd really like to get my hands on the original again. There's a lot happening on the canvas, and I don't feel I've got the technique perfected, not quite. I'm thinking about making a visit. If I knew that this new deal on the Portnoy were destined to fall through, then I'd switch my Portnoy for his. He'd never know the difference. With just a bit of hype, I'd create an eager market for Portnoys. Rather than work on any more Gentileschi, we could work on some Portnoy sketches tonight. For old times' sake," Nathan added.

"Okay, we might as well work while we talk. I'll get ready," Chloë said. She then began to disrobe while Nathan set up his easel and collected the canvases he had prepared for the creation of mid-nineteenth-century Portnoys.

"This back room gets so cold. I keep telling you, and you've done nothing about it!" Chloë complained.

"I have; I bought a space heater. You'll be fine," he assured her. "I have some historical clippings—photographs, engravings, and whatnot—we can use as a source of inspiration. For the first one, I was thinking something like 'dead, discarded, raped woman holding a child's toy' so suddenly she's a mother, not merely a woman, and that heightens the horror of the scene," Nathan explained.

"You're sick, you know," retorted Chloë. "I like it, but still . . ."

"There's not much to draw from on Portnoy. There just isn't all that much available. Now, I had all sorts of ideas for Gentileschi; she was easy. Just pick a story where a woman is subjugated by a man and turn the tables, but make her particularly vindictive. See? Easy. I saw you as Eve defying God. It would have been great!"

Soon they were responsive to their old rhythm, artist and model sharing a single muse: money. Chloë assumed the various poses requested by Nathan. He sketched, then took copious quantities of photographs for each pose, intending to complete the actual paintings at a later date.

Chloë was an ideal model. Her alabaster skin presented as a blank canvas. Thinking aloud he said, "I'd really like to paint your skin . . . use *it* as a canvas."

She glared at him. It didn't matter; he wouldn't know where to begin anyway. She was comfortable sharing her body and sufficiently fit to tolerate the various poses for extended periods of time. He did what he always had.

"I have an idea!" Nathan announced suddenly, directing Chloë to a mattress on the floor. "Lie or fall down as if you've been thrown down." As usual, he did a quick sketch, then a series of photos. "Now, throw a pillow on the mattress and once again, throw yourself down but atop the pillow this time." Nathan followed with a quick sketch, drawing Chloë's body atop the previous one. "And throw the bolster onto the pillow and again, toss yourself on top of them and hold the pose." This was repeated numerous times, gradually building toward the desired end product: a pile of female bodies. The rest of their time together was spent in this fashion—Nathan the artist drawing from his model's poses.

When Chloë left later that night, she reiterated her plan to follow Gil to Toronto, abandoning this life she had enjoyed for the past five years. She didn't know that Nathan was already in the process of securing another contact in Toronto: Yoichi Song.

With sadness revealed in his eyes, Nathan watched her depart. Now that Chloë was leaving, he'd need to find another model and partner, or change his modus operandi and continue his work alone.

CHAPTER 9

It was mid-morning on Saturday when Lucy came upon Kent packing his gym bag. "Where are you off to?" she asked.

"I've got a competition."

"Huh?"

"I'd been hunting for a *Savate* or *Boxe Française* club—"

"Ah, *that's* the secret you've been carrying since we arrived!"

"Yeah, I really wanted to give it a try. I found a club that welcomed me and gave me some very pointed lessons. There's a competition today, and I've been permitted to register as long as I have all the required equipment."

"Ah, the shoes and the pants that you picked up in Montmartre. You were going to show me when we returned, but the whole Bellamy thing dominated our conversation."

"Yes. There's no substitute for the shoes, nor for the pants. They've got a stripe down the side of each leg, and in savate, a kick is supposed to be completed with the leg fully extended, as revealed by the straightness of the stripe down the leg. If you want, you're certainly welcome to come with me and watch. I just don't think you'd enjoy a sweaty gym; the ventilation isn't the best."

"No, you're right. Enjoy yourself. I wish you luck in your matches, but I won't be watching. Have you found much overlap with the karate training you've done with Albin?"

"Yes and no. In the heat of the moment, my reflexive movements are karate, not savate. This competition is point-sparring, not contact, but it will be fun nevertheless."

"See if you can get someone to video your matches and send them to me. You'd probably like to review them as well," Lucy suggested.

"I was thinking; the sky is supposed to be clear tomorrow morning, and Sainte-Chapelle opens at nine. We could check it off your list if we visited tomorrow. But plan to dress warmly; according to the forecast, it'll be chilly," Kent advised.

After their visit to Sainte-Chapelle, Lucy and Kent made their way from the first to the sixth *arrondissement*, hoping to catch the entertainment offered at the bandshell in the Jardin du Luxembourg. Today a dance band performed. Its members were dressed in a variety of outrageous and creative homemade costumes. Their musicality was impressive, and people in the audience were moved to dance wherever there was room to do so.

When the dance band had played its final number, people dispersed, and Lucy and Kent headed out with the crowd, eventually finding a small table and a couple of chairs on the sidewalk outside a popular bistro.

"Espresso?" Kent inquired. Lucy nodded. "*Bonjour, monsieur, puis-je avoir un espresso pour madame et pour moi un espresso double, s'il vous plaît.*"

"Your French has really improved, Kent. I'm impressed. Your conversations with Serge and at the savate club have probably had a lot to do with the improvement. Talking about something you're particularly interested in helps, I think."

"I think so. And sitting here, one can work on developing a good ear."

"You mean *eavesdropping*, I presume."

"I do."

"Careful. That cuts both ways. You may be overhearing and overheard at the same time." Lucy reminded him.

"Okay, so I'll be cryptic: What do you think is actually going on with that gallery owner?" Kent asked, sipping his espresso.

"There are several ways that he might be 'maximizing his profit'," Lucy answered, providing air quotations with her fingers. I know he has the skills to be a good forger. It's considered a forgery if the intent is to pass it off as an original; otherwise, it's just a copy and sometimes that can be legal. The Portnoy is definitely a forgery, assuming that Serge retains the original and they haven't been switched. Nate could sell either one, but my guess is that he'd want to make a substitution and hold the original for sale himself. But there's also the challenge he'd face in demonstrating provenance. Serge likely has the documents in a safe, unless he's already shared the ones for the Portnoy with Nate. Without unduly upsetting him, perhaps you could find out. If the switch has already been made, we should inform Serge before he sullies his own reputation by trying to sell a fake."

"Tomorrow, after we tour Nôtre Dame—I'll ask him then."

"There are other scams, but I think Nate would rely upon his own talent in painting for whatever scheme he's concocted."

Nathan spent all of Sunday working to reproduce Portnoy's style in the painting of the pile of women's bodies. The bodies nearest the bottom were blue-black, with the colour changing gradually until the final body at the top of the heap, in a paean to Chloë, had alabaster skin and a slit wrist. The bodies located mid-pile were more grey-blue, evocative of her favourite colours. The work still needed a title. He applied Portnoy's signature, a bold scribble, to Opus One.

CHAPTER 10

"What's the weather forecast for today?" Lucy asked Kent when he returned from the *pâtisserie* with croissants, having left her to prepare their coffee for breakfast.

"Cool, but dry. There's a wee bit of rain expected for tomorrow, but then it stays dry and gets progressively warmer over the rest of the week," he answered. Not bothering with the bread basket, he tore open the paper bag containing the croissants and placed it directly on the table. As he took his seat, Lucy brought his Americano.

"So, I guess it's good we're doing Nôtre Dame today rather than postponing it for tomorrow like I considered doing. I dislike carrying an umbrella, but I hate getting wet even more," she said, stirring her latte.

"My, my, aren't we picky!" Kent responded teasingly.

"So, we meet Serge at Fontaine de la Vierge in Square Jean-XXIII at five-thirty this afternoon, right? It'll take us at least ninety minutes to walk, so we leave here at four. Or, do we leave earlier and eat elsewhere, closer to Nôtre Dame?"

"What's with all the details suddenly? Where has my free and easy Lucy disappeared to?" Kent asked, somewhat concerned. Something seemed to be bothering Lucy.

Lucy took a moment and didn't respond immediately. "It may be stress due to Nathan Bellamy. Yoichi came so close to working with him, and Serge came so close to dealing with him . . ."

"Yeah, but neither actually experienced anything bad—they just came close. They both felt the heat from the fire, but they didn't get burned. When do you think we should tell Serge about Nathan Bellamy? Or, perhaps, you now think we shouldn't?"

"Oh, I think we should tell him. At the very least, it'll confirm for him that he's right to trust his intuition about people. I don't want to detract from an enjoyable tour of Nôtre Dame, so perhaps shortly after, when we're done there, or even tomorrow."

"I think Serge is looking forward to this as much as either of us. I've really enjoyed talking with him. It's not really talking shop, but it would be understandable if it seemed like that to you. It's a bit like being re-energized by a really great conference program."

They left their apartment on Murat early, walked for ninety minutes, and enjoyed a leisurely light meal at a bistro. At precisely five-thirty, they were seated on a park bench, waiting near Fontaine de la Vierge in Square Jean-XXIII, behind Nôtre Dame. Serge arrived moments later.

"Bon après-midi, mes amis," Serge declared in greeting, gesturing with his cane, his signature cravat, hat, and cape worn with panache. "We shall go to meet my friend and then begin the tour without delay."

They followed Serge away from the cathedral and toward a small building nearby, which reminded Lucy of a kiosk. The building was a carved-limestone construction and well-hidden by lilac bushes, their intense scent being somewhat overpowering. Serge's friend, Albert, was the project director, the official overseeing the lengthy restoration currently underway at the cathedral. Albert emerged from the lilacs and sneezed. Embarrassed, he nonetheless quickly composed himself and welcomed Lucy and Kent. Lucy found his face fascinating. Strong features lay beneath the wrinkled and weathered skin. He was younger than Serge—but not by much—and, like Serge, appeared fit and energetic.

"We shall enter through the crypt," Albert informed them.

Once they had entered the small vestibule, Albert keyed the lock, securing it, then directed them to follow him down the stone steps into the dank environment of a basement level. Already the tour was unlike what the average tourist would experience. Lucy could tell from Kent's expression that he was simply delighted.

"It is, of course, very damp at this level. We are but a small island in the middle of a significant river, and these stones and the water have been fighting their battle for many hundreds of years. We are constantly repairing, and while we do that, we also research, trying to uncover more of Nôtre Dame's secrets. Sometimes the repairs done in the past were respectful of the history and sometimes they were not. There is much we do not know and cannot know without doing damage to the materials; that we cannot and do not permit. We try to stop time, you might say. As you know, that is impossible. So, we who work on Nôtre Dame de Paris try to do the impossible! It is a labour of love."

"When was the current work begun?" Kent inquired.

"It was 1963 when a cleaning of the façade was first ordered by the minister of culture. Hundreds of years of accumulated soot and grime were removed. Remember that Nôtre Dame is built atop the Church of St. Etienne. Some excavations were performed, and in 1965, the catacombs dating from Roman and medieval times were revealed. In 2018, just last year, we began what is to be a long-term renovation project and have erected scaffolding to facilitate the work. It is an attempt to make subtle adjustments in support structures and the like in order to secure the building and as much as possible prevent further deterioration. Our work honours those who have laboured here over the past eight hundred years, and this is the only recognition we seek: acknowledgment that we respected the past."

"It must be difficult to work with the tourists milling about," Lucy suggested.

"Yes, and yet they are here to admire and learn about Nôtre Dame de Paris, so we do not fault them. We welcome them."

"From where was the stone sourced?" asked Kent.

"In most cases, we really don't know, even now, after so many years. Much is said to have been quarried in Montparnasse, but I suspect that, given the various construction projects carried out over the years to modify the cathedral, other quarries were also used; for example, there is a significant quarry in a forest an hour northwest of Paris, known as the French Vexin. While the cathedral was begun in 1163, it was about forty years later when the famous flying buttresses were completed. What you will see here is a cathedral that was generations in the making. To attempt to designate any particular aspect as more worthy than another, especially basing the decision solely on age, is inappropriate."

They continued to follow Albert, with Kent and Serge sometimes pausing to have a quiet exchange concerning a specific detail. Moving upward like cicadas, they eventually emerged from underground.

The air was sweet with incense, and the vast space was lit by sunlight filtering through the rose window at the end of the transept. The structure drew one's attention upward, toward the heavens, and the light itself represented a heavenly presence.

"The clerestory is one of the most dematerialized areas; it has the largest expanse of glass and allows in the most light. That would have been essential in the twelfth century."

"I understand there were modifications made throughout the ages, but when would you say the cathedral would have been considered finished?" Lucy asked.

"The mid-fourteenth century is generally considered to be when the cathedral was completed, so two-hundred years after construction began, but it was much different then from what it is now," Albert explained.

Their tour continued in this manner. They were able to examine all of the cathedral's treasures up close and were provided as much time as Kent required, becoming immersed in the history and lore of Nôtre Dame de Paris. Every question was answered fully and accurately, even though sometimes the answer was "we don't know." The tour provided by Albert was intimate as well as informative. Time passed quickly.

Over an hour into the tour, they were well-beyond the range of tourists and high above the nave, examining the structure between the roof and the vault. Lucy wasn't comfortable on the scaffolding, but her limitless curiosity helped her overcome her fears. Kent, Serge, and Albert seemed fearless. Workers continued in their labours, ignoring their presence as if it were just another day at the office.

Suddenly, there was a sharp sound, a shout piercing the usual drone of workers' conversations. Kent looked at Serge and Albert as the two men carried on a brief and highly animated conversation. Lucy sensed their agitation, then she detected a scent that frightened her. One that demands attention: fire!

Workers shouted and moved en masse to exit the area after doing what they could to extinguish the burning, ancient wooden structure that supported the roof above the vault. Acrid smoke billowed toward them. Quickly, Albert gathered their little group and ushered them back onto the metal scaffolding and down to ground level, all the while on his phone, speaking with a sense of great urgency. They could tell it was serious, though they didn't realize at the time just how serious.

Kent and Lucy quickly thanked Albert and left with Serge as soon as the construction elevator affixed to the scaffolding returned them to ground level. Expecting the rapid arrival of emergency services, the area was cleared of people with the help of anyone with a commanding presence. Both Serge and Kent barked evacuation orders at tourists who were far too intent on minimizing the significance of such an event and taking selfies to be posted on social media for the benefit of their friends back home. In short order, the threesome crossed Pont au Double to claim a bench in Square René Viviani and watch the drama unfold from the left bank of the Seine. All that they had just been shown, they might now watch being destroyed.

"You know, the bridge we just crossed, Pont au Double? There has been a small bridge there since the mid-seventeenth century. This is its third incarnation and was constructed in 1883," Serge informed them.

They watched, and Serge explained what they were seeing. "You will see . . . *les pompiers* . . ."

"The firefighters," Lucy offered, noticing that stress was causing Serge to lose his facility with English. While she could switch to French, that would leave Kent in the cold since the stress would in all likelihood make it more difficult for him to recall his vocabulary. Besides, they'd not had occasion to use the word *pompier* prior to this.

Serge continued. "Yes. They will be removing artwork. There is an order established by which the works of greatest significance are removed first. This will occur while others begin to fight the fire. You will also notice that they will not use high pressure to spray the water. That would be damaging to the structure. They will use a lot of water, but at lower pressure than you might expect. And they will not spray water on the stained glass for fear of shattering the glass."

As flames engulfed the roof, Lucy thought she saw a tear streak Serge's cheek. There was a tell-tale streak on Kent's cheek as well.

"Remember the lead vault, that false ceiling of the nave? That is how Gothic architects sought to protect the contents when the roof catches fire. It is not unheard of, so the original designers anticipated such an occurrence. When the Communards attempted to burn the Cathedral in 1871, they failed." He paused, then said, "I think I shall pray to Nôtre Dame."

The trio sat on the bench, riveted by the spectacle as it unfolded before them. Just over an hour later, the spire collapsed into the vault. The spire had been added in 1859. The Gothic architects had not been consulted about the wisdom of such an addition.

They departed shortly thereafter, walking along the left bank of the Seine to the Tour Eiffel, and then across the Pont d'Iéna to the Trocadéro before winding their way to Serge's apartment. Being of one mind, they were silent. It would be nearly eight hours before the fire would be brought under control.

CHAPTER 11

The building was old—grand, but old—and as such, it had only a rudimentary security system. Nathan watched as the old man departed late in the afternoon, and although he didn't know how much time was available, he thought he'd take his chances. The old man had appeared dressed for dinner, though with an elderly individual, it was often difficult to tell. Such individuals rarely dressed in casual attire. Patient surveillance and a good pair of binoculars helped to reveal the passcode for the entry. Once he was inside, Nathan eschewed the elevator and made his way up the stairs to the top floor where the Portnoy was housed.

Located at the top of the stairs, the penthouse door was not in a high-traffic area. He tried the various tricks he had learned to manipulate locks, but without success. So far, he had been lucky. No one had seen him climb the stairs to this upper level, or try to gain access. After another fruitless attempt to pick the lock, he slumped against the door, and his attention was drawn to the long window providing natural light on the landing. He checked the window and was able to open it; it was actually a set of French doors. Someone must have considered it an appropriate fire exit out onto the penthouse terrace. Although locked to the outside, the doors were no challenge from the inside.

Once on the terrace, there was little concern for noise or mess. Nathan broke through the glass in one of the apartment's doors to the terrace and gained entry into the apartment.

Although the contents of the posh apartment distracted him, he was able to locate the Portnoy, hanging on the wall in what appeared to be the guest wing of the large residence.

The first step was to remove the canvas from its frame. He unhooked the painting from its mount and placed it facedown on a bed in one of the rooms. There he carefully removed the small square nails and pocketed them. When he had released the canvas, he rolled it and placed it in the cardboard tube from which he had earlier removed his version of the Portnoy. Then he began to place his own Portnoy within the frame, using the original nails. So far everything had gone smoothly. His confidence was heightened by his success. His Portnoy now hung in place of the old, which was now rolled and secured within the protective tube.

Rather than leave, Nathan decided to search for the documentation on the Portnoy. Given their interactions regarding the resale of the Portnoy, it was possible that the documents had not been returned to their proper secure location and might have been placed in a drawer as a temporary measure. Nathan sometimes did such things; it was always possible that Serge had as well.

Nathan's focus was on obtaining the documentation. He had to work carefully so as not to leave any hint that the Portnoy had been tampered with. He was blissfully unaware of the passage of time until the door to the apartment was unlocked, and Serge returned home— with guests.

After briefly berating himself for his inattentiveness, Nathan secured the tube now containing the original Portnoy and cautiously made his way toward the entrance. Although he had not seen them, by their voices alone he determined that there were at least three people. They all sounded familiar to him; he winced, trying to concentrate so he might distinguish among the voices and identify them.

With the voices seemingly originating from one end of the apartment, Nathan determined the feasibility of exiting the way he had entered—through the French doors onto the terrace. The building was only six stories in height, which meant he might be able to exit into the garden directly from the terrace. It was an odd structure; every floor had a terrace, creating a step-down formation that could provide a safe egress from the property for him.

As he made his way across the room and toward the penthouse terrace, a voice suddenly called out.

"Hey! What the—" Kent grabbed at Nathan, knocking the tube containing the original Portnoy from his grasp. "Serge, call police!" he called out.

While Kent enjoyed point sparring, his real interest lay in full-contact savate. A martial art originating from the streets of Paris and the sailors of eighteenth-century Marseille, savate was born from savagery. Real savate, *la danse de la rue,* was comprised of *lutte Parisien* or street wrestling, and English boxing. It was known for its devastating kicks. It was fast, powerful, and deadly—as Nathan was about to learn.

Lucy and Serge rushed into the room, with Serge still on the phone to the police. Lucy looked over at Nathan and studied him carefully. She determined that he didn't appear to have a weapon. She gave herself two tasks—one, stay out of Kent's way, and two, move Serge's valuables out of harm's way. Nathan would be incorrect if he assumed Kent wasn't armed.

Not only is he armed, he's legged as well, Lucy thought. She had missed seeing him compete in the savate competition, but she was keen to watch him take down an adversary in real life.

Nathan should have run; he should have made a break for it, running in whatever direction seemed feasible. However, he'd been so focused on the original Portnoy that he couldn't bear to leave it behind; it seemed to have a hold on him.

Desperate for the Portnoy and frantic about the situation he was now in, Nathan made his second mistake. Foolishly, Nathan threw a haymaker with his right, aiming at the left side of Kent's head. Unfortunately for Nathan, Kent's skill and training gave him the ability to anticipate his opponent's moves. Kent knew what Nathan would try. Stepping toward him as Nathan launched his punch, Kent simultaneously high-blocked the haymaker and delivered *un coup de coude*, an elbow strike, to Nathan's chin. Nathan stumbled backward. As he tried to recover his footing, he felt a sharp pain deep on his right side. In that moment, Kent had delivered a powerful roundhouse kick to his liver, just below his rib cage.

Nathan collapsed to the floor, powerless to retaliate. As he lay there, gasping in agony and incapable of sustained movement, he appeared bewildered by this turn of events. Lucy and Kent were not.

As Serge brought cording to secure Nathan while they awaited the arrival of the police, Lucy took a photo of the bad boy and sent it to Yoichi.

CHAPTER 12

A heavy April fog enshrouded the base of the CN Tower as Chloë's flight arrived at Toronto's Pearson International Airport. Little of the sprawling city located along Lake Ontario's north shoreline could be seen from the air. She deplaned and followed the other passengers as they snaked their way through the terminal, eventually arriving at their destination: customs and immigration. Clearance and entry into Canada went swiftly, and then things ground to a halt as Chloë waited with others at a luggage carousel. Time seemed to stand still. Chloë took her cellphone in hand.

"*Bonjour!* Gil, I'm here in Toronto. Will you be a dear and come fetch me?"

Chloë craned her neck to see whether the baggage carousel designated for her flight was beginning to move. While people crowded about, none of the passengers on her flight from Paris appeared to have obtained their suitcases.

After listening to his instructions, she nodded. "I understand, Gil, dear." He had arranged for ground transport to his current address at the Gillespie estate. He told her to exit with her suitcases and take a left in the corridor. She was to walk a great distance straight ahead until she reached a desk dealing with ground transport. There she would find the company called Blue Limousine Service.

"You're sure they know where to take me? I don't have your address written down. Oh! I've got to go. The luggage is coming."

It was apparent that several of the younger male passengers had noticed her, yet none came to her assistance. After struggling with her luggage, Chloë's cart was finally loaded with all three of her items, and she exited the baggage area on her way to the car which Gil had assured her would be waiting.

The rest of the trip went smoothly. The limousine ride was longer than expected, as the car parted from the dense traffic on the westbound highway and found a quieter roadway to follow to her destination. This provided her with the opportunity to repair her hair and makeup. She checked her breath and freshened it with a quick spritz of something minty, then applied a bit of Gil's favourite perfume to her wrists, throat, and cleavage.

"The driver says we're still about five to ten minutes out," Chloë explained when she phoned Gil a second time. "You will be there for me, won't you, Gil dear?"

The traffic thinned, and she soon found herself in a wooded community of upscale homes high on the bluffs overlooking Lake Ontario. A view of the lake was apparent from the roadway intermittently during this part of the drive, and she was afforded only a quick glimpse of the houses, each a unique architectural masterpiece.

"Very nice," Chloë murmured as the limousine turned left and entered through the gate of the Gillespie estate. She checked the mirror and practised her smile—nearly forgotten during the long flight she'd spent in the economy section. She had tried for a last-minute upgrade in Paris, but had been informed that none was available. No amount of flirting could convince the airline's personnel to give her special consideration.

The architecture of the Gillespie home was distinctly modern yet somehow organic, with much glass and stone. The car followed the tear-shaped driveway and came to a halt under a dramatic portico that sheltered the main entrance from the elements. A fine spring rain began to fall just as the driver exited the limousine, taking full advantage of the portico's protection.

Chloë collected her personal items from the back seat and approached the massive, solid walnut door set into the stone structure of the entrance. The driver deposited her luggage by the door, then departed—all with barely a nod in her direction. And then Gil opened the door.

"Welcome, Chloë dear," Gil said, holding the door open and encouraging her to enter. "Just let me get your luggage." While Gil brought the luggage into the house, Chloë looked around the space, devouring the details.

She had entered into a small stone anteroom with a grate and drain recessed into the floor and two long and narrow panes of glass set near the top of the side walls, against which long bench seating was installed. Opposite the entry was another set of doors that had been left open, revealing a large foyer just beyond. Once he had again secured the outside door, they moved through the doorway and into the foyer. Gil turned toward Chloë and swept her into his arms.

"I was hoping you would come. I have so missed you, *mon trésor,*" he cooed, pressing his body tightly against hers. Coquettishly, she snuggled in close to him and looked into his eyes, batting her eyelashes in completion of the cliché. They kissed; his eagerness was apparent. The corners of Chloë's lips curved upward. They embraced, yet again, and over his shoulder she continued to survey the interior of the house.

To the left was a short hallway with two doors facing one another and a third at the end. The purpose of the rooms behind them was not readily apparent. To the right was a wall of glass overlooking a small patio with an avant-garde cascading fountain, comprised of polished-stone balls on a rough-hewn plinth. The area had lain hidden behind a stone wall and had not been visible from the driveway or entranceway. She could see that the glass continued at a ninety-degree angle where a main hall intersected the foyer. The small patio, therefore, was enclosed by glass on two sides and stone on a third while the fourth continued as an L-shaped garden in front of service rooms at the far end of the house.

"Are you ready to play, *ma minette?*"

"Oh, Gil, *mon bébé* . . . I am here to play . . . that is why I have come! But I am so sorry to say that your *minette* needs to unpack, and I would very much like to take a bath. Travel is such an ordeal. Do you not feel sorry for me, *mon nounours?* You could join me, or at least keep me company if the bathtub is too small for both of us."

In Chloë's presence, Gil regressed to adolescence. He was guileless, smirking as if on the verge of exploding and all the while hovering at the precipice of a giggle. He should have been embarrassed, but this was the effect Chloë had upon him, and he was in her thrall.

He wheeled her luggage to the elevator, located at the end of the foyer, and they ascended to the upper floor. Chloë was wide-eyed, her eyes darting about. There was a staircase encircling the elevator, and to one side, she could see the dining room. To the other side was the living room with a back wall made entirely of glass, providing a view across the pool deck and toward the pool-house with Lake Ontario off in the distance. She noticed that the walls were covered in sheets of stone containing large fossils. A black grand piano gleamed in a corner.

Chloë couldn't play piano. She couldn't play any musical instrument. Nor could she sing or dance particularly well.

And she wasn't well read. But none of this had ever been a hindrance. Chloë had other skills . . . and she was persistent. Chloë had been born in London to her French mother while her father, originally from Oldham, had been involved in some sort of self-employment before being forced by the Crown to take a long break in HMP Birmingham. As a result, Chloë was fluent in both English and French, but had little formal education. She had further honed her street smarts when she and her mother returned to France and lived in Lyon for a while.

Sometime later, Chloë had gone to Paris to seek her fortune. Chloë acquired certain skills there, and though she'd never hit the big time, they do say that persistence eventually pays off. Such people eventually get what is their due.

Gil brought Chloë to a guest bedroom next to his own. Just in case Elsa were to make another surprise visit, there at least would be no chance of her discovering something of Chloë's in his room. "If you take this room, you will have your own bathroom and plenty of room for your clothing. And you will be close to me; I am in the room directly beside yours."

"I thought we would be using the master bedroom, *mon nounours*. This room is lovely, but it is not the best, is it? And you deserve the best, *mon nounours,*" she said, gently stroking his cheek.

"Remember, my dear, this is not my estate. I am simply using it for the year while the owners, an old school friend of mine and his wife, are travelling abroad. They're currently staying in the Paris apartment. The arrangement works well for us both. Unfortunately, the master suite is locked, as are a few other rooms. I know, as I've tried their doors. They've even stored away all of their artwork. We have use of everything that isn't locked though, and if you think it is warm enough some day that you would like to swim in the pool, then let me know. I just need to contact the handy-man who tends to such things. But there is a swim spa in the pool house, and it's available to you at all times. The kitchen is in the great room on the main level, and the games room is on this floor, just down the corridor. There's even a full gymnasium on the lowest level."

Chloë shook her head. *"Non, non, mon nounours,"* she declared. "We'll get our exercise in other ways! Let me take care of my clothes and freshen up; then I'll join you. I know I'll be hungry, so why don't you prepare something for us."

Gil left to carry out her wishes. With him gone, Chloë began to draw her bath, secure in the knowledge that he wouldn't make a surprise visit. Gil was obedient, if nothing else. She disrobed and entered the large bath, easing herself into the hot water.

She enjoyed her time alone.

The next morning, Chloë awakened to discover that Gil had already left her side. She rose, catching her reflection in the full-length mirror of the wardrobe. She admired her naked form and posed, trying out various facial expressions and the subtleties in the tilt of her head. She loosened her shoulders then stretched as she moved them backward. She was pleased to see that her breasts, still perky, were lifted front and centre by her practised good posture. She turned to admire her *derrière*: firm, smooth, round. Then she heard the sound of the elevator rising.

Gil exited the elevator with the breakfast tray he had prepared for Chloë. He opened the door to her bedroom and stood for a while just inside the doorway, holding the tray and watching her. Her naked figure was crouched catlike upon the bed, stretching out as if searching for something under the bedding, near the foot of the bed. Finally, she located her prey and seized hold of it, extracting a pair of pale pink, lacy G-string panties from under the covers. She held the pose for a moment, giving Gil another opportunity to admire her body, then gracefully stepped into the lacy intimate and pulled it into position before acknowledging his presence.

Gil placed the tray on a small table and crossed the room to Chloë. The touch of her smooth alabaster skin beckoned to him, yet again. He caressed her bottom and she responded by turning her back toward him. He nibbled at the nape of her neck as he cupped her breasts in his hands. Chloë sighed audibly as they coupled and fell onto her bed. And so they passed the days.

CHAPTER 13

Kent Gillespie drew back the heavy drapes and welcomed the morning sunlight into the apartment overlooking Boulevard Murat. As the rays of sunlight brightened the room, illuminating the dust motes and causing the breakfast table settings to sparkle, he joyfully announced the start of another new day in Paris. Then he took his seat at the table and waited patiently for his wife. While he waited, he entertained thoughts of how they might celebrate their twentieth anniversary, though it was several years into the future. Kent liked to plan ahead.

"And here are our coffees: Americano for you and for me, a latte," Lucy said, taking her seat at the table. "I haven't quite got the hang of the coffee equipment in this apartment. I guess coffee isn't a priority item for your friend, Bert."

"*Merci*," Kent replied, taking the cup into his hands. "And here are the brioches and croissants, fresh from the *pâtisserie*," he said, pointing to the warm pastry nestled in a bread basket. "Well, what he may lack in coffee, he makes up for in art, doesn't he?" Kent said, nodding in the direction of the various Picassos adorning the walls. "And he does seem to love Belle Epoque furniture."

"The Belle Epoque furniture may well suit this apartment but these Picassos are not as they seem, unfortunately. You might want to advise Bert to have them properly examined, though they already should be—assuming they're insured. Then again, perhaps he knows and doesn't care."

"Oh, before I forget: I'll be phoning Albin later," Kent said. "Is there any message you'd like me to pass along?"

Albin and his sister, Helen, were long-time employees of the Gillespies and considered family. They and a more recent employee, Elinor, were charged with the maintenance of both the Gillespie estate and the summer house on L'Orté Island. Helen and her partner, Elinor, resided on the estate while Albin lived with Eve, their ageless Swedish neighbour. Although Albin and Eve's relationship had gotten off to a rough start, the subsequent four years had brought contentment to both of them.

"I can't think of anything right now, but if I do I'll let you know," Lucy answered, stirring her latte and lost in thought. "Your friend's name is Matthew Gilbert Espie. Why does he call himself 'Bert'? I could see 'Matt', or 'Gil' before 'Bert'."

"I don't know. It was a very long time ago, but I think he identified himself that way when I first met him at university. It wasn't until graduation when I learned that his first name was Matthew and not something like Bertram. Perhaps his mother called him Matthew or Matty so he decided to use something completely different for school. Kids try out all sorts of things when they're off to uni. You remember . . . " Kent sipped his Americano and wiggled his eye-brows, his eyes smiling at Lucy.

"But he calls her 'Gun,' and that is terrible!" Eve protested. "Her name is Gunilla, not 'Gun.' Gunilla is the name of my favourite Swedish ballerina." Eve was the acronym used by

Euphrosyne Vighild Ek, the Gillespie's widowed neighbour and Lucy's dear friend.

While Kent was on the phone with Albin back in Canada, Lucy passed the time chatting with Eve on her cell . . . getting her side of their ongoing saga.

"You're going to have one very confused dog, I suspect, Eve. Which name does she respond to: Gunilla or Gun?"

"Neither. I am told that golden retrievers can be stubborn. She is so sweet and lovable—just like Albin, I think. But then he goes and calls her 'Gun'!"

"Have you met your temporary neighbour's wife?"

"No. Perhaps she is invisible. I liked it better when you were home, Lucy. When are you coming back?"

"We'll be along the Mediterranean during the summer and re-evaluate for September, I guess. I'd like to visit Ireland, and Kent would like to get some suits made. He's considering a bespoke Savile Row tailor, something like that. We haven't given it much thought, but it's safe to say we'll also be heading to London at some point. It'll all depend on the progress Bert Espie makes on his house really, allowing him to live there instead of in ours."

"I've rarely seen him and I haven't talked with him since he arrived—not once in all these many months. Of course, Albin has seen him and spoken with him. He's kept a good eye on your place for you, my Albin. Did I tell you that Bert declined my invitation to dinner? So far, neither of us has seen any woman there. Are you sure his wife's coming? I think you said her name was Elsa."

"At this point, Eve, I don't know what to think. We just assumed, based on what Bert told Kent, that the house he's building up the street is for himself and his wife. So, I would have thought you'd have seen her by now."

"Gunilla visits your property often, but Bert doesn't keep your gate secured, so I'm afraid she'll get out through the open gate."

"I don't understand. How can she get onto the property in the first place? You always have your gate secured."

"Oh, Albin made a bridge, a wooden one that goes over the wall between our two properties. It looks rather like one of those classic step-bridges, the kind with an extreme arc liket you frequently see in Chinese-style gardens. He built it in a heavily-treed section, so you wouldn't notice it unless you knew where to look. It's so he can do quick checks on your property without having to go the long way around. But now Gunilla has decided to use it as well. I think maybe Gunilla likes him more than me, even though he keeps calling her 'Gun'!"

"It always comes back to that, doesn't it? What about a name the two of you can agree upon?" Eve didn't answer, so Lucy decided to switch topics. "I understand that your ornithological group spent a few days out at L'Orté Island recently. How did that go?"

"Oh, everyone enjoyed their time there. Your island house works very well for such a retreat. Albin came out as well. I think he wanted to visit with his sister. She and Elinor took good care of us, and we completed a thorough survey of the birds you have on L'Orté Island in the early spring. The OA—that's what we call our club—is arranging another visit later in the year as well. I took Gunilla, but she was on-leash when she was outside. I couldn't have her disturbing the birds we'd come to survey. When the others left, Albin and I stayed a few days longer to visit with Helen and Elinor, and then I let Gunilla run. But she stayed close by me anyway. Strange dog, but very sweet. I think Albin's influence, especially calling her 'Gun,' *makes* her strange."

"Well, you let me know when you finally meet Bert Espie's wife, okay? I'm curious. Kent has said only positive things about her, and I thought the two of you would enjoy each other's company, since I understand she's Swedish too. I have to go now, but I'll talk to you again soon. Say 'hi' to Albin for me!"

"I'll do that. Have fun. I'm going to chase squirrels with Gunilla. Bye!"

When Lucy disconnected from her call, she sat back and chuckled to herself. She heard Kent approaching from the other end of the apartment, laughing aloud.

"What's up?" Lucy asked, her face still flushed from stifling her laughter during the conversation with Eve. "Gunilla or Gun? Whose side are you on?"

"Oh, those two and that dog. Poor thing doesn't have a real name yet!" Kent exclaimed. "But I don't think you've heard the whole story, primarily because Eve doesn't actually know the whole story."

"Okay, I'll bite. What's really going on there?"

Kent plopped himself onto the most comfortable chair in the room. "It's all part of a ploy by Albin to get Eve to give up on calling the dog 'Gunilla.' He calls her 'Gun' just to irritate Eve."

"Well, he's certainly succeeded in doing that!"

"He'd rather have her called 'Nilla' as in 'vanilla,' but he really wants her named 'Cookie.' He just thinks that Eve wants to select the name herself, so he doesn't want to suggest it outright in case it gets rejected. She's a rescue pup, and her problems have been reduced to the matter of her name. I think she's going to be okay, no matter what name they finally use. She'll probably answer to 'hey you'."

"Remind me not to let you name our dog when we get one, at some point, maybe."

"He gets her to follow him over to our place when he goes to check up on things there. Then he trains her to come, calling out 'Cookie,' and treating her with dog cookies."

"That explains it. Eve was telling me that the pup crosses into our yard over a wooden bridge Albin has built over the wall, and I couldn't figure out what was so interesting on our side. You know, Eve hasn't seen Bert's wife yet. She doesn't think she's anywhere around. Have you spoken with him?"

"Yeah, I don't think that is going as we'd hoped. I should have known. Let's just say that Bert's not well-organized. I thought that perhaps he'd matured as a businessperson, but that doesn't seem to have been the case, unfortunately. His construction of the house up the street is going slowly, as if he hasn't got a clear vision of the project. That's acceptable only because this is his personal house that's being built, but it doesn't translate well when you're constructing something for a client. I can't see selling him my business. I'd rather become increasingly exclusive in the projects I agree to take on than see the company damaged by Bert biting off more than he can chew."

"I thought you knew him."

"I did too. But this update, this new Bert, is definitely not a 'new and improved' version. He was always the kind of guy who would do creative, quirky designs. Unfortunately, they were rarely of the type to translate well in the real world. He'd have been better as a Hollywood set designer maybe. He could do a good job designing for a big theme park or a themed hotel in Vegas, I think. As far as single-family dwellings are concerned, I'd limit him to fun dwellings, like cottages or second homes in remote, exotic locations. I can see him building Hobbit houses, ultra-modern igloos, tree-houses, or some of those overwater bungalows like where we stayed after leaving New Zealand. Or perhaps a garden residence like in Bali. But those tend to be built as part of a larger project. Personally, I think he's building a white elephant in our neighbourhood, but it's not my place to tell him."

"Have you ever actually met his wife?"

"Yeah, a few times, though briefly. And that was years ago. She seemed very nice, though shy, I thought. I understand they've got a couple of kids in university now. Her name is Elsa Carlsson—I thought I told you all this—very white-blonde. She's an MD, and she also has a PhD in Pharmacology. She established her own pharmaceutical firm in Gothenburg which is doing very well. I really don't understand how the two of them got together. Then again, the same thing could be said of many couples."

"Well, you can't see inside their relationship, can you? I'm sure people wonder about Eve and Albin, or Helen and Elinor—probably even you and me. I was just wondering because Eve was looking forward to meeting her as a kindred Swede, but months have come and gone and there's no Elsa."

CHAPTER 14

The day had a leisurely start. It had rained during the night, and the morning sky appeared undecided about whether it might continue periodically during the day or choose instead to clear and permit some sunshine. By mid-morning, it was decided; the sky cleared and the sun brightened the world—at least the portion in the north-west corner of Lake Ontario.

"Feel like a walk?" Albin asked. Both Eve and Gunilla responded positively to his suggestion, and it wasn't much later before the three of them were ready to set off to enjoy the freshness of the morning.

Eve was adjusting the dog's collar and preparing to secure the leash. She was chatting away to the golden in Swedish. About what was anyone's guess. Eve was convinced that Gunilla was very intelligent, because she understood Swedish. The rest of the world seemed quiet. Albin smiled, content in that moment and patient with Eve's fussing over the dog.

Suddenly both Albin and the golden froze, their attention riveted upon something they'd apparently sensed nearby. Then Albin took off running toward the wooden bridge, over the wall and into the Gillespie's yard. After a long moment, he called, "Gun!"

Eve watched as the golden broke away from her and took off after Albin. "Nilla, come back!" she called after them. "Where are you going? And why?" she cried out, exasperated with both of them. "And don't call her 'Gun'!"

Eve followed, crossing the little bridge and entering her neighbour's yard. It took but a moment for her to determine that both Albin and Nilla had gone toward the front of the house, so she did as well.

The front door was wide open and just inside the threshold, lying with his back on the floor grate in the anteroom and his feet nearest the door, was Matthew Gilbert Espie, dead—the two gunshots in his chest and one in his forehead were a dead giveaway. A slender young woman with long black hair and alabaster skin, wearing grey tights and a thin blue pullover, stood transfixed in the foyer just beyond.

Eve quickly recovered from the shock. "Let me take hold of Nilla. I'll take her home and then come back. Albin, you'll make the call to 9-1-1?" She attached Nilla's leash and took care to remove her from the scene of the crime. Eve was always efficient when under stress; it seemed to help her focus. It was the minutiae of life that sometimes confounded and overwhelmed her.

Albin phoned emergency services and kept an eye on the woman with the black hair and fair skin. She was not familiar to him. As he spoke with the 9-1-1 operator, he carefully entered the anteroom and approached the woman standing in the foyer. He tried to speak with her but she seemed too shocked or confused to answer, or perhaps she was merely unwilling. Other than the body of Matthew Gilbert Espie lying dead in the anteroom, everything within view seemed neat, clean and tidy. Albin snapped a series of photos of the crime scene, making certain to include the woman in many of the shots. She wasn't panicking—there was no emotional out-pouring at all—but she also wasn't saying anything. It was as if she were deep in thought.

It wasn't long before Eve returned. She remained under the portico, keeping near to Bert Espie's body and the woman while Albin entered his sister's apartment, located above the triple garage. Although Albin no longer lived in the apartment—and hadn't for several years—he retained full access to the residence. The apartment was empty; his sister, Helen, and her partner, Elinor, were currently in residence at the Gillespie's summerhouse on L'Orté Island in Lake Erie.

Eve watched as blood continued to drain, albeit at an ever-decreasing rate, from the body of Matthew Gilbert Espie, pooling under the floor grate in the anteroom. It seemed to take ages, though Eve's watch would disagree, before the emergency services vehicles arrived. When the police had taken her statement, she moved to the side to wait for Albin. Eventually, she decided to place a telephone call to the Gillespies in France.

"Lucy? Eve here. Bert Espie is dead." Eve wasn't inclined to mince words.

"What?? How? When?"

"Just now. Minutes ago. He was shot to death just inside your front door."

"I'll go find Kent."

"Albin will call him soon, I expect. He's just gone off into the apartment," Eve explained. "There's a woman here too. Mid-twenties, tall, lithe. She's got very white skin and long, black hair—not like how you described Elsa, the wife. I'll send you a photo. The police are already here. We'll secure the house for you, of course. I saw Albin a moment ago, but he's gone back inside now with one of the officers."

"Yeah, Albin has Kent on the phone now," Lucy informed her. "Sounds like they're viewing the security logs. Albin sent a copy of it to Kent already.

"Then you know as much as I do, maybe even more," responded Eve. "I'll give you a call again when I know something more." Eve disconnected from the call, and while keeping an eye on the woman, she waited for Albin to return.

When Albin and the officer concluded their examination of the video available in the security office, they exited and Albin secured the doors once again. "Mr. Espie hadn't been granted full access to the house," he told the officers, "as he was just staying here temporarily. Many rooms were left locked. I would like to check that the situation has not changed, that those doors that should be locked have not been tampered with." In the company of a junior officer, Albin was granted access to the house in order to verify security on behalf of the owners, Kent and Lucy Gillespie. Then he was directed by the police to leave the property. Although he was curious, he didn't learn what the police questioning of the woman had revealed.

"It was as if you and Nilla both heard something, but I heard them say that they think a silencer was used. How could you hear it?" Eve asked when the two of them returned home to an enthusiastic welcome from Nilla.

Albin smiled at her use of 'Nilla' and commented on how the two of them—he and Nilla—had dog-hearing, "My military training, I guess. Both Nilla and I detected the sound. I saw her ears perk up. It was just a different sound and shouldn't have been there. Took me a little while to figure out what it was that I'd heard. It's not the sort of thing you expect to hear, but I was sufficiently familiar with it. I called out to you when I had identified it, but I guess you misunderstood and thought I was calling Nilla by that other name. You don't like it, so I won't use it anymore."

"What's happening now? Surely, they're not going to let that woman stay in the house." Nilla brought her head under Eve's hand, so Eve stroked it gently as Nilla rested against Eve's thigh.

"No," he said. "Kent and I have our suspicions, though no one seemed interested in our opinions. Fortunately, because Kent and Lucy are the owners, they could require that woman to leave the residence and take her belongings with her. I think the police prefer to have everyone off the premises anyway. They'll stay while she packs up and goes elsewhere. The police weren't willing to share any information they obtained from her, so we don't know what she's told them. I noticed in the security log that either she or Bert had attempted to enter nearly all of the locked rooms."

"How inappropriate!"

"I agree, but that's a discussion we need not have. He's dead, and she is gone. It's a matter for the police."

"But what did the security cameras show?" Eve asked, continuing to badger Albin for more information.

"A sports car—a Ferrari, I think—drove up. The passenger got out. He was about my age I guess, so definitely older than Kent. When Bert answered the door, the passenger and he had a few words. You could see Bert nodding his head. I wish I could read lips. I've already told Kent we should upgrade the system to get audio as well. Anyway, Bert nodded, and the guy fired twice into his chest and then a third time into his forehead when his body had already fallen onto the floor grate. It looks like what I imagine a mob hit would look like. But all that mob stuff was over and done with four years ago, so this just doesn't make sense." Albin poured them each a small glass of aquavit and then sat on the sofa, beside Eve, drawing her in close. "Cookie," he said. Nilla turned to receive her treat, then resumed her position, her head resting contentedly against Eve's thigh.

Chloë packed up her few possessions, adding a few things of Gil's to her bags in the process. She secured the Benedictine and the Chartreuse Jaune, as well as the chloral hydrate and a few other drugs he'd acquired. She swiped any keys, credit cards, or money she found—things that might be of use to her. Lastly, she called for a cab. While she waited, she phoned Nate.

Her call went to his voicemail. *"Bonsoir, ç'est moi.* I've got something happening here, Nate. I need to tread carefully, but I think it'll be worth taking a chance. I have access to a house containing a variety of significant works of art. I haven't seen them, but the owners have money, and one is actually a professional artist of some renown apparently. I can just imagine the art work they have in storage! The rooms are locked; I just need to get beyond the locks and then clear them out and re-lock. Do you have anyone in Toronto you could trust with this? I've claimed to be Gil's wife. Oh, he's dead by the way—shot, but not by me. Gil's building a house up the street from the one with the artwork. I'm going to try to get his house turned over to me as his widow, and then I'll quickly sell it for cash. I may need some documents. Give me a call when you get this. I need help here. I've never done anything quite like this before, certainly not on my own. I want this, Nate; I need it. It's a great opportunity. Make it happen for me–us, *bébé!"*

CHAPTER 15

After her tests and the Mnimi treatment were completed, Elsa left Astrid in the lab and returned to her own office, beside Juji's and accessible to it by means of a door connecting the two offices, as well as from the corridor. She lay down upon the sofa to relax and could hear Juji and Leo in Juji's office, talking and laughing together. Juji's phone rang and their conversation abruptly stopped.

Elsa focused her attention on the call. *"Hallå,"* she heard Juji say, and then she continued to listen to Juji's side of the call:

"Juji Abebe . . . Elsa Carlsson's lawyer . . . I am empowered to act on her behalf in such matters . . . No, Ms. Carlsson is in the office today, but she is not available at this time. As I said, I am empowered to act on her behalf in such matters. I could forward the documents supporting this, if it is necessary . . . Yes, Matthew is Ms. Carlsson's husband . . . Matthew Gilbert Espie. Yes . . . He's been going back and forth between his apartment in Paris and a personal project near Toronto. He doesn't inform Ms. Carlsson each time he travels . . . Oh! When? . . . Did you catch whoever did it? . . . Alright . . . Alright, what is it that you need from Ms. Carlsson? . . . I can take care of that. I'll get over as soon as possible . . . Yes, I've got all the information: Homicide, Detective Inspector Patrick Brennan, your address is . . . Okay, I've got it. Thank you for calling. I'll see you soon, within the next few days most likely," Juji said.

When Juji concluded her telephone conversation, she looked across her desk toward a concerned Leo, "What's the matter, Juji?" he inquired. "You look like you've seen a ghost."

"Matthew, Elsa's husband, is dead."

"How?"

"He was shot to death in the doorway of the house where he was staying in Canada, some community just west of Toronto. They don't know any more than that at this point. I need to go over and make arrangements for the body. They'll be ready to release it by the time I arrive."

Elsa was so stunned by what she'd just overheard that she sat back up on the sofa, trying to absorb it all, but she made no move to enter Juji's office to inquire further. Numb, she tried to regain her clarity and focus.

"Are you going to tell Elsa now?" Leo asked.

"I need to tell Astrid first, then the three of us can discuss it before I decide when and how to tell her. She's been doing so well. I just don't want to stress her. However, I don't want to keep anything from her, especially news such as this. I'm not comfortable informing the children. It's nearly *fika,* so why don't we meet in the break room? I'm going to the laboratory to tell Astrid, and then we'll join you and Elsa. We can tell her after *fika*, when we've returned to her office."

When Juji and Leo exited the lawyer's office, Elsa entered and copied out all the notes Juji had taken in response to the phone call. Then she opened the safe and removed a few items she thought she would require. Leo had left his bag on the sofa, and she quickly rummaged through it, locating what she needed. Then she left.

Initially, things went well for Elsa. It was a mere ten-minute drive from Nanovo to the Gothenburg airport. Unfortunately, there were no suitable commercial flights available. The morning flights had departed already, and the afternoon flights tended to require at least one connection, the best of them involving a three-hour wait in Amsterdam. Other flights offered longer waits, often several.

Elsa had experienced such difficulty in the past and remembered there were executive jets that could be chartered. She had done so before, and this was the means she chose to transport her to Toronto. Although she would need to wait for the jet to be readied, it would nevertheless require less of a wait than she would have had at Schiphol Airport in Amsterdam. *Problem solved.*

Elsa had given the matter a lot of thought during the flight from Gothenburg. The first place she wanted to go once she landed in Toronto wasn't the police station. She wanted to see the house Matthew had been building. She even remembered the address. The Mnimi had given her mind back to her.

The taxi ride was longer than she had anticipated. The address was a considerable distance outside the city proper. The area was wooded, and the houses appeared to be architecturally designed estate homes on large lots. The taxi delivered her to a property on which sat a large, modern home displaying some rather quirky architecture—as if the architect had set out to break every rule in the book. There was no landscaping, and it wasn't apparent whether or not the house was ready for occupancy. She dismissed the car, planning to order another when she was ready to leave.

Gingerly, she picked her way through the remaining construction debris that littered the property until she arrived at the front door. She had a general idea of what to expect regarding the styling of the home's interior. Matthew had shown her the plans on one occasion. She tried the front door, but it was locked, and she didn't have the key. She wondered if the trip had been foolish. *Probably.*

Reflexively, Elsa knocked on the door. She detected movement within. When the door opened, she was greeted by a slender young woman about twenty-five years old. She had alabaster skin, piercingly blue eyes, and long, black hair. She was everything Elsa was not.

"Yes?" the young woman queried.

"I am here about Mr. Espie," Elsa responded.

"Yes?" the young woman repeated. "Do you know that Mr. Espie died recently?"

"Yes, I do. Did he die here?"

"No, at a house just down the street," the young woman said, her words tinted by a French accent.

"And what are you doing here?" Elsa asked.

"Well, I couldn't very well continue to live in that house, could I? This one isn't quite finished, but all the necessary things work, so I moved in here."

"And you are . . . ?" Elsa coaxed.

"Oh, my name is Chloë. I'm Mrs. Espie," the young woman claimed.

"Well, I think there is some confusion here, Chloë," Elsa replied. "You see, I'm the registered owner of this home: Elsa Carlsson from Gothenburg, Sweden. You can call *me* Mrs. Espie."

"Oh," Chloë responded tersely. "Perhaps you should come in then." She led Elsa into the great room. Growing tension accompanied them.

The furnishings were rudimentary and likely from an economical Scandinavian warehouse store. Elsa saw only a sofa, a television, a table, and two chairs. Someone, likely Chloë, had a love of black, grey, and blue, the colours of the upholstered furniture and Chloë's apparel.

"Would you like a cup of coffee?"

"Please. That would be nice. I've not had breakfast yet, so coffee would be very welcome," Elsa said.

She noticed bottles of Benedictine and Chartreuse Jaune on the countertop. While Chloë proceeded to make the coffee, Elsa wandered about the space. It felt like Matthew: empty.

While wandering about, she happened upon a feature she remembered Matthew mentioning. The two-metre section of wall was convex and clad in stainless steel. On either side, there was a stainless panel inlaid with seemingly random pieces of blue granite.

"I hope you don't mind your coffee black. I wasn't expecting a guest."

"I guess not," Elsa mumbled under her breath. "No, black is just fine, thank you," she said aloud. She had given the matter some thought and had questions to ask Chloë, but first she really wanted a cup of coffee.

With her back turned to Elsa, Chloë poured the coffee, then placed a cupful on the kitchen island for her. Elsa took a seat on the black upholstered sofa and sipped her coffee. The beans were Robusta, typically Matthew. As she drank more of the potent black liquid, eventually finishing her drink, she became aware of something she wished she'd noticed earlier. The coffee tasted of chloral hydrate, its bitterness well beyond that of mere Robusta beans. *Of course.* She had given Matthew the Morpheus in Paris, and he had evidently brought it with him to share with Chloë in Toronto. It was all starting to make sense to her.

Quickly, she tried to determine how much time she had before the drug took hold. She had no way of knowing how much Chloë had transferred to the cup. She also had no way of knowing if her own use of the substance many years ago—early in her relationship with Matthew—would provide her with any tolerance for the current dose. What she did know, what gave her confidence, was that she understood the effects of the drug and that they were heightened when the drug was consumed on a full stomach. Most people would have assumed the opposite. Elsa knew that, whatever the reaction, the extent of it would be lessened because she'd not eaten breakfast and had taken only a light meal on the plane.

Elsa's greatest concern, which she was forced to ignore presently, was the negative impact the chloral hydrate would have on the success of her Mnimi treatments. She knew it wasn't a good situation; nevertheless, it was the reality of the one in which she found herself.

Assuming that the chloral hydrate would eventually kick in, Elsa had to take action quickly. "So, we are the two Mrs. Espies. I married Matthew's father not so long ago. How long have you and Matthew been married?" Elsa inquired, hoping that Chloë might feel less threatened by her presence if she thought Elsa was her step-mother-in-law. It didn't seem to matter to Chloë. She took no note of what Elsa had said. Chloë had concluded—erroneously it seemed—that Gil, who Elsa called Matthew, had no family. As such, her situation was still complicated by Elsa's existence and the fact that they had met.

As a result of Chloë's indifference to Elsa's claim of being the step-mother-in-law, Elsa chose to behave as if the chemistry of the chloral hydrate was taking hold. "Oh, I'm sorry, I'm quite light-headed suddenly. I must be more exhausted than I thought, or perhaps it's just that I haven't eaten today. Where is the toilet, please?" Elsa queried. Chloë pointed down the hall.

Having seen the floor plan for the house and with her unique memory still relatively sharp due to her recent treatment, Elsa knew where the room was located but had thought it best to ask. There, she relieved herself then tried to induce herself to vomit in an effort to further reduce the amount of chloral hydrate in her system. When that failed, she slurped a generous quantity of water from the basin faucet in order to swallow a potassium tablet she had taken from Leo's kit back in Gothenburg. Then she returned to deal with Chloë.

"I have a second cup of coffee for you," Chloë said upon her return. Elsa thanked her but only pretended to drink. No matter, a moment later, the chloral hydrate finally kicked in, and Elsa lay sprawled on the floor, semi-conscious yet aware. She was unable to get her body to respond with any meaningful movement. Chloë stood above her. "Well, this hasn't gone quite as I had planned," she said, then disposed of the second cup of coffee in the kitchen sink.

Leaving Elsa sprawled on the cold floor, Chloë walked over to the panel on the left side of the curved, stainless-steel-clad section of wall and depressed one of the blue granite shapes nearer the bottom. The wall panel suddenly came alive and a curved pocket door automatically slid to the right, revealing a doorway opening into a partially finished room resembling a wine cellar of modest proportions.

Chloë was slender but not athletically so. She grabbed hold of Elsa and struggled to drag her into the small room, which was cluttered with the odds and ends needed in the final stages of finishing construction. In the awkwardness of the struggle, Chloë's elbow bumped a red button mounted on the inside panel. The door quickly slid shut, securing the two women inside the small room.

"Fuck! Okay, keypad . . . " Chloë said, speaking aloud yet to herself. "He said something about his name G-I-L . . . nope. E-S-P . . . nope. M-A-T . . . no." Chloë was becoming increasingly stressed, and rightly so. She was trying to remember what Matthew—or Gil, as she called him—had said about the panic room because that's what this room was. "C-H-L-O-E . . . oh for fuck's sake, already! E-L-S-A . . . it's not your name either. A-B-C-D . . . Nothing works!" she hollered. The panic room was soundproof. Chloë cried out in frustration and fear. She had worked herself into a heightened, nervous state which interfered with her attempts at guessing the correct code. She was wasting time trying the same codes again and again, as if a second or third try using the same input would suddenly yield a different result.

Elsa was only mildly aware of Chloë's panic. The small room was air-tight and would eventually be equipped with air and water sources, but those had yet to be installed. Chloë began to suffer a panic attack. She no longer selected numbers or letters on the keypad; she pounded at the pad with her fists until she was exhausted. Her breathing became impaired and stress consumed her. In the end, she simply fainted.

Meanwhile, Elsa completed her surrender to Morpheus and spent the time asleep on the floor of the panic room. Her own symptoms were gradually lessening, but until she was fully recovered, she needed sleep. She knew there was sufficient air—for now.

The persistence of memory is elusive. We don't always remember those things we're expected to consider the "big things." Sometimes our minds choose to remember the little things instead. Perhaps that's why we take photos of the big things, because at some level we know that without a formal record, the event will pass into oblivion. But a child may develop a positive sense of security, warmth, and roundness—memories of being nursed. Or the willingness to accept stories about fairies and sprites—memories of the tricks the light plays on reflective surfaces.

Since her parents' medical problems had first surfaced, Elsa had read voraciously, studying neuroscience, brain physiology, and the impact of various pharmaceuticals. Coupled with the work in which she was involved at Nanovo and the treatment and testing carried out by Astrid, she was well-aware that her own memory was now in jeopardy. There was no way to know precisely how the chloral hydrate might have interacted with the Mnimi, perhaps critically impairing the outcomes noted in the nascent treatments as the hypnotic interacted with the new drug. Their current theory was that new memories could not be successfully established in the presence of the chloral hydrate. This was only conjecture, of course, as they weren't prepared to jeopardize Elsa's treatment in order to study the repercussions of chloral hydrate interactions more closely.

There was music. Her favourite Chopin. In her Morpheus-induced dreams, Elsa tripped lightly over the notes, admiring their mathematical precision. There was logic in the creation of beauty. The big things were merely collections of smaller, more precise things, and they in turn were comprised of even smaller things. It was much like life. There are no big lives, no grand lives. We are born; we die. And in between, for whatever time we have, we live and interact with the world. Would the world remember each individual life? Was the world even aware of our existence? Sufficiently so to remember us? And if we were remembered, would it be accurate? Would it be a flattery or a belittlement? And what would it matter anyway? Each of us is but one note of a symphony, and it is the interplay of many notes that creates the beauty, not a lone note, especially one devoid of markers—instructions about how it is to be played.

When Elsa awakened some time later, she was initially disoriented. Then she remembered that she was in Matthew's panic room in the house in Toronto, Canada—and she had to get out. She moved deeper into the room, pushing past the construction materials, which had been left there. Finally, she located what she had trusted would be there, in the floor, the second hatch. She located the corresponding keypad and used the head of a screw to enter the code Matthew commonly used for such things: B-E-R-T. The hatch opened, and she climbed out and down the ladder into the basement. Just as her head cleared the floor, Elsa reached inside the room with a piece of wood and depressed the red button, moving quickly to toss the wood aside as the hatch slid closed above her.

During the time the hatch had been open, oxygen-rich air had entered the room, resuscitating Chloë. As her vision cleared, her eyes took in the keypad that had frustrated her, and her gaze fell upon the spot where she had last seen Elsa. She was no longer there! For a moment, this gave hope to Chloë. In her weakened state, she struggled to her feet and stumbled through the construction debris cluttering the room. In desperation, she looked for the exit Elsa had used. When she found it, it was sealed as thoroughly as the main entrance. Her eyes fell upon the second keypad, the one on the wall near the floor exit. In an excited panic, Chloë again began to enter all the variations she could think of for a passcode, but without success, yet again, and again, and again . . .

Elsa made her way from the basement level of the house and returned to the washroom she had used earlier. After drinking so much water, and with the diuretic effect of the high-caffeine Robusta coffee, her bladder was ready to burst. But this also would help to rid her body of the chloral hydrate and its metabolites. She paused to ingest another potassium tablet and washed it down with a minimum of water.

Elsa backtracked through those rooms she had wandered earlier, being careful to wipe down anything she might have touched. She identified the cup she had used, washed it, and found a place for it in the cupboard. She gathered her belongings and exited the house, retracing the steps she had taken when she first arrived.

Feeling slightly dazed by the lingering reaction to the chloral hydrate, Elsa wandered back up the roadway, until she found herself standing in front of the house whose address Matthew had given her in Paris, saying this was the house of a friend, the friend who would stay at the Paris apartment for the month of April. *The apartment will be empty soon,* Elsa thought as she called for a car to fetch her at that address.

At nearly two o'clock in the morning, traffic was light during Elsa's return to Pearson Airport in Toronto. Soon she was there, in a safe and comfortable place to think and decide what to do next.

Suddenly, it occurred to her that today was special—the day the representative from Nanovo would be guesting on "News and Notes" with Lars Andersson. Using her cellphone, she logged into the feed from 96.7 Radio Sverige.

"Good morning, Gothenburg! Lars Andersson here at 96.7 Radio Sverige. It's eight in the morning, so this must be 'News and Notes.' Why is it I feel like I'm forgetting something . . .

"Nanovo Group is researching Alzheimer's disease, bringing jobs and health to Sweden and across the EU. Don't forget: Nanovo.

"We'll meet our guest very shortly, but first I'll give you a hint about today's main topic. Let's kick things off this morning with a song from 2014 by Glen Campbell: 'I'm Not Gonna Miss You'."

Already the memory of Chloë was gone from her mind. Chloë: young, lithe, beautiful—and entombed for the foreseeable future. Elsa listened to the words of the song and smiled when she remembered Matthew. *How true*, she thought. *I'm not gonna miss you.*

Hours later, with the chloral hydrate cleared from her system, Elsa sent the messages that needed to be sent to those she had left behind at Nanovo two days earlier. Her timing was most fortuitous. Their commercial flight was just touching down in Toronto, and she received three replies all saying the same thing: "Where are you? Stay there!"

They all met in the main hall on the departure level near the Scandinavian Airline's check-in, and the foursome left together, arranging to take two adjoining rooms at an airport hotel. Without Elsa's knowledge, Juji contacted the detective inspector and arranged to meet with him and deal with whatever paperwork might be required to take Matthew home. Astrid and Leo remained at the hotel with Elsa to evaluate and treat her as best they could without resorting to a hospital.

"I think I was poisoned again with chloral hydrate, Astrid. But . . . I don't remember how or . . . when . . . or by whom? It's all gone!" Elsa was understandably upset.

"Why did you come here, Elsa?" Astrid asked.

"I happened to overhear much of Juji's conversation, enough to know that I needed to be in Toronto. I'm sorry that I upset you. And Leo, I'm sorry I took the fob for the car, but my need was too great, and I couldn't resist. I was compelled to come here, but I'm really not sure why."

"How did you get here so quickly?" Leo inquired.

"Oh, I contracted an executive jet. We can all return together when Juji returns," Elsa answered, producing a document that she gave to him. "Where did she go?"

"You took the potassium from my bag as well, Elsa. Did you ingest any?" Leo asked, readily avoiding her question.

"I don't know," came Elsa's honest reply. "Here's my bag; see what you can find." She handed her bag to him. "There's a big chunk of the day during which I can't account for my actions or whereabouts. Not knowing is such a devastatingly empty feeling!" When she said the word "empty," Elsa felt the echo of a distant memory, but it was faint.

"Well, it seems you did take some of the potassium, or perhaps you lost some. I think you took some, and it has helped you deal with the stress. That's excellent," Leo answered, his expression revealing that he was pleased that Elsa was doing so well, yet concerned that she suspected another poisoning.

Astrid appeared pensive. "Elsa, I'm going to take a blood sample. I'll test it when we return home, and we'll deal with any findings then. I have a dose of Mnimi. I don't think it would cause any problems if I administered it to you, and it may help." Astrid was doing her best, but there was little more she could do safely without taking Elsa to hospital and prolonging their stay in Toronto.

They needed to get Elsa back to Sweden, back to Nanovo.

Juji presented her passport and other credentials to Homicide Detective Inspector Patrick Brennan, a bald and stocky man with intelligent brown eyes. "How did you know to contact Nanovo about Matthew, Inspector Brennan?" she asked.

"There was a business card in Mr. Espie's wallet. We were actually surprised to learn that his wife was in Sweden, Ms. Abebe. I have a few questions, and then we can do the identification. Would you please describe *Mrs.* Espie for me?"

"Well, Mrs. Espie goes by what you would call her maiden name, Elsa Carlsson, and she would refer to herself as Dr. Carlsson."

"She's a physician?"

"She is a researcher with a medical degree as well as a PhD in pharmacology. She is the CEO and President of Nanovo Group, a pharmaceutical firm that she established about twenty years ago in Gothenburg."

"And a physical description, if you wouldn't mind."

"She is of average height and weight for a Nordic woman in her mid-forties. Her hair is a very pale blonde, nearly white, shoulder length, and usually worn up. Her eyes are a very pale blue. Why do you ask?"

"I can't really discuss that, but let's just say that it seems this office has more work to do. Do you happen to have a photo of Dr. Carlsson?" Brennan asked, and then added, "Oh, and they are—or were—actually married, right?"

"Yes, Elsa and Matthew were actually married. One of the documents I gave you is their marriage certificate. They have two children, both attending university in Gothenburg. The eldest has just completing his PhD in pharmacology. Now, for a photo . . ." Juji looked through the photos stored on her phone, hoping to find one of Elsa with Matthew. "Ah, here's a good one: Elsa with Matthew and the children."

Brennan looked at the photo. "Would you please forward a copy of that to this email address," he said, showing her the email address on one of his business cards. "Now, Mr. Espie's full name was . . .?"

"Matthew Gilbert Espie. Elsa always called him Matthew, so those of us who worked with her called him Matthew as well."

"What about 'Gil'?"

"I've never heard that diminutive used in reference to Matthew, but it's always possible. For the past several years, Matthew lived and worked primarily in France while Elsa has continued to guide the work of Nanovo in Gothenburg, where she lives on her family's old estate." Juji paused. "I have a request, Inspector Brennan."

"Yes, Ms. Abebe, go ahead," Brennan responded.

"I'd like the address and contact information for the party who owns the house in which Matthew was living when he was shot. I understand it was the home of a long-time acquaintance of his, and I'm hoping the individual might be able to assist us in dealing with the house Matthew was building—just up the street, as I understand."

Detective Inspector Brennan was taken aback. This was news to him. And it seemed to contradict some of the information that had been obtained by police when they'd responded to the call.

"Okay, like I said, we've got more work to do here before we're done with the investigation; however, if you can confirm the identity of the body for me, I see no reason to prevent you from returning to Sweden with it." Brennan rose from his chair, then asked, “By the way, why is Dr. Carlsson not able to do the identification?”

“Elsa has been ill and stress can be lethal to someone in her condition. She is under doctor’s care.”

Detective Inspector Brennan accompanied Juji to the morgue for a formal identification of Matthew’s body and then left her there to deal with the rest of the arrangements, promising to forward to her the information she had requested as soon as he could.

With assistance from the pathologist on duty, Juji was able to arrange for an immediate cremation. Elsa, Astrid, Leo, and Juji would remain in Toronto just long enough for it to be completed, then return to Gothenburg with Matthew’s cremains later that same day. They would be in Gothenburg for breakfast and at Nanovo for *fika*.

“Rashid,” called Detective Inspector Brennan upon returning to his office, “let’s bring that woman in here, the one from the Espie homicide. Pale, long black hair, said her name was Chloë and that she was his wife. Now!”

CHAPTER 16

The Air France flight out of Orly was only ninety-minutes long but delivered Lucy and Kent a world away from Paris. On its approach to the runway at Nice–Côte d'Azur Airport, the plane flew in a broad arc over the Mediterranean, Cannes in the west, then the Lérin Islands and Cap d'Antibes, before landing on the tarmac abutting the sea. The air was warm, the breeze gentle, and the sun was set ablaze in a blue sky with nary a cloud in sight.

Lucy saw that a broad smile had developed across Kent's face, and when she caught a reflection of herself in the windows of the terminal, noticed that she wore one as well and that it was equally broad. *Can't get any better than this,* she thought as they made their way through the small airport. Mark Witherspoon, their host, had suggested they send their luggage ahead, and they had followed his advice in this matter.

As they left the secure area, they paused to locate their ride. "Lucy, over there, by the doors," Kent exclaimed as he made eye contact with the tall black man displaying a card in his hand that read 'Titan,' the name of Mark's company. The man was dressed in greige walking shorts and deck shoes and wore a short-sleeved greige polo shirt. His belt and the monogram on the shirt were indigo. Given his posture and the musculature apparent on his arms and legs, he was very fit.

"Welcome to the Côte d'Azur, *Madame et Monsieur Gillespie.* Please call me O. Monsieur Witherspoon is waiting for you on board the *Theia."* His voice was deep, rich, and warm; his eyes were dark and unrevealing.

O escorted them from the airport terminal to a pristine black luxury sedan parked nearby. As O took care of their carryon luggage, placing the items in the trunk, Kent opened the back passenger door for Lucy, who clambered in so he could follow. There were several bottles of cool water waiting to quench their thirst. They each grabbed one. O made a quick telephone call, and they set off.

"Do you happen to know if our shipped luggage has arrived?" Kent asked.

"Yes, it was delivered earlier today, and the items have been placed in your stateroom. The earlier shipment of art supplies was delivered to your studio on board the *Theia.* We were uncertain whether you'd like someone to unpack for you, or if you would prefer to do that yourself, so everything has been left untouched," O explained.

"That's perfect. Thank you." Lucy chirped, her eyes absorbing the view through the darkened windows of their vehicle. The Mediterranean—its blues different from the cerulean blue of the sky but just as glorious—was dotted with small sailboats and large yachts. While there were some personal watercraft, Lucy noticed that they kept far away from shore. The greatest number of people seemed to be involved in sunbathing, swimming, and bobbing about on various inflatables.

Many of the beaches they passed offered loungers, beach umbrellas, and various amenities for a flat rate. Such sections were adjacent to beach restaurants and bars providing the sun-worshippers with food and drink during their day at the beach. Since the sections were commercial enterprises, the beach umbrellas were part of their colour scheme, and up and down the coast, clustered rows of colourful umbrellas could be seen, rather than a random assortment of people on beach towels.

"Is there sand or pebble on the beach?" Lucy asked.

"It depends. Some have had sand brought in, but other beaches have been left as shingle. There are people who prefer one over the other. The proprietors try to keep everyone happy."

Twenty minutes after leaving the airport in Nice, O announced, "To your left, you can see Le Fort Carré, which marks Port Vauban, where the *Theia* is currently berthed. Over the next four months, you likely will become very familiar with Antibes."

The roadway curved left around the harbour and approached a large plaza dotted with sculptures. Beneath the plaza, there was subterranean parking and many of the cars adjusted their position in the flow of traffic in order to access the garage space. At one end of the plaza was a massive ferris wheel. It wasn't as large as the one called the Eye of London, but it was still impressive.

"What's the ferris wheel called?" Lucy asked O.

"I have only heard it referred to as 'the big wheel.' I don't think they have named it."

At the far end of the plaza, the roadway split. One lane allowed one-way entrance to the old city through an arch in the rampart while the other remained two-way, and followed alongside the quay, an extension of the city ramparts bordering it on the sea side. Lucy noticed that the further they drove down the quay, the larger the vessels became. As their vehicle approached a gate in yet another old stone wall, Lucy caught just a glimpse of an interesting white form off in the distance on the right, amid a collection of walkways and terraces. Before she could ask him about it, O said, "Off to the right, this area is called Bastion Saint-Jaume. There, on the upper level, you can just see part of a very large white sculpture, *Le Nomade.*"

When their vehicle reached the gate in the wall, O acknowledged the security attendant, and they were waved through. The yachts here were incredibly massive and reason for the enhanced security. The *Theia* was in the fourth berth, her stern facing the dock. When they saw her, Lucy and Kent both gasped in amazement.

The motor yacht reminded Lucy of a multi-layered wedding cake. The *Theia* was both beautiful and massive, a floating island. White with indigo-blue accents and lettering, she was dazzling in the bright Mediterranean sun. She would be Lucy and Kent's home for the next four months.

O opened the car door to assist Lucy. She hoped that her gasp for air had been inaudible. It wasn't. O smiled, understandingly. Kent joined her while O retrieved their carryon luggage from the trunk. They paused for a moment to take in the awesome beauty of the *Theia*—her seven decks, one-hundred-five-metre length, and eighteen-point-five-metre beam, pristine and glistening in the sunshine. She was sleek yet possessed graceful curves. Lucy and Kent proceeded toward the gangplank jutting from the *Theia* to the quay.

As they stepped from the gangplank and onto the teak decking at the beach-club level, they were met by Mark, sporting impeccable casual attire consisting of a designer-label plissé-effect shirt in taupe with indigo splotches, indigo walking shorts, and taupe deck shoes. He wore aviator sunglasses that he removed to greet them and introduce them to the staff members gathered on deck.

Lucy had never before met Mark, so she compared her impression of him with the descriptions Kent had provided to her over the years of the men's friendship. Kent had said that Mark was about seventy-five-years old, and while the man sported a head of white hair, there was little else to suggest such an age. Thirty years Mark's junior, Kent was already greying a bit at the temples, and Lucy wondered if perhaps she were looking at *him* at some time in the future. Both men were of a similar build and very fit, though Kent was slightly taller and Mark slightly heavier.

His voice deep and booming, Mark welcomed them warmly, then introduced them to the senior staff, the command level on board the *Theia*: Captain Holm Fisker, Chef De la Cour, Bosun Anglio, Chief Engineer Walker, and the Interior Manager, Madame Papadopoulos. "You've already met O, our Head of Security. Now, a toast to welcome our guests to their new home!" And that would be the first of many glasses of champagne Lucy and Kent would enjoy on the Côte d'Azur.

After brief conversations with the executive staff, it was time for Lucy and Kent to get settled into their stateroom. "When you've got things organized as you like them and have freshened up, meet me in the lounge on this deck, and we'll show Lucy to her studio. If there's anything you need, just let Madame Papadopoulos know," Mark said, nodding to the wiry black-haired woman clutching an e-tablet. "And if, for any reason, the stateroom isn't suitable for you, well, there are others available, though eight of them are on a lower deck."

Lucy and Kent followed Madame Papadopoulos up one of two staircases flanking the infinity swim spa two decks above, through the lounge and down the hallway. The small woman walked with purpose; she was clearly in charge of such matters. "Your stateroom is on the same deck as Monsieur Witherspoon's stateroom. His door is at the end of the hall, the door on the left. And you are here," she said, stopping in front of a door on the right side of the corridor. "Actually, two staterooms have been prepared for you. There is a door linking them."

The door was opened, and Lucy was shown into the most wonderful space. The ceiling was an interior design marvel; in part a tray ceiling, in part a coffered ceiling, it combined warm sand-coloured teak with sculptural elements to define specific areas, including the sleeping area, the dressing area, and the sitting area. While the colour scheme favoured taupe and greige, the accent colour of the room was indigo. The pale carpeting, a deep-pile bespoke Chinese textile, was sculpted to resemble the patterns made by gentle waves rippling the sand. It defined the sleeping area, encircling the platform bed. Architectural features of the room were highlighted by a cladding of pale beige fine-grained marble. In some cases, the marble was sculpted by controlled sand blasting, forming distinctive shells and fish in contrast to the polished stone used elsewhere. It reminded Lucy of the fossils in the stone-clad walls of her principal rooms back home in Toronto.

They spent a moment just getting a sense of the space. The room was eight metres in width and in its length contained a lounge area, a dressing area with a safe, a full whirlpool bath, a large glass-enclosed rain shower, and a super-king-size bed. A large terrace lay just beyond the abundant and generously-sized glass doors that provided access along the starboard side.

Kent opened a door at the far end of the room, discovering his own suite beyond. It was similar to the first but with slightly different decor. "I had mentioned to Mark that we each have our own suites at home, largely due to our somewhat conflicting sleep habits. I guess this gives us the option. Why don't I move my stuff into this other suite and leave you to this one?"

Lucy's curiosity led her across the room for a peek into Kent's suite. The layout was similar, as was the impressive size, but the colour scheme was quite different. Instead of taupe and indigo, Kent's suite featured a rich Hawaiian koa wood with inlaid malachite green accents, the silky lustre of the stone melding perfectly with the highly-polished koa. The bespoke Chinese carpeting around the super-king-sized bed used the two colours in combination, creating a pattern inspired by the movement of seaweed in the currents. The sculpting of the carpet fibres enhanced the effect established by the colours. The taupe and greige continued into his suite as well, though with the abundance of koa in the suite, it did not take on the lightness of Lucy's.

"Quite honestly, Madame Papadopoulos, I'm overwhelmed by all of this," Lucy admitted. "Do you have any suggestions?"

"Please, call me *Papa*," she said, smiling. Papa suggested that it was probably best if they simply considered themselves the only guests in a particularly luxurious hotel. "Would you like me to assign a personal assistant to each of you?" she asked. "Do you have any preferences: gender, language, personality?"

"A PA sounds like a great idea, Papa. I'm rather an introvert and get lost when I paint, so someone compatible with that—not too chatty or bubbly. And female, I guess. Is that doable?" Lucy asked.

"Yes, certainly. I have someone in mind already; her name is Alice. She speaks English, French, and Swedish, which is her mother-tongue," Papa said while checking her e-tablet and making an entry. "Please excuse me while I find out what your husband may prefer. I'll return shortly."

Lucy continued to transfer her personal items to their appropriate locations within the dressing room. Soon Papa was back from Kent's suite and began to assist her.

"I'd like to continue to work on my French and my Swedish—I have a close friend and neighbour at home whose mother-tongue is Swedish, and it would be nice to improve—but I was also considering German," Lucy informed her.

"I could assign you a PA who spoke German proficiently, or just suggest you speak with O, who *is* German. Monsieur Witherspoon said you'd likely be using the fitness centre. O does training for self-defence. That way you might combine the language training with the physical training," Papa advised her.

"Sounds like a good idea, Papa," Lucy agreed. "I'm curious. What is the size of the *Theia's* crew?"

"Currently there are fifty crew members," Papa responded. "We've been over seventy upon occasion."

"Fifty! What does everyone do?"

"As I've said, just think of the *Theia* as a luxury hotel with very few guests. Most of the crew deal with engineering and systems maintenance, matters for the bosun and the chief engineer. The next largest number deal with providing for those on board, both guests and crew, so that's the operation of two galleys and two laundries, for example. And the more flexible number would be those who provide for care of the guests. O is in charge of security, and I am in charge of house-keeping matters. Your PA can show you the fitness centre, spa, sauna, massage room, beauty salon, and health centre. Remember that those rooms aren't necessarily where you need to take your treatment. The masseuse and the staff of the beauty salon can come to you here if you wish, rather than you go to them."

"I think I'm still shocked by the number in the crew. Is there a range of nationalities?"

"Oh my, yes, indeed! We must have twenty different nationalities on board."

"Does everyone speak English?"

"For the most part, yes. And many speak French. But Monsieur Witherspoon has made certain that there's always someone who can converse in the language of the ports we're visiting and the various nationalities of our guests. Over the years, that has resulted in a rather diverse crew. It's nice. Many are both multi-talented and multi-lingual."

When everything had been assigned a spot, Papa tapped her e-tablet to arrange for the transfer of their suitcases and the disposal of packaging. Then she nodded to Lucy and disappeared down the corridor.

Lucy poked her head into Kent's suite but found it empty. She suspected that he must have been more efficient and completed his tasks earlier, choosing to exit his suite directly to the corridor, rather than coming through Lucy's suite. She freshened-up quickly, changed her clothes and shoes, then went in search of Mark and his promise to take her to the studio.

By the time Lucy met Mark in the lounge, he and Kent were already deep into a discussion of the structural and functional engineering aspects of the *Theia*. ". . . and her beam is eighteen-point-five metres. You're looking at a tonnage of 7,700. She can hit twenty-two knots, but our usual cruising speed is between seventeen and twenty knots," Mark explained. "And the thing I'm the proudest of is that we have a fully-contained onboard sewage treatment plant."

"Hello, gentlemen! Lucy said in greeting. "Mark, the *Theia* is simply gorgeous! And I've been enjoying the art—all female artists so far."

"Yes, my late wife, Theia, collected art by female artists, or more accurately, *not male* artists. I've concentrated them on the decks I frequent so that I can enjoy them each day. Grab your drink, and come with me. You too, Kent. I want to show Lucy to her studio."

There was an elevator, but since the studio was on the next deck above, they opted to use a set of stairs.

"This had been a conference room, but as I'm no longer directly involved with the operation of Titan, I no longer need a conference room. What do you think, Lucy? Will this be okay for you? You'll have natural light from three sides and access to a terrace as well," Mark said as he opened the double doors to what might have been the forward lounge on some yachts. There were full-length windows along three sides, and sliding doors provided access to a private terrace that ran outside those windows. Mark had installed a Nespresso machine and some comfortable seating, but most of the room remained empty save for the crates of art supplies Lucy had arranged to have delivered.

"Oh, Mark, this is fantastic! I think you're going to be hearing lots of superlatives from me, but truly, I am simply blown-away." Lucy beamed.

Mark breathed a sigh of relief and became visibly more relaxed. Lucy had found the room suitable to her needs. He was pleased.

"I think I should unpack in here, Mark. Why don't you and Kent return to what you were doing before I interrupted you and continue with your technical discussion of the *Theia's* attributes. Engineer meets architect—it'll be days before you're all talked out. Probably involve Bosun Anglio and Chief Engineer Walker as well, I should think."

"Sounds like a good idea," Mark said. "It's nice being able to discuss these things with someone who knows and appreciates the issues."

"As opposed to those of us who just repeat the mantra, 'ooh, pretty!' I guess," Lucy said, teasingly.

"I didn't mean to suggest—" Mark began.

"I'm just kidding, Mark. Whereas Kent steps forward, toward the details, I step back and try to get a feel for the whole," Lucy offered in explanation.

"Okay, then. Enjoy your time. Do what you want, whenever you want. Just let your assistant know if there's any change in your schedule that requires accommodation, or if you leave the *Theia* for any reason. Who is your assistant?"

"Alice."

"Ah, she's a quiet one, but efficient. And you, Kent?"

"Fabrice."

"Ah, 'Fab the Fabulous.' He's quite the character. We'll leave you to it then, Lucy. Dinner is at eight tonight—casual dress, aft lounge near the swim-spa. I thought we might take a short dinner cruise, just up and down the coast between Cannes and Nice. We can go down to St. Tropez or up to Monte Carlo another day. In the meantime, if you need something, anything, just contact your assistant."

She had sensed that Mark was a bit of a father figure for Kent, and while the age difference between the two men supported that assessment, it also appeared to be unimportant to their friendship. As Mark and Kent turned to leave, Lucy caught Kent's eye; they smiled at one another and nodded in agreement. *This is perfection,* thought Lucy.

CHAPTER 17

Time passed quickly as Lucy organized the space to become her temporary studio. She contacted Alice to arrange for the removal of the packing crates and then prepared several canvases with gesso.

Lucy usually ate earlier than seemed the norm in France, especially on the Côte d'Azur. As a result, she found herself getting hungry, and with the evening meal still hours away, she decided to contact Alice with a request for a light snack.

"Hej!" Alice called upon her arrival. She brought coffee and a variety of cakes and biscuits onto the terrace where Lucy was seated, enjoying the view of sixteenth-century Fort Carré across the harbour.

"Hej!" Lucy answered. "Do you have time to sit with me and chat, Alice?" With encouragement from Lucy, Alice poured herself a cup of coffee and selected a couple of the pastries before taking a seat on the terrace. "I know about *fika*," Lucy assured her, as she selected a financier. As much as possible, Lucy kept the conversation in Swedish and used the opportunity to find out everything she could about the *Theia* and Antibes. When her Swedish failed her, she relied upon her French to communicate, eschewing the use of English in order to improve her language skills.

When their extended *fika* came to an end, Alice departed with the cart, now laden with their empty coffee cups and plates. Lucy secured the doors to the studio and returned to her stateroom to grab a shower and dress for dinner. Meanwhile, the *Theia* began her departure from Port Vauban in preparation for the dinner cruise Mark had mentioned.

The evening meal featured Lebanese dishes, providing a variety of flavourful, fresh, and visually beautiful food. The beverage was a fresh lemonade with limoncello and just a touch of rosewater. It was the perfect way to unwind and stimulate conversation—eating, drinking, and talking for hours, all the while enjoying the evening along the Côte d'Azur and the lights of the various communities they passed.

"Tell me, Mark, how did you happen to select Titan as your company's name?" Lucy asked.

"In a manner of speaking, it was named after my wife. Theia is, of course, my wife's name. We had just married in 1969, September third actually, when I incorporated Titan. We lived in Atherton, California, and she was working on her PhD at Stanford. Her area of study was the history of science, medicine, and technology, and eventually she took a position within the history department there. Shortly after meeting her, I had researched her name—in order to impress her, of course—and learned that Theia was a Titan goddess, specifically the goddess of light and shining and all things that shimmer. It is the goddess Theia who gives value to jewels and precious metals, gives them their lustre and sparkle, and makes them so appealing. The Greek poet Pindar exclaims that the most valuable entity is Theia, and after her, gold comes in at a distant second place."

Lucy smiled, enjoying Mark's detailed story. Not only was he handsome and gregarious but he was also a classicist and clearly well read.

"While I couldn't see naming my company 'Theia,' naming it 'Titan' was the next best thing. Theia was the academic. I never finished a degree. I never flunked out, but I couldn't stick with any course of study. I did engineering for a time, then computer science, business, and earth sciences. Titan grew rapidly, especially after we focused more on mining for rare earth metals. And, of course, we've been very much into the development of highly specialized electronics."

Lucy was somewhat surprised that Mark was giving the long answer to her question, but found herself interested in the information.

"And now my boys have Titan, and I have the *Theia*, though I've lost the original, *my* Theia."

"I'm so sorry, Mark." Lucy paused and after a moment added, "I understand you have two sons?"

"Yes, they're both married and with their own children. As a matter of fact, I attended a grandson's graduation at the University of Glasgow just last year, and he's now gone to work at Titan as well."

"We were shocked and saddened to hear of Theia's passing, Mark." Kent offered. "I feel fortunate to have met her back when we were discussing the Monroth project, and I was trying to get the two of you to come for the project party back in 2015."

"Thanks for your kind words, Kent. We should have; *I* should have. Theia was available. She had resigned her position when she turned sixty-five, and I think she would have especially enjoyed meeting Lucy. But I was still pretty wrapped up with Titan back then." Mark sighed.

The evening air was gentle, and Mark suggested that they move out of the lounge and onto the deck. He pointed out various landmarks as they skirted the coastline, travelling westward around Cap d'Antibes and then cruising between two of the larger Lérin islands: Île Sainte-Marguerite and the Île Saint-Honorat.

"There's a monastery that was established in the Middle Ages on Sainte-Honorat. The order, Cistercians I think, value hospitality. So, this being France, that means they make wine and more recently—as of about 150 years ago—a liqueur as well."

They lifted their glasses, delivered a spontaneous toast to France, and enjoyed a group chuckle.

"Did you ever read Voltaire or Alexander Dumas? The other island, Sainte-Marguerite, is the site of the seventeenth-century fort that housed the man in the iron mask for a time during the reign of Louis XIV. If you want to visit, just let me know, and I'll have a tender drop you off for the day. The tour is interesting, but even better, the rest of the island is covered with Aleppo pine and eucalyptus forest with all sorts of walking trails. Take a picnic lunch, and you'll have a pleasant day."

Lucy and Kent caught one another's eye, confirming their mutual interest in such an outing.

"As interesting as the story of the man in the iron mask is, the story about the guy who was imprisoned in the same cell subsequent to him is also interesting," Mark said, enticing them. "It's been a while, so I hope I get the story straight. Let's see . . . this chap, an Irishman as I recall, is doing very well financially and marries a French woman who—with the help of her brother—seeks to get rid of the Irish chap and control all his wealth. They start a whispered campaign that he's actually a threat to the king. Well, the king is rather paranoid about such things so he issues a letter with his seal, a *lettre de cachet*. Therefore, without charges or any evidence of wrongdoing, the guy is imprisoned for life, and his wife is granted free rein over all his finances. Apparently, when restoration work was being done on the cell, they came across the guy's writings. They were coiled and shoved into a crevice."

"That's simply horrible," Lucy said. "There's so much beauty here, and then to hear of something so horrible . . . somehow it just makes it seem even worse, if that's even possible."

They sat and continued to chat, the *Theia* eventually changing course to move eastward. When they again reached Cap d'Antibes, Mark began to explain, "The rocky coast here has lots of paths or *sentiers,* which have been used for many generations to provide quick and sheltered access to the water. They were very popular with smugglers, so the customs officials used to frequent the paths, trying to catch them. As a result, you'll see that many of the paths are identified as *sentier du douanières,* or customs trails.

There are some really nice walks along here and elsewhere along the coast; Cap Martin and Cap Ferrat are both good. There are numerous other shoreline walks you may enjoy as well; I understand you both like to keep active. You might want to climb the Nietzsche path, up the mountain to Eze. Theia was particularly partial to the perfumes produced there and in nearby Grasse, so that's where we get the toiletries that we stock on the *Theia*. Theia actually helped develop the bespoke scents we provide. It's not the vessel's name you see on those items, it's actually hers.

"And before I forget, the red Ferrari on the dock is at your disposal as well. Just let O know that you're planning to take it, so you're sure to have a full tank. He's got the key. O tells me that you've both requested self-defence training and that you, Lucy, are planning to work on your German. I hope you find time to paint!"

"Good point, Mark. And perhaps it's time I called it a night, gentlemen. I'm fading rapidly. I think all this fresh air is going to result in a very good night's sleep." Lucy wished them both a goodnight, moved to kiss Kent, then left the two men to continue their conversation.

CHAPTER 18

Vincenzo took the telephone call from his nephew, Carmine, who was still at work at the border checkpoint in Ventimiglia.

Vincenzo had arrived only recently in Ventimiglia, visiting with his youngest sister, Gina, and her children; Carmine was one of them and Vincenzo's favourite. Many years ago, having been born and spending his childhood at the foot of the volcano on the island of Stromboli, Vincenzo's family had moved to Messina, a town on the island of Sicily, facing the strait bearing the same name. Later, as a young adult, he had left Messina for Brindisi to find employment. Now he called Naples his home. But his plane had landed in Genoa, so he thought he would spend some time with Gina and the family on the coast, near the border with France.

"*Si*, Carmine, what is it?"

"Uncle Vincenzo, I remember when we were talking about your trip to Toronto; you said something about a Canadian by the name of Kent Gillespie? I have a good memory, so I am sure I heard right."

"Perhaps, but why do you ask about this Kent Gillespie?"

"I have a red Ferrari here, and it is being driven by a Kent Gillespie. His wife, Lucy Gillespie, is with him. They are Canadian. I have detained them entering Italy. What would you like me to do?"

"Good, Carmine. Good boy. Find out as much as you can, and slow things down a bit. If this is the Kent Gillespie I hope it is, then I need to be able to follow the car and find out where he is staying." Vincenzo ended the call and quickly made arrangements for a car.

Fortunately, the car was a blue Lamborghini. It moved like the wind. Soon, he was with Carmine at the border checkpoint—but not soon enough.

"Here are copies of their passports. And this is where they are currently staying until the end of August," Carmine explained as he handed Vincenzo a sheet of paper containing all of the pertinent information. "Today, they are spending time in Latte, but they will be returning to Antibes later today. I'm sorry I could not delay them long enough for you. If you stay close by, they will pass this way again. The Ferrari they are driving is red, and this is its registration number," he said, pointing to the information on the sheet in Vincenzo's hand. They chatted awhile longer, and eventually Carmine went back to work the rest of his shift. Vincenzo pulled the blue Lamborghini off to the side.

To pass the time, he turned to the photocopy of Kent's passport and studied it, preparing himself to follow Kent Gillespie across the border. *You look a lot like the last guy who said his name was 'Gillespie,' except he's dead now,* Vincenzo thought. He reached for his gun, but it occurred to him that he did not have it, and the one he'd used in Toronto had been left there. No matter, Vincenzo was skilled.

Sooner than he expected, the red Ferrari was in the westbound lane, waiting for a border security spot check. Vincenzo indicated to his nephew that he was ready. In short order, the red Ferrari was cleared to re-enter France. As the blue Lamborghini with Vincenzo at the wheel sped through the checkpoint after them, Carmine called out, *"In bocca al lupo!"*

"Crepi il lupo!" Vincenzo called back in reply.

Vincenzo liked to have a plan, as they had in Toronto, but this time, he'd get the right guy. If the opportunity presented itself, he would take care of Kent. If not, he would collect information, then tail Kent and take care of him another day.

He missed his old friend, Fortunato. Without Fortunato, Vincenzo would need to plan, watch the traffic, and keep an eye on Kent—all at the same time. With the many years of practise that he had accumulated, Vincenzo was confident that he could deal with this pretty boy from Canada. Although others might have expected that their ten-year age difference would give Kent an advantage; Vincenzo scoffed at that. Ultimately, *he* was the professional, not Kent.

Vincenzo and Fortunato had known the Canadian called Guilio. Vincenzo had been his partner during his days in Brindisi and Bari. Gradually, they had both begun to spend more time in Naples, and Guilio had branched out into men's fashions while Vincenzo opened a restaurant in Naples: Pomodoro del Sole. They were a good team.

Then Guilio had returned to Canada. They hadn't been as close after that, but Vincenzo had loved him like a brother. Vincenzo had contacted Guilio early in 2015 and learned that he had a few things to take care of near Toronto. He'd mentioned his frustration with someone called Kent Gillespie, who had become the bane of his existence. Guilio hadn't been too clear about it, since he was a bit drunk at the time, and so was Vincenzo, but it was clear to him that this Gillespie was a dog that needed to be put down.

And then he'd heard via the grapevine that Guilio was dead, killed in a Canadian jail later that same year. Vincenzo was incensed. Guilio had assured him that Gillespie was the root of all his troubles. Therefore, it was clear to Vincenzo that Guilio's death in jail was the fault of this Gillespie. *It was obvious.*

Vincenzo had thought about this injustice ever since then. One night in Naples, after Pomodoro del Sole had closed for the night, he and Fortunato had hatched a daring plan over a shared bottle of *grappa*. They'd fly to Canada, visit this Gillespie at his home near Toronto, and deal with him once and for all—in honour of Guilio. Fortunato would do what he did best; he would drive. It was always good to have luck on your side, and that's what Guilio had called the driver: "Lucky." They had sealed their plan with a toast to Guilio, declaring: "Hail Caesar!" Whether they were motivated by the boredom of the newly-old or by an honour quest was difficult to determine.

The plan and its execution were perfect. They'd picked up the car, a blue Ferrari, and taken a little drive to obtain the gun and silencer from contacts in Toronto who also provided them with fake identification. It was important to be prepared. When everything was in order, he and Fortunato had driven to the Gillespie estate and entered through the open gate. Fortunato referred to it as "accepting an invitation."

They found the Gillespie house set well back on a large, heavily treed lot. The driveway was in a tear shape and passed under a portico, before continuing back to the gate. The house itself was a multilevel glass and stone structure. The modernity of the building did not appeal to either Vincenzo or Fortunato.

Fortunato positioned the Ferrari to the far left on the driveway and kept the motor running while Vincenzo went to the front door. Fortunato had provided good luck. A man, who Vincenzo guessed to be in his early forties, answered the front door. Vincenzo had inquired, "Gill–es–pie?" He had said it to him slowly, clearly.

The man had distinctly said, "Yes, I am Gil Espie."

That's when Vincenzo shot him—two taps into the chest, one parting shot through the forehead, directly into his third eye. This man who had been such a thorn in the side of Guilio was finally dead. The pair of visitors rapidly departed, using the GPS system of the Ferrari to get them to the airport as efficiently as possible. The drive should have taken them thirty minutes, or less since they had a Ferrari. But Fortunato never made it—and Vincenzo missed the first plane out.

It had happened so quickly that Vincenzo remembered little of the accident itself or how he had come to know that Fortunato was dead. Having grown up on Stromboli, he had learned how to deal with life under such circumstances. Self-preservation was key, so Vincenzo had grabbed his travel bag and moved quickly to collect all of his possessions. While everyone at the accident scene was in shock, he would disappear. If he moved quickly enough, he could put critical distance between himself and this accident. No one would even know he'd been there. Soon the accident would generate interest from police services, hospital services . . . and the media.

Vincenzo quickly moved away and managed to catch a ride to a point closer to Pearson International Airport. Eventually, he arrived at the airport and moved to the next step: cleaning himself up. He had to make certain he looked pulled together and that his documents were in order.

As his head began to clear, a thought suddenly occurred to Vincenzo: the gun! He couldn't remember whether he had taken the weapon and silencer or left them behind. He searched through his fine Italian leather weekend bag and even patted himself down—twice—just to be certain. He didn't have the gun, not in his luggage and not on his person.

Now he just had to remember whether or not he'd worn gloves at the time. *Cazzo!* Had Kent Gillespie cursed them in his final moments? No wonder Guilio had hated him; now Vincenzo hated him too! He was so angry that he could have killed him a second time.

Vincenzo had scrolled through the news stories from Canada. He found no article mentioning the death of Kent Gillespie, though there had been a shooting reported in the neighbourhood he and Fortunato had visited. The article said that a Matthew Espie had been shot dead at the home of Toronto architect, Kent Gillespie, who was travelling in Europe.

Vincenzo found a report of a traffic accident on Highway 403, occurring the same day as he and Fortunato had been on that very highway, bound for Toronto's Pearson International Airport. He searched, but there wasn't much available—certainly nothing to suggest that a second person had been in the blue Ferrari. He'd gotten away successfully.

The news story appeared to be focused on the fact that the blue Ferrari had been destroyed. Although the article mentioned that next of kin were being contacted, Fortunato himself had received little attention beyond that. On the one hand this was good, yet on the other this was a slight to Fortunato. The headline of the news article referred to the twist of fate as a "boating accident." Vincenzo shook his head as he read the details. A speedboat being transported on a trailer pulled by a utility vehicle had come loose from its bindings. The utility vehicle was travelling on an overpass, angled across Highway 403. The boat had become free and momentum had propelled it off the trailer and over the guardrail. Gravity had taken care of the rest. Its narrow bow had pierced the windshield on the driver's side of the blue Ferrari, resulting in Fortunato's sudden death. Neither he nor Fortunato could have predicted that he would die in such a manner.

The first available flight back to Italy out of the Toronto airport had deposited Vincenzo in Amsterdam, and his connecting flight had delivered him to Genoa. It wasn't ideal. He'd hoped to have returned directly home to Naples. Instead, Vincenzo decided to make the most of it. He arranged to spend time with his little sister, Gina, at her home in nearby Ventimiglia. He even considered opening a second Pomodoro del Sole in nearby Sanremo. That was how he had come to be available some time later to act on Carmine's information. He was being given a second opportunity to wipe Kent Gillespie from the face of the earth. *Guilio, then Fortunato—Kent Gillespie is dangerous!*

CHAPTER 19

Vincenzo tailed the red Ferrari driven by his target. After a disappointing experience in Latte, Kent and Lucy had decided to do the touristy thing and see the sights in the old city of Menton. Lucy wore a long silk scarf about her head, its ends trailing in the warm breeze as Kent sped along the roadway. Despite the letdown that Latte had been, she was having a good time. She felt like a movie star from a bygone era and enjoyed a sweeping sense of freedom from behind her dark sunglasses, the scarf securing her fiery tresses.

Vincenzo noticed Kent move to say something to Lucy. She responded by quickly removing her scarf. He followed them on the drive along the waterfront, travelling westward on a stretch of roadway designated "Porte de France." He hoped they wouldn't stop to walk on Quai Laurent or along the beach. Neither would provide him with sufficient opportunity.

It was worse than that; they were headed for the old city. That meant that they would be climbing the stone steps and roadways up the mountain to the Basilica of Saint Michael Archangel and perhaps to the top of the hillside town and the Cimetière du Vieux Château. His hope for an opportunity to kill Kent evaporated—for the moment. Instead, he would settle for eavesdropping on their conversations, aiming to gain information which would allow him to devise a specific plan to be implemented at another time.

Lucy and Kent parked their vehicle in the newly-constructed underground parking at the Vieux Port de Menton and failed to notice a blue Lamborghini driven by a well-dressed older man with a sun-kissed complexion. When they exited their vehicle, they remained oblivious to the fact that they were being followed. They were focused on each other, and although Latte had not been the fun outing they'd hoped, they were confident they would find other experiences to fill their day.

"Perhaps you should google 'Isadora Duncan'," Kent suggested to Lucy as they walked hand-in-hand through the gate to the old city. "Specifically, her death."

"Why? Who was she?"

"She was a dancer who socialized with the likes of Gertrude Stein, Hemingway, F. Scott Fitzgerald, Picasso, and Henri Matisse here on the Côte d'Azur. She too liked to wear long, flowing silk scarves, and probably dark sunglasses, just like you. While she was a passenger in a sports car, her scarf got caught around the axle of the rear wheel. She was pulled her out of the car and strangling by her scarf. It happened in Nice, 1927," Kent explained, adding, "I didn't want to chance that happening to you!"

"I love you too," said Lucy. Kent raised their clasped hands to his lips and gave her hand a kiss.

"Okay, I've got the angel in the shot . . . if you just move your right arm a bit higher, you'll be pointing directly at Latte—or at least, I think you will," Kent advised, and Lucy did as he suggested while continuing to secure her sunhat with her left hand. He took a series of photos, then handed back her cellphone. "Sorry that Latte was disappointing for you. The town itself has been swept into Ventimiglia it seems. It's not as if we had to drive deep into Italy though, merely six kilometres, so it was no big deal in that respect. I really hoped you'd find a distant relative, or at least someone with the surname *Sarto."*

"Well, we were in the area so I thought it might be nice to see the town where my grandfather's family came from but when I've tried to search for someone using the surname, Sarto, I end up with lists of tailors instead, which I guess is understandable, since a *sarto* is a tailor." Lucy took a few moments to select the best photos and deleted the others Kent had taken. "The view from this cemetery is incredible; no matter which direction I'm looking, there's a magnificent vista. Every view is a postcard. Too bad the permanent residents up here can't enjoy it."

"I'm surprised that so many of those buried here many years ago have Anglo names. I'd have expected French and Italian, but not so much English. I wonder why," Kent said, puzzled.

"The name translates to 'Cemetery of the Old Castle.' The old castle itself must have been quite the labour-intensive build, but the view would make it well worth the effort," Lucy said.

"Yeah, for those who survived," opined Kent. "I guess it was a good location for a fortress. You can keep an eye to the east and watch what's approaching from Italy, or you can keep an eye to the west and watch what's approaching from Monaco and France. I understand that the residents of Menton have quite an independent streak, and somehow it's all due to lemons."

Lucy turned her attention away from the east and Italy, looking in the opposite direction. "What is that off to the west, just beyond Menton?"

"There's the town of Carnolès, adjacent to Menton on the far side. Then you can see Roquebrune-Cap-Martin beyond that. We could walk the path around the cape another day. Would you like to do that?"

"That sounds like a great idea. I've enjoyed our walks on the paths around Cap d'Antibes and the Nice to Villefranche-sur-Mer walk, and the one around Saint-Jean-Cap-Ferrat. All of them! How about we do that the day after tomorrow? Take a walk, maybe bring a picnic lunch?" suggested Lucy. "If we leave Antibes promptly in the morning, we can avoid a bit of the heat of the day. You think we should aim for nine?"

"Sure, but what would you like to do now?" Kent asked.

"I could use a dish of ice cream or gelato about now. Let's return to that *gelateria* we passed before we trudged up here."

"Actually, I could do with a full lunch. So, let's go down toward the Jean Cocteau Museum you noticed before we came up here. That'll take us past the old shopping district with all the little restaurants and shops, including the *gelateria.*"

They made their way back through the various levels of the terraced cemetery with its raised family plots and crypts, eventually finding themselves in front of the Chapelle des Pénitents Blancs, about halfway down the hillside. "This was a location they used in an episode of 'Poirot.' I remember this plaza in front of the church and the steps and the view . . . such fun to have recognized it!" Lucy declared.

Vincenzo followed them as they descended the slippery cobblestone walkways. He was pleased. The day after tomorrow, he would be waiting at the start of the trail, at the little monument to Le Corbusier. They would need to pass him; there was no other way to begin the path. For now, he would be content to remain and watch.

Having returned to the main plaza, Lucy secured two chairs at a small table near the fountain while Kent selected their treats. As she waited, she snapped a few photos of the crowd and considered how she might use the day as inspiration for a series of paintings. She had ideas, but they hadn't as yet achieved clarity.

Kent soon returned with dishes of limoncello gelato. "I ended up bowled over by all the flavours available, so I decided on the limoncello, because Menton is known for its lemons. I got chatting with a local, and he was telling me that Menton used to be part of Monaco, but they levied a high tax on lemons, so Menton aligned itself with France instead and has been part of France since the mid-nineteenth century."

"Oh, your French must be improving if you caught all that. Seems a bit odd to be having dessert first, doesn't it? Instead, we'll call it a palate cleanser or a frozen digestif," Lucy suggested. "Then we can have dessert later."

"What a sneaky way to rationalize getting two desserts! I approve," Kent enthused. "I also thought I'd pick up some of those kouignettes. I think they're like the *kouign amann,* those Breton pastries that Chef De la Cour served and we both really enjoyed."

"Remember, those are the fattiest dessert pastries on the planet, Kent. I'm not disagreeing at all though. Sounds yummy. I'd like one of the salted caramel and a Cointreau as well."

"I saw O here too. I don't know if it's his day off or if Mark sent him to be our bodyguard—probably the former. I was paying for the gelato, so I couldn't speak with him. Besides, on his day off the guy should be given his own space and I wouldn't want to impose. There he is now," Kent said, nodding in the direction of a shop selling limoncello."

"Nope. Sorry, that's not O. From a distance, it sure looks like him, but it's not him."

"I still think it is, but we can just ask him when we return to the *Theia.* What would you care to bet? I propose we bet one euro."

"I think I can handle that. You're on!" While she enjoyed spoonfuls of the luscious lemony gelato, Lucy examined the photos she had taken. A face in the crowd caught her attention, and she enlarged the photo to examine it more carefully. "Who does this look like?" she asked, as she turned the screen toward Kent. She could tell that he found the face familiar as well, but likely hadn't placed it. "Think back a few years ago, back to 2015."

"She looks a bit like . . . let me think . . . it's coming to me . . . Oh! The lawyer you had dealings with regarding your grandaunt Gracie's estate. Yeah, I can see the resemblance now. Perhaps Gracie was right—once you've seen a lot of people, they start to look alike. So, Juliette Garner has a doppelganger in France, though she might be a tourist here, like we are. I'd heard she disappeared from Toronto after the guy who murdered your grandaunt was killed in jail. Do you think she did it and she's on the lamb now?"

"You don't think that's actually Juliette then. Is that what you're saying?"

"Well, I don't know, but I doubt it. You don't actually think that's her, do you?" Kent inquired.

"Why not? We're here. There's nothing stopping Juliette from being here as well. If I'd noticed earlier, I'd have walked over to find out, but I was just taking random shots of the people around the fountain at the centre of the square and didn't notice the resemblance to Juliette soon enough. I'll look out for her while we're here, just in case. She probably didn't see me either . . . or it isn't Juliette." But Lucy could feel the hairs prickle at the back of her neck.

Having eaten the gelato, and now feeling cooler and rested, they resumed their leisurely stroll, first stopping to pick up the pastries and then visiting a shop to taste the limoncello being sold there. "Perhaps it's the heat and the exertion, but the liqueur tasting has really knocked me for a loop. What percentage of alcohol is it?"

Kent checked the information on the bottle of limoncello he'd purchased. "Thirty percent alcohol. And the samples were very generous. You definitely need some food. We spent so much time earlier trying to find the way to the cemetery that we're going to end up having a rather late lunch."

They selected a restaurant with a large dining terrace. Lucy ordered *moules et frites* with a bottle of sparkling mineral water; Kent decided on a slice of quiche with a small salad and a glass of *rosé* wine. The meal provided Lucy with additional time to gaze over the crowds milling about the carts on the cobblestones covering the square. She didn't see Juliette, or her doppelganger. And she took no notice of Vincenzo, always close by and attentive to their every word.

Vincenzo didn't recognize the name "Juliette," but he did recognize "Garner." His old friend, Guilio, dead already four years, had mentioned a Canadian lawyer by the last name of Garner rather frequently over the years that Vincenzo and Guilio had worked together. He planned to share that information with the old bosses after he'd taken care of Kent. He sensed that they would be interested and perhaps appreciative.

CHAPTER 20

There was a light knock at the door to the studio, as if the party knocking didn't want to intrude yet had need to do so. Lucy called out, "*Entrez*!" put aside her brushes, and wiped her hands, readying herself to deal with whatever was coming her way. It was Mark.

"Well, hi there! Have you come for a coffee?" Lucy said, already moving toward the Nespresso machine.

"I've got something to discuss with you, Lucy, but I will have that coffee. I'll take an Americano, straight up.

"Sure, Mark, just take me a few minutes here. Take a seat. They're all yours!"

Mark appeared to be in a more serious mood and didn't pick up on Lucy's comment. "Do you happen to know who said, 'When someone you love becomes a memory, the memory becomes a treasure'?" he asked.

"Nice sentiment. But no, I don't."

"Yeah, I sure can't remember—and I hate not giving credit where credit is due."

When the coffees were ready, Lucy presented Mark with his, then picked up her espresso and sat opposite him. She was going to comment further, but Mark began, "I have my memories of Theia, and it's time the various things she owned were transferred into someone else's possession." He took a sip of his Americano, then continued. "I'm talking about the collection of paintings she assembled over the years. If there is a suitable gallery, which could provide security, access . . . and is appropriate to this collection of artists, that would be ideal. I had already made some initial queries and was working with a gallery owner in Paris by the name of Bellamy, but I was never fully comfortable with him. More recently, my calls have not been returned. As far as I'm concerned, I've had it with him."

Lucy was relieved to hear that Mark was no longer dealing with Bellamy, the shady dealer and old acquaintance of Yoichi's. She thought it best not to mention that Nathan Bellamy was having legal difficulties involving art theft and forgery. And that she was somewhat responsible for his legal problems—and Kent for his capture.

"I'd be very honoured to take care of that for you, Mark. I have some ideas even now and can put out feelers to see if there are others that might be suitable. You're sure you don't want to offer it to your sons?" As the last words spilled from her mouth, she regretted asking. His reasons were his own—whatever they might be.

"No," was all he said.

"I know that I'll need all the existing documentation and authorization from you to discuss the matter and make arrangements on your behalf. What are some of the things you need to have happen to the collection, and what are some of the things you most definitely do not want to happen to it? I'll need some direction on that."

"I can get all that put together for you in short order, since it's been something I've had on the back burner awhile already. I do need to get them out of here—even if they're put into storage for a while—sometime in August, so you've not got much time, I'm afraid. I'm planning to make some security changes on the *Theia,* but I don't want to find myself easily targeted by thieves. You can have me billed for any transport costs, insurance and storage fees—whatever is required. I'll put that in the authorization." He handed Lucy a list of the works in the collection. "This list orders them according to their acquisition date," Mark said in explanation.

She began to read from the list and couldn't help but speak their names reverentially. "Carr, Slater, Goncharova, Morisot, Kahlo, Gentileschi, Kittredge . . ."

Rendered speechless, she looked at Mark with tears in her eyes—and he knew he had chosen the right person to oversee the rehoming of his late wife's priceless collection.

Lucy had not been able to return to her own creations after Mark departed from the studio. She hoped she could connect with Yoichi. The six-hour time difference would work in her favour this time, unless Yoichi was out of the studio, having a business meeting.

"Bonjour, Lucy! Gosh, I'm surprised to hear from you. Our brunch call isn't scheduled until next week—or am I wrong?"

"No, you're right. Something has come up, and I require your input."

Yoichi was intrigued. She could tell by the tone of Lucy's voice that this was somehow different. "You're alright, aren't you?"

"Yes, yes—nothing like that, but it's nice of you to ask. I have just now been put in charge of a large collection of works by a variety of artists, none male, and I need to find a home for them. Since that will take time, I need the name of a good company to handle the shipping of the items and their storage until I can arrange a suitable home for them. I'm looking for companies that would be trusted by the National Gallery, Louvre, Guggenheim, Tate . . . places like that."

"Who are the artists, and how many works are we talking here?"

"I'll email the full list to you, but we're talking Rocio Amozurrutia, Georgia O'Keefe, Annie Pootoogook . . . At quick count, I'd say twenty-four different artists."

"Ah, yeah . . ." And then Yoichi sat down. Even six-thousand kilometres away, Lucy could tell. "So, not Nate then?" Yoichi said wryly.

"Interestingly enough, Mark was considering dealing with him on this but has since changed his mind. I think Nate has a few legal problems occupying him at present," Lucy said, her tone dripping with sarcasm.

"That's an understatement," Yoichi quipped.

"I am so very relieved that I happened upon that Portnoy forgery in Nate's studio—what a coincidence, eh? You know, that Gentileschi I saw in his studio is also a fake, just as I suspected. The original is here; it's part of the Theia Witherspoon collection. I'd suspected Nate's was a fake when I first saw it but didn't know for certain. Then today, Mark spoke to me about the collection, and later I saw the original."

"I heard that they've confirmed that Nate Bellamy's 'Gentileschi' *is* a fake, but no mention was made of who owns the original. Small world. At least Nate didn't get around to making a switch of the paintings like he tried with Serge. Well, he's not the only one out there up to something, so let me look into it. Send me the information you've got, and I'll get back to you as soon as I have something. Where are they currently sitting?"

"Here, in Antibes, on board the *Theia*. Oh, another thing—it's got to be done quickly, meaning they've got to be taken into secure storage no later than August of this year. I don't understand why, but that's a requirement."

"It would be nice to bring them to Toronto, but I think it's only fair that we see what would be best for the collection and the public." They chatted awhile longer, then said their goodbyes, planning to talk again very soon.

CHAPTER 21

Two days after their first trip to Menton, Kent and Lucy returned for their planned walk and picnic. Kent found parking for the red Ferrari a short distance from the start of the seaside path which began at a monument to Le Corbusier. It was another beautiful day on the Côte d'Azur—cloudless skies, a gentle breeze off the Mediterranean, and summer temperatures. He watched as Lucy slathered on additional lotion with a high sun protection factor. Being a redhead, that was just part of her regular routine for a day in the sun. Sunglasses and a floppy sunhat completed her preparation.

They both worn featherweight hiking shoes and cargo shorts. Kent carried a small backpack filled with two bottles of cold water, apples and protein bars. It wasn't a traditional picnic; these were provisions for a trek. "Got your phone?" he asked her.

"Yup, all set," she replied, enthusiastically.

They took no notice of the older man dressed in a hooded track suit. Some people used the path as a source of challenging exercise and timed a return run. For others, it was a casual stroll or a picnic outing with plenty of stops along the way for photos. Although pleasant and polite, people tended to mind their own business.

The path was much like others they'd discovered, often related to a long history of smuggling and government attempts to counteract the illegal activity. Although they'd learned from Mark that the general term for such a path was *sentier du douanières*, certain sections tended to have acquired other names in honour of local celebrities. They had been told that the first section of today's path was called 'Sentier Le Corbusier', in honour of the architect-designer who had drowned offshore in 1965. (Lucy expected that Kent would provide her with Le Corbusier's biography during their walk.) Eventually this path merged with another, Sentier Massolin, which passed by the Cabanon of Le Corbusier, and then provided a route to Monaco.

They followed the rocky path along the western edge of the cape. Waves broke harshly against the sharp, rocky outcroppings. The clarity of the water revealed a rocky bottom and the variability in depth resulted in a variety of blues. Lucy found herself mixing paint colours in her mind to match what her eyes detected in this reality. High on a flat rock promontory in the distance, they could see the government buildings of Monaco, the principality reigned over for the past seven-hundred years by the Grimaldi family. The scene beckoned, and they increased the pace of their footfalls.

Vincenzo felt challenged by the walk. His apparel was too warm for the activity. His new athletic shoes irritated the side of his toe and the heel of his left foot. Already he was running short on water. He hoped for a public-access tap somewhere along the route. The path repeatedly involved climbing up and down rocky stairways in no discernible pattern. Other people would appear suddenly either coming toward him, or coming up behind him, having accessed the path at a different point, or merely moving at a greater speed. The opportunities to deal with Kent were not as great as Vincenzo had expected.

Nevertheless, he was highly motivated. He had been able to match Kent Gillespie's passport photo with a published photo of him in attendance at a charity function. This time Vincenzo *knew* he had the right man.

Kent and Lucy stopped for a snack just before the Sentier Massolin from the roadway atop the cliff merged with the Sentier Le Corbusier.

The area provided sufficient privacy that Vincenzo could keep an eye on them while not having to interact with them. It was a piney glade, which had developed on an old rock ledge and provided considerable space for picnickers. Waves crashed around the rocks further down the cliffside at the water's edge. Vincenzo was well-aware that he needed to act soon, or formulate another plan. The opportunities were sudden but so brief that there was no action he could take that would have been satisfactory. He watched them snacking on apples and protein bars—and water. Vincenzo was thirsty. And his feet hurt. Dehydration was exacerbating the tremor in his shooting arm. He'd need to get close to Kent in order to guarantee a kill shot.

As he wandered about the glade, Vincenzo saw that the path ahead would soon begin to follow an even more interesting route. There was a sheer cliffside up ahead. The cliffside had become unstable, and when maintenance had been carried out on the path, the entire cliffside had been covered in concrete panels to provide stability and ward off further erosion. It reminded him of the photos he had seen of the Hoover Dam project in Nevada. The path itself had been replaced by a metal walkway located about one-third of the way up from the water's edge. Below, large rocks jutted forth from the seabed. He noted the way in which the path wound around the coastline, assessing whether or not this area would be the best location for the execution of his plan—and Kent. However, he couldn't use his gun, except up close and with the silencer; there would be too great a chance of an echo in that area. He identified the direction he would plan to run during his escape after doing the deed. It was all coming together for him—except for the irritating presence of the odd runner on the path.

Lucy retrieved her cellphone from a pocket in her cargo shorts and moved toward the second path, Sentier Massolin. She asked Kent to pose near the edge of the cliff in order to get both the glade and the rocky seaside in the shot.

Vincenzo seized upon the opportunity. During the time Lucy and Kent remained focused on one another, he rushed toward Kent while simultaneously reaching for the gun he had tucked under his hoodie.

Kent detected movement and a sound which was different from that produced by the crashing surf. The distinctive sound alerted him to the approach of another walker. Out of the corner of his eye, he saw Vincenzo pull a gun from under his hoodie. Instinctively, he turned to face his attacker while simultaneously downward blocking Vincenzo's hand with force and knocking the gun from his grasp. Kent immediately snapped a front kick of his rear-positioned right leg to Vincenzo's solar plexus. Overflowing with adrenalin, Kent followed that with a powerful left rear-leg sidekick to Vincenzo's right knee, hyperextending and possibly breaking it. Having lost the use of the limb, Vincenzo also lost his balance, stumbling awkwardly toward the edge of the cliff side and falling backward over the edge. His backward descent followed the path his gun had taken onto the rocks below. A brief, muffled cry could be heard as Vincenzo fell, landing head first; his crumpled body sprawled facedown in a tidal pool refreshed by the waves.

Lucy and Kent embraced. He was physically spent, but still on an adrenaline high. They were both relieved—and confused.

Lucy had it all on video. Immediately, she contacted Mark by text and attached the video she had taken. Meanwhile, Kent phoned Mark and asked him to contact the police in Roquebrune on his behalf. There was nothing they could do for the attacker without putting their own lives in jeopardy.

Neither Lucy nor Kent noticed that another runner had happened upon the glade just as Kent had been attacked. Fortunately, he had witnessed the entire incident. He too was on the phone, and Lucy detected that he was speaking with the police.

It wasn't long before members of the various services arrived, including police and rescue. A policeman took statements from both Lucy and Kent. In his excitement, Kent lost all his French, so he was relieved that the officer was able to converse in English. However, Lucy remained completely proficient in French and arranged to provide the police with the video of the attack. The runner and the policeman with whom he had been talking took the side path toward the roadway and didn't return.

Within ninety minutes of having called Mark, he and a lawyer were present on the scene to offer assistance to Kent, should that be required. Apparently, it wasn't. The four of them watched as the attacker's body was retrieved from the rocks below, transferred to the glade, and from there to the emergency transport vehicle, parked up on the roadway.

"Well, Monsieur Gillespie, you are free to go. At some point, you may be contacted to make a formal statement, but everyone seems very clear about what occurred and that the attacker's actions directly led to his demise. It's a police matter now, and I wouldn't be concerned any further."

"Why would anyone want to harm Kent?" Lucy asked, puzzled. "Do you think this has anything to do with the shooting of Bert Espie? Perhaps it wasn't some random attack or someone intending to shoot Bert; maybe they intended to shoot Kent!" The possibility sickened her. "I'd really like to know who the attacker was. Actually, anything the police learn. Is there any hope of that?" she asked the lawyer.

The lawyer merely shrugged. "Best just to leave it alone. Trust me on this," she said, then turned and followed the departing emergency personnel to the roadway, leaving Lucy standing in the glade.

CHAPTER 22

The days passed pleasantly, though Mark could detect a heightened awareness on the part of his guests. Lucy said that she sensed someone was watching every time she and Kent went out about the area shopping or sightseeing anywhere from Cannes to Monaco. She expressed considerable concern upon returning from a seaside walk from Villefranche-sur-mer, around Cap-Ferrat, to Beaulieu-sur-mer, claiming that the two of them had been followed. Mark thought she might be suffering from a bit of paranoia, which was understandable. They weren't inclined to revisit Roquebrune-Cap-Martin.

"O is being assigned to you folks, to keep you safe and out of difficulty. Kent tells me that you've got another walk planned for tomorrow morning. You do whatever you were planning to do. If you see O, ignore him completely. And if you do notice him, let him know that upon your return, because I don't think he expects to be seen."

"We're going to walk all the way from here, down along the ramparts of the old city and beyond, following the shore all the way around Cap d'Antibes to Plage de la Garoupe. Then we'll walk the Sentier du Littoral to Avenue Mrs Beaumont on the far side of Villa Eilenroc," Kent explained.

"I'm impressed!" Mark declared. "Myself, I'm planning to enjoy a bit of Crown Royal and a baseball game on television. To each his own."

Shortly after breakfast, Lucy and Kent readied themselves for another lengthy walk. Kent sent off a quick text to O to let him know what time they were departing, and to remind him of their route. He sent a quick message off to the ever-attentive Fab as well, letting him know he was free to tend to his other duties.

O responded, his text simply saying: *OK.*

Fab responded as well, his text saying: *THNX! :)*

Once they were geared up and double-checked that they had left nothing important behind, Kent and Lucy took off on foot. They walked down the Quai des Milliardaires and through the security gate in the old wall. They waved to the attendant on duty and continued their walk along the Quai Julien Baudino, passing the smaller yachts berthed to their right. To their left, Plage de la Gravette, a sandy public beach surrounded by medieval ramparts, was already welcoming bathers, eager to spend time in the sun and bathe in the sheltered, cooling water.

Having cleared the port itself, they continued along their way, walking atop the old city ramparts, dotted with metal sculptures. As they passed behind the Marché Provençal at Cours Masséna, Lucy suggested that they purchase a few apples from a market vendor there. Their little detour led them past the Picasso Museum, and soon they reached the Archeology Museum situated inside an old seaside fort. The men playing pétanque in the nearby park remained focused on positioning their boules close to the cochonnet, and paid no attention to the two curious observers.

"There's O," Kent said, nodding his head in the direction of a nearby bench. "When we get back, I guess I'll need to tell him that we spotted him. It is O, isn't it? I mean, I already lost a euro to you in our last bet."

Lucy paused to assess the person Kent identified as O. "Nope, not O," she announced as the man stood and stretched. "Just a lookalike doing his morning Tai Chi."

"I'm still going to mention it to him—but I'm not betting you!" Kent declared, feigning his upset at having lost their Menton bet. "Oddly, whenever you've declared that it's not O—like when he's walking down the quay toward the *Theia*—you've be wrong, but whenever it happens, like now, and we ask O once we've returned to the *Theia*, then you've been right. I will say that you have been consistent."

Having rounded Pointe de l'Îlette, they proceeded along Plage de Ponteil. Shortly thereafter, they passed the sailing school. For a while they paused to watch a column of students in Sunfishes follow their instructor's boat into deeper water to catch the wind; it reminded Lucy of ducklings following their hen. They picked up the pace again, as they followed the beach promenade along the length of Plage de la Salis. For a time, they used a narrow sidewalk on the sea side of the Boulevard de Bacon, which curved around the cape to become Boulevard de la Garoupe. Finally, it was onward to Plage de la Garoupe and the Sentier du Littoral, which lay beyond. Although they had already walked several kilometres since leaving the *Theia*, it was only *now* that their walk would officially begin.

Once again, there were a great variety of people enjoying the day in a similar manner. Some ventured onto the rocks and fished, though without apparent success. Others located nooks and crannies among the rocks, which offered a bit more privacy for sunbathing, or a picnic later in the day when they would be eager for some shelter from the sun.

"I feel like there's someone watching us, Kent," Lucy said. She looked around, but saw no one suspicious. Nor did she see O, or the man Kent thought was O.

"Perhaps you're just feeling O's presence," suggested Kent, hoping that he was correct yet lacking in confidence. "I wonder if we'll hear anything much about the guy I slammed onto the rocks at the bottom of the cliff on Cap Martin."

"He tripped and fell, Kent."

"Not quite. I definitely broke his leg."

"While defending yourself and protecting me. Would you rather have lost the fight? Because that's the only alternative I can see."

"Yeah—I mean no—but it still feels like something other than self-defence. And I keep waiting to get called back to talk to the police. In that event, I'd better call Mark's lawyer to accompany me. Otherwise, I'd probably manage to dig myself a hole and crawl right into it. I just feel so guilty. I mean, the guy *died*."

"You have absolutely no reason to feel guilty, Kent. I think you should have a little talk with O. Perhaps he can help you form a clearer and more positive perspective on this. He's the one who trained you in those moves."

The path reminded Lucy of the yellow brick road from "The Wizard of Oz." A repair crew had worked to improve the path itself, but it was set amid very rough terrain, a clear path through mayhem. It traversed relatively flat surfaces and then suddenly required one to climb a collection of steep rock steps, some up, then a few down, then a turn and another step down, followed by numerous steps up and along a cliff face dense with plants—pomegranate, agave, mimosa, fig, and several types of palms—all vying for space. The variation was exhilarating.

"I've seen people run on this, but I don't really understand how they manage it. I'd trip and fall; I'm sure of it," Lucy admitted.

The path passed beneath a stone lookout platform, the platform itself forming a sheltering roof over the path. The lookout was part of one of the many large estates on Cap d'Antibes. As Mark's guests, Lucy and Kent had attended a pool party there shortly after their arrival in Antibes, meeting the philanthropist art collector who resided at the estate during the height of the summer. Lucy remembered the party primarily because of the number of celebrities she had recognized. It was a carefree and light-hearted party, and she'd had fun. Now it was a brief respite from the sun that she longed for, and the shade and seating were very appreciated, as was the water she carried—even though it was warming ever so slightly.

The sun was approaching its zenith, and Lucy was glad she'd slathered lotion on all of her exposed skin. She wore a fine white cotton outfit she had purchased locally. The proprietor had called the pants "harem pants," but all Lucy cared about was that they were comfortably loose fitting and could be secured at the ankles. The blouse she wore was voluminous and as long as a tunic. It too could be secured, at the neckline and the wrists. Whether or not the outfit was fashionable was not her concern; it was cool and helped filter the sun. *Redheads and sun have a difficult relationship.*

She had selected her footwear with the terrain in mind. They were light but supportive hiking shoes and featured several shades of blue. Mark had complimented her on her shoes, probably because they were blue and that reminded him of

Theia. With her large, very dark sunglasses and wide-brimmed floppy white sun hat, there wasn't much exposed skin at risk of burning. The sun was reflected by all of her white apparel, and O had no trouble locating them. Lucy literally glowed.

The path appeared to end at an outcropping, near the dead end of Chemin des Douaniers; however, the gate on the other side of the street was open and the pathway continued there. Lucy and Kent were familiar with the path and were pleased that the portion beyond the gate was also available, as that was not always the case. Delighted with their good fortune, they happily continued along their way.

"Honestly, Kent, I feel as if we're being followed."

"We are. By O."

"No, I don't think it's just O, though I don't see him either. I think there's a guy, but I don't see him now.

"Maybe he thought *we* were following *him,* so he's cut his walk short."

"Wouldn't that be ironic!" Lucy tittered.

They continued their walk, now along the shore of L'Anse de l'Argent Faux, and watched the boaters, swimmers, and snorkelers enjoying the sheltered bay. This location had been the subject of many of Lucy's recent paintings, and as she enjoyed the scene again, she was thankful for the inspiration it had provided her.

Soon they reached the far point on the perimeter of the Villa Eilenroc, built during the Belle Epoque by the architect who'd also designed the Paris and Monte Carlo opera houses, Charles Garnier. The villa was designated a listed property and its park a managed conservation area. Lucy and Kent located the cobble walkway and followed it upward and further inland to reach Avenue Mrs Beaumont. They continued along Avenue Mrs Beaumont, intending to connect with Boulevard de la Garoupe again and return home by reversing the route they had used on their approach. What they considered "the walk" was now done, and all that remained was a cool-down stroll back to the *Theia*, though given the heat of the day, actually cooling down was most unlikely.

Before they had walked even thirty metres along the avenue, they detected a slight commotion behind but within proximity to them. When they looked back, they could see O struggling to secure an individual who was clearly resisting. Kent hurried back to see if he might assist, but a look from O told him to stay away. He did. Moments later, O had the man in handcuffs. He was now under his control and sitting on the edge of the roadway, looking dejected. Then O used his cellphone and sent a text.

Soon, O motioned to them to approach. "He claims to be Interpol." Then he addressed the man. "Where on your person might I find identification?" He asked in French, then English, then German . . . The man indicated to O where his identification could be found, and O retrieved it. After examining it, he showed the items to Kent, then unlocked the handcuffs and returned the identification to the Interpol agent.

At that moment, Mark came running through the gate from a nearby villa and stood near O. An attractive, somewhat younger gentleman, casually though expensively dressed, and an even younger but larger and distinctly muscular and trim man stood close by. Mark spoke with the well-dressed man while the muscular man spoke a few words to O. Both men spoke in Russian to each other.

Without even talking to one another, Lucy and Kent agreed to let the others sort things out. The Interpol agent exchanged business cards with Mark and the well-dressed man.

Kent decided he wanted one as well. "Please, your card; here's one of mine," Kent said, removing a slightly battered business card from his wallet and offering it to the Interpol agent in exchange for one of his.

As the Interpol agent was handing his card to Kent, Lucy blurted out, "You're the one from Cap Martin! Kent, remember? This is the guy who witnessed the attack on you and then spoke to one of the policemen at the scene, and then the two of them seemed to just disappear. This is the same guy!"

This information merely added to the confusion over the incident.

"I think we need to have a little chat, don't you? Why don't you come see us?" Mark asked and then, looking directly at the Interpol agent, commanded, "Tomorrow afternoon at two."

The Interpol agent, Matteo Gallo, nodded and walked toward a black sedan, which had just arrived. He didn't run with his tail between his legs, but moved thoughtfully and with recognition that he was in no position to argue with a couple of billionaires and their security detail, not without the support of the agency.

"I guess that's his transportation," Lucy mumbled. She had a new and increased admiration for Mark. She had never before seen him in his business mode—this Mark was quite a different animal. And his approach seemed to be successful, even with an Interpol agent.

"Mark, by what miracle are you here and not on board the *Theia*, watching baseball and drinking Crown Royal?" Kent asked out of curiosity.

"I *was* watching baseball and drinking Crown Royal—with my friend Roman here."

Lucy sensed Kent wince a bit at the mention of "Roman." She knew it reminded him of his kidnapping experience four years earlier because that had been the kidnapper's surname.

"Lucy, Kent, this is my good friend Roman Volkov. Roman, this is the Canadian couple I promised to introduce you to, but under different circumstances," Mark said. Handshakes were shared and cheek pecks exchanged.

Roman was magnanimous and welcomed the couple into his villa, a massive structure with several sprawling outbuildings: pool house, tennis pavilion, guest house . . . The landscaping on the immense property was very precise, and the trimming of the shrubs and trees was meticulous, achieving postcard perfection. They approached the front door by following the long driveway, lined by Mediterranean cypress. Towering umbrella-shaped Aleppo pines dotted the landscape.

Kent identified the architectural style as yet another Neoclassic—lovely but in its own way predictable. Discretely, he shared with Lucy his prediction of what the furnishings would be like. "Louis d'Azur," he whispered in her ear. That was what he had come to call the style consisting of elaborate gilt French antique furnishings paired with a pale and sun-kissed Mediterranean colour scheme rather than the tapestries and elegantly patterned luxurious wallpapers, drapery, and carpeting found in similar residences further north. He was right.

CHAPTER 23

Mark had arranged for one of the rooms on board the *Theia* to be cleared and outfitted with a small conference table with seating, and by two in the afternoon of the following day, the room was ready. It was important to him that the Interpol agents *not* be provided a tour of the *Theia*, his home. The room he selected was on a lower deck, at the stern. It provided privacy from prying eyes and was soundproof, as were many of the rooms of his vessel.

At precisely two o'clock, gate security notified the *Theia* that their guests had arrived. With their car parked on the quay, the Interpol agents approached the gangplank to the *Theia*. O stood on board to receive them, check identification, and accompany them to the room.

Lucy and Kent, Mark and O, and Mark's attorney, Simone Gagnon, were already in the room, espressos in hand. The individuals took seats, with Mark's lawyer taking the chair at the head of the table. In turn, each identified themselves to the others.

The agents, Luc Anouilh and Matteo Gallo, looked uncomfortable—just as Mark hoped they would. "Monsieur Gillespie, we have some questions for you regarding your murder of Vincenzo Rizzo—" Agent Gallo began, only to be cut off by the lawyer.

"You have clarified your prejudicial stance, Agent Gallo. If you wish this situation to be clarified for everyone's benefit, I suggest you approach your questioning with an open mind. Now, are you accusing Monsieur Gillespie of murder, or was that description merely due to a lack of language skills on your part?" she said, her expression one of contained superiority, bordering on disdain.

Agent Gallo made an attempt to gain control of the situation, saying, "There is no need for either of you gentlemen," referring to Mark and O, "to be present. We'll call you if we require anything from you."

"I don't think so, Agent Gallo. Kent and Lucy are my guests, and O here provides security in accordance with my wishes. While they are my guests, I am most certainly participating in this discussion."

Agent Anouilh must have known that their options were limited; he picked up the thread of the questioning while Agent Gallo sat beside him and scowled. "Monsieur Gillespie, did you know or know of Vincenzo Rizzo?" Agent Anouilh inquired.

"No," Kent replied, tersely.

"How did you come to be at that location upon that day?"

"My wife and I had decided two days prior to walk the seaside paths around Cap Martin."

"What caused you to make this decision two days previous?"

"Her grandfather's family immigrated to Canada from Latte and she knew very little about them, so she was interested in finding out a bit more. We drove across the border into Italy two days earlier and visited Latte, but there wasn't much to see, and we didn't even find anyone with the same surname."

"And what surname would that be?"

"Sarto."

"And how does that lead to the death of Vincenzo Rizzo two days later?"

"I don't know. But after we spent time in Menton, we decided that we'd like to return to walk the path around Cap Martin two days later."

"Where were you when you made this decision?"

"Well, we discussed it during lunch in Menton."

"And where did you have lunch?"

"I don't recall the name of the place. There were tables set outside, in the plaza. If it's important, I could bring up the credit card transaction for you." Kent outlined, in as much detail as he could, his actions that day in Menton.

"Madame Gillespie, is this description provided by your husband complete, or is there something you would like to correct, or add perhaps?" Agent Gallo inquired, urging Lucy to speak.

"Everything he's told you is precisely what happened, but of course, I can't speak to those parts where I wasn't present," Lucy said.

"And during that time, what is it that you were doing?" he asked.

"Ah, I was very hot and thirsty, so I was just waiting rather eagerly for him to return."

"And that's all that you did?"

"Well," Lucy said, thinking back to that day, "I watched the crowd, and took some photos of the crowd. Being an artist, I take a lot of photographs, most of which are then deleted as junk."

"Do you have any of those photographs?" Agent Gallo asked.

"I don't know. I may have deleted them. They'd be on my phone," Lucy said, then checked the files on her cellphone. "I've found the ones from Menton. What is your number? I'll send them to you." Lucy saw nothing wrong in providing the agents with those photos, which would show random individuals, but she wasn't prepared to hand over her phone to Interpol agents.

When Agent Gallo received the photo file, he immediately forwarded a copy to Agent Anouilh and the two agents examined the photos. There appeared to be something—or someone—in certain of the photos that excited them.

"Do you recognize any of the people in these photographs?" Agent Anouilh inquired.

"Well, I thought I did. But Kent and I agreed it was just someone who looked a bit like someone we'd known over several months in Toronto four years ago. We've not seen or heard from her, or anything about her, since then."

"And can you point her out in your photos?"

Lucy located a photo containing the person she thought looked like Juliette, enlarged it, and showed it to the agents.

"Who was she to you, this person in Toronto?"

"Her name was Juliette Garner; and she was my grandaunt Gracie Hogan's lawyer. My grandaunt was murdered, and Juliette was the lawyer who settled the estate."

"Murdered? Such things occur frequently within your circle of acquaintances?"

"Agent Gallo!" Simone Gagnon admonished him with tone more than words.

"Did you speak with her?" he asked.

"No."

"Why not?"

"Because I first noticed her in the photo while I was reviewing them, waiting for Kent to return to our table. By the time I looked at the crowd to see if she was still there, people had shifted position, and I couldn't spot her. I had been uncertain anyway."

The agents talked quietly to one another for a time, then Agent Anouilh asked, "Who murdered your grandaunt?"

"The man was arrested, but died while in custody. He had several names. I knew him as Caesar from when I was a very young child, and Kent knew him as Julius Roman—he was Kent's tailor, actually. He called himself some other name as well when he dated a friend of ours, but I don't recall what that was," Lucy explained. "Why do you ask?"

"Did you ever hear the name Giulio Roman?

"No. Why do you ask?"

"Vincenzo Rizzo was an acquaintance, or perhaps we should say a business partner, of Giulio Roman. In Italy, Giulio and Julius are the same," Agent Anouilh explained. "So Giulio Roman is the same as Julius Roman."

Shocked, Lucy and Kent looked at one another in silent communication.

Then Agent Gallo asked, "Can you think of any reason that Vincenzo Rizzo would have recently returned to Italy from Canada?"

"No. Like I said, I don't know the man." Then it occurred to her. "What if he meant to harm Kent?"

"Well, that is what you claim occurred on the path at Cap Martin, isn't it?" Agent Gallo said, an attitude creeping back into his voice.

"No, you don't understand," Lucy said, trying to clarify. "We let a friend stay in our home while we've been travelling, and he was shot and killed at our doorway. What if that was this Vincenzo, and he thought that Bert was Kent?"

"So," continued Agent Gallo, "the name of this victim in Toronto—so we can verify this with the police there—is Bert—"

Kent interrupted at that point. "His full name was Matthew Gilbert Espie, and he was approximately my height, build, and colouring."

"And his occupation?" Agent Gallo queried.

"Architect and interior designer."

"Why was he living in your home?"

"Well, we plan to be travelling for about a year, and Bert is, or was, building a home for himself and his wife on a property nearby. We stayed at their apartment in Paris in April."

"So, he lived in Paris then?"

"Well, part of the time. His wife, Elsa Carlsson, is the head of Nanovo, the pharmaceutical firm, and they also live—or lived—at her family home near Gothenburg, Sweden," Kent explained, rapidly tiring of the unproductive back and forth with the agents. "Look, I'm willing to help you do whatever it is you are trying to do, but this is rapidly becoming tedious and frankly, irritating."

Agent Anouilh took over from his partner. "Madame Gillespie, can you tell me why your name has come up recently in an Interpol file?"

Mark was taken aback by the question.

"How would *I* know? Perhaps *you* could tell *me!*" Lucy responded, much to Mark's delight.

"Do you recognize the name Yoichi Song?" Agent Anouilh asked.

"Of course. I'm an artist, and she's my agent. She owns the Song Gallery in Toronto."

"Yoichi Song mentioned your name in conjunction with a man currently in our custody, Nathan Bellamy." Mark's head snapped in Lucy's direction at the mention of Bellamy.

"Yes, Yoichi had dated him when we were in school many years ago. He studied art as well and had opened an art gallery in Paris. He'd contacted her recently with a business proposal. She didn't feel she knew him well enough and wanted me to provide an assessment of the man and his business—just a sense of the situation—to help her make a decision. While I was there, I happened to see some things that suggested improprieties at the very least. I reported my findings to Yoichi, and she took care of the rest. Actually, Kent foiled an attempt by this person to steal a painting from Serge Proulx, a friend of ours in Paris. Although the local police were investigating the attempted theft, I understand from Yoichi that Interpol is now involved in that case as well. Perhaps that's the source of my name in your files. Why on earth would that be something worth your mentioning at this time?"

Lucy was irritated that the agent had identified Nate Bellamy by name in Mark's presence. She didn't want him to be on edge about the re-homing of Theia's art collection. Later, she and Kent would need to share with him the complete tale of Nate's attempted theft of Serge's Portnoy. While Kent had been finding the questioning tedious and irritating, Lucy had officially reached the end of her patience with the entire process.

"Look, I thought we might clear the air and bring clarity to whatever has been going on, but that doesn't much appear to be happening. So, gentlemen, I am leaving," Lucy announced.

Agent Anouilh stood and spoke directly to Lucy, "Madame, I understand. Truly I do. But just give me a moment, please." Then, with a nod to Kent, he said, "I shall send you each the same message now, to your phones. Please read it carefully. It will answer many, perhaps all, of your questions. The message will delete automatically within five minutes of being sent. It is for your eyes only. I must insist that you do not share the contents of the message with anyone else, including those present with you today, as it could jeopardize the lives of others. I cannot stress this enough."

Mark, O, Simone, and Agent Gallo withdrew from the room. Lucy and Kent were left at the table with Agent Anouilh, awaiting the message. It arrived; they read it. They looked at one another and understood. Then it was gone.

"I never told her, Kent, but I knew some of that already," Lucy said quietly.

Lucy, Kent:

Juliette Garner here; remember me?

I was surprised to see you two in Menton, and I guess you were surprised to see me as well. You seemed to have recognized me, Lucy. Since you're reading this, I guess that has been confirmed.

Please—I implore you both—do not mention my name to anyone at any time, concerning any matter whatsoever. I need to be forgotten. The Interpol agents are merely trying to protect me from harm.

I don't know why or how, but it appears that you've become, or remain, entangled in the disreputable activities of certain members of my family's law firm. Lucy, your grandfather used the alias 'John Taylor,' which Bennett Garner created for him. That alias was reserved for dealings with the American gangsters who had contracted to receive liquor being smuggled through L'Orté Point and into the USA during Prohibition.

Bennett's son, Clarence, began to work for the mob. He acted as their lawyer in matters other than the liquor smuggling operation and was actually the person who facilitated Julius Roman's movements between Canada and Italy. I don't know who at the firm continued that sort of work after Clarence retired and finally died.

Someone definitely did, but I don't know who. I wasn't able to figure that out, just that someone among us was still involved. Therefore, I decided to leave the firm and offer my services to Interpol. It's amazing what you can find when digging through old files. This has put me on their hit list, I guess. Nevertheless, I think I sleep better at night now than if I'd merely continued working for Garner & Garner.

I don't know what happened to Julius Roman in jail; I don't know who killed him, or had him killed. My guess is that it was someone well-placed who cannot afford the negative publicity Julius' accusations might have delivered. I doubt that person has any interest in the two of you. Who knows why Julius was so fixated on you, Kent? And I really don't understand the attack by Vincenzo Rizzo near Menton either. Makes no sense to me.

I just wanted you to know a bit about what's happening . . . or at least why it's happening. You're not seeing things after all!

But please, for my safety—and apparently yours as well—just forget about me. And if you should happen to see me again sometime, don't acknowledge me. I'm a stranger in your life, and you are strangers in mine.

I'm trusting you both with my life.

I wish you all the best,

Juliette

CHAPTER 24

O had been sent by Mark to collect Lucy and Kent and escort them to his office, just off his stateroom and near O's stateroom and the security office. This was clearly unusual and, as a result, caused them some concern. Lucy wondered if it might have something to do with their recent discussion of Nathan Bellamy; the revelations may have unnerved Mark. O said nothing as they approached Mark's office.

The door was wide open, and Mark seemed pleased to see them. He arose and crossed the room to a grouping of five comfortable chairs gathered about a low table. Their preferred beverages were clustered at the centre on the table. He gestured to them to take a seat. "Please, make yourselves comfortable. You're probably wondering why I've asked you to my office for this little meeting," he said, smiling. "I think it's time we had a little chat. I wasn't certain this would be necessary, but it appears that it is. Usually, we can get away without such a gathering—"

Mark's phone rang and interrupted him. He checked to identify the caller, then announced, "Sorry about this. Please, just give me a moment to take care of something."

Mark rose from his chair and crossed back to his desk, but portions of the conversation were audible to Lucy and Kent. ". . . No, I'm ending it . . . You're young. Find someone else, or do something else . . . I'm sorry you feel like that . . . It's not as if we haven't talked about this before . . . I told you how I feel about it . . ."

Finally, having ended his call, he returned to his guests, grabbed his beverage, sat down, and simply stated, "Just some fun on the side that was time to bring to an end." The silence was deafening. Lucy and Kent each sipped their drinks, neither one knowing what to say. Mark looked at them, apparently confused, then bemused. "Oh my, you didn't think . . . you couldn't have!" Mark began to laugh, and O, usually stoic, smirked.

"That was Rayan. He's a young chap, an engineer I met at a conference a few years back, and I've been funding a mining venture he's been working on in his native Pakistan. Apparently, the Chinese are interested in buying the mine and the permits need to be updated periodically, and that requires money and more money. But you see, the Chinese tend to play a long game—a very long game—and I'm no longer interested. I think it would be best if Rayan just pulled out and found something else to do. This is his first project, so it'll break his heart, I know, but that's better than spending the rest of his life waiting for this one deal to pan out. No matter how long he lives, the Chinese company can wait even longer, and they very likely will do just that. As soon as he pulls out, they'll snatch up all the permits and get on with mining the site," Mark explained. "Like Kenny Rogers says in that song, 'Ya gotta know when to hold 'em, know when to fold 'em'." Mark sang the last bit, and his voice wasn't half bad.

"None of it would have been our business anyway," Kent said. "Still, I must say, you had me going there."

"Me too," Lucy chimed in, sipping her limeade.

"Well, that turned out to be an amusing interruption. Let's see, where was I? Ah yes, the reason for this little gathering.

Lucy, you've got a good eye. No one else has ever noticed what you have." Lucy looked at Kent and he at her, but that brought no clarity to the matter, so they waited for Mark to continue.

"Several times you've commented that O wasn't O—"

"I'm sorry, but—" Lucy began, feeling a need to defend her perception.

"Just bear with me, okay?" Mark urged. "You've based this on what, precisely?"

"Body language, I guess. The way he walks sometimes isn't the way O usually walks. It's especially apparent when there are no other identifying features. But then, when he gets close, it turns out I'm wrong, and it's O."

"No, in these instances, you've been right each and every time. Amazing." Mark glanced over at O and shook his head in wonderment.

Now Lucy and Kent were clearly confused.

"You've met O, here," Mark said, acknowledging O, but have you ever wondered why he's called O?"

"Actually, no. It feels like prying to ask. If someone wants me to know something like that, I assume I'll be told," Lucy explained.

"Well, you are now going to be told. O's full name is Oko Owusu."

Mark nodded to O, who picked up the thread of Mark's explanation. "My name, Oko, means 'elder twin'." He paused for the words to sink in. "The person you have identified as *not me* is my younger brother, Ebo. Ebo means 'Tuesday,' the day we were born. Ebo, *kommen sie,* brother!"

Ebo, his identical twin, entered through the security office, smiling. "Surprise!" he said cheerily to Lucy. "I too am called O."

"How wonderful!" Lucy exclaimed. "You probably work very well together, being twins."

"Yes, it has its advantages in our line of work. We were both in the KSK, that's Kommando Specialkrafte, the German Special Operations Unit, and I think that the various injuries we've sustained over our careers has led to the slight physical differences between us. Also, I am more handsome than my much older brother, don't you agree?" Ebo said.

"But I am smarter," suggested Oko.

"I am not getting involved in that kind of a discussion!" Lucy said, laughingly. "Well, it's nice to know that I'm not bonkers. Thanks for clearing that up for me. For us. But I guess that we should now forget what we've just learned, right?"

"Yes, Lucy, I'm afraid so," Mark instructed. "The fewer people who pick up on this, the better. Actually, I considered just telling you, Lucy, and not Kent, but I didn't like asking you to keep a secret from him."

"Please remember, Madame Gillespie, that Oko and I share what in German is called *hellsehen*. Oko, English word?"

"Ebo is referring to what you might call a sixth sense, telepathy or clairvoyance," Oko clarified. "Twins do connect on a level that defies explanation but is nevertheless understood by the other twin. We have no desire for you to refer to us by our individual names. It is appropriate to refer to us together, or separately, as O."

"Thanks, Mark. Thanks . . . O," Lucy said, nodding to each of them in turn. "Speaking for both of us, we promise to keep *stumm.*"

CHAPTER 25

Lucy had risen early, and she had already spent several hours painting when she heard Kent's knock at the door of her studio.

"Good morning. Sleep well?" he asked in greeting as he entered, careful not to sneak a look toward her works in progress.

"Good morning to you too! I felt so inspired this morning, I thought I'd get an early start."

"Sorry if I disturbed you, but I wanted to check in with you before we leave. Mark and I are taking a drive up the coast, toward Monaco. It's another gorgeous day, and Mark wants to show me something."

"It's time for me to take a short break and grab some breakfast. I'll come down with you. What is it Mark wants to show you?"

"Not sure, but it sounds like a construction project of some sort. Guess I'll find out when we get there."

As they left the former conference room turned studio, Lucy realized that she actually felt at home on the *Theia* and in this place and time. She suspected that her new series of paintings would reflect this. Life was good, and she was confident her paintings would convey that sense.

"Good morning, Mark. I hear I'm to be abandoned by you two gentlemen."

"Good morning, my dear. Abandoned but for the crew and O, who will keep you safe. But may I suggest you see us off? I want to show you my toy."

They left the deck of the *Theia* and stood awhile on the quay while O brought a car out of the secure storage unit set on the quay. "The car is carried with other tenders, and it takes time to position it back on land, so I arrange for secure storage whenever we're berthed," Mark explained.

This wasn't just any vehicle. Lucy thought she heard Kent gasp; she could sense his excitement. Although she didn't consider herself a car person, she had to admit that this vehicle was impressively beautiful. The two-tone Mediterranean blue Corsini Arion left her bedazzled.

"I ordered the Arion when I decided to retire. My sons thought I was crazy, but I could tell they were already wondering which of them would be the one to inherit it one day. I told them that neither of them would—I'm taking it with me!"

"Your car is gorgeous, Mark—I mean it—it's simply amazing. The two of you have a great day, and I'll see you when I see you. I'm going to enjoy a croissant and a latte while I breathe in this glorious air, and then I'm returning to my work." She kissed Kent goodbye and waved as the coupe exited through the security gate defining this section of Port Vauban. She was aware that all eyes were on the men in the Arion.

Lucy decided to take her breakfast on the deck just outside the studio and near her paintings. Kitchen staff transported the necessary items, including a small table, upon which they arranged a ramekin of goat yoghurt, another of Perigord strawberries, and a basket of butter croissants, still warm from the oven. The staff member poured Lucy's latte, then departed, leaving Lucy to her thoughts and the new day.

Lucy's canvases were large, the scenes inviting the viewer to step into them. They were light, delicate, and bright—reflecting her sense of the Côte d'Azur. The style evoked one of modern impressionism, suggesting sparkling water and the movement of hot air. Over the past four years, her brushwork had become increasingly free and less fastidious than it had been earlier in her career, and both she and Yoichi agreed that the change was for the better. It was also very likely due to the resolution of things concerning her past.

So far, she had produced only coastal paintings, focusing on the crystal blues and greens of the Mediterranean Sea and the pale-coloured, jagged dolomite and aragonite rock cliffs at the seaside. In some, there was a suggestion of an umbrella pine's green needles or the red of its bark. Others hinted at the flowering shrubs abundant in the region—the fuchsia, magenta, purple, red, orange, white, and yellow of bougainvillea.

When I complete this lot, I may play with flowers awhile, she thought, not planning to paint them realistically, as that had been done so often before, but instead to paint their exuberance, to capture and then share their joy of existence. She felt she now more deeply understood Picasso's *Joie de Vivre.* Creative ideas swirled in her mind, rising—it seemed—from the depths of the magical Mediterranean. *C'mon, first things first, time to focus. These all need finishing touches.*

In some cases, the paintings included bathers in colourful swimsuits, and she was pleased with the transparency she had achieved in distinguishing those body parts above water from those below. One could appreciate the appealing clarity of the water and sense its coolness in contrast to the heat of the day. In some, there were people she had painted standing, sitting, or lying on the rocks, sunbathing, the heat expressed as a shimmer on their bodies. Just as one could sense the coolness of the water, the warmth of the sun on the bathers' skin was palpable. She was pleased with the success she'd had in depicting children with their beachballs. She was delighted with everything. It occurred to her that her adults communicated a sense of childlike joy and playfulness, yet her children, filled with wonder, appeared more content and serene than any parent might think possible for the younger set.

She was pleased with the boats she had included in some of the paintings—just small boats, often sailboats, the kind an average family might have for a Sunday outing. Often, they were depicted at odd angles, as she had viewed them from above while standing at the edge of a cliff.

Somehow the paler shades worked, even when the hues were vibrant and, in some cases, nearly neon. Lucy was very pleased with herself. Generally very self-critical, this was a relatively new sensation for her. She took a dagger striper in hand and dipped it in the black acrylic on her palette. "Awen," she said aloud as she signed the painting with a flourish, announcing its completion. She then went on to sign all the others that she considered complete. She looked forward to sharing her accomplishment with Kent when he and Mark returned later in the day.

CHAPTER 26

Mark exited through the security gate defining the more exclusive section of the port, the area reserved for the berths of the mega yachts such as the *Theia*. The roadway snaked around the port, initially following a portion of the old city wall, a small public beach to the left and the berths of smaller yachts to the right. Mark continued past the large plaza that formed the roof of a subterranean garage complex and featured sculptural installations, some of which also dotted the Antibes' ramparts at various spots along the old walled city. The massive ferris wheel, providing tourists with views of the town, was already doing a booming business in advance of the rising temperatures expected later in the day. It wasn't long before Mark connected with a major roadway and turned eastward.

Traffic remained light despite the season. It was still early in the morning and a Tuesday. Kent could tell that Mark wanted to let the Arion run as free as he suspected it could. Whenever it was possible, Mark would accelerate, achieving speeds beyond that permitted, ever mindful that the French police would enforce the speed restrictions—unlike the Italian police, according to Mark. The Arion remained in the passing lane.

As they sped along, Mark said, "I know you're not as much of a car person as I am, Kent, so let me summarize a few things for you here. The interior is completely customized. The wood detail you see is Hawaiian Koa. It's protected. The tree must be on private land and fall naturally—can't be harvested—before the wood can be taken and sold to be used. The rest is pretty much self-evident. I take it, you're comfortable?"

"Yes, very. The ride is smooth and amazingly quiet. There's quite a bit of koa used in my stateroom. Is it a favourite of yours?" They had already cleared the northern portion of Nice and were approaching Villefranche-sur-Mer. Cap Ferrat jutted outward on Kent's right, and Beaulieu-sur-Mer lay just beyond.

A Lamborghini suddenly appeared behind them, but Mark remained in the passing lane. He chuckled. "Unless he's a tourist with a rental, he knows we're faster. There's only so fast you can go here with speed limits and a roadway cluttered with sensible people, unlike us." The Lamborghini appeared content to remain directly behind them. "I think you said that you have an Escalade; that's a V-8, probably about 400 horsepower, maybe a bit more. The Arion is a sixteen-cylinder vehicle, producing just a smidge over 1500 horsepower. The Lamborghini behind us tops out with a V-12, producing upwards of 800 horsepower."

Kent looked at him and grinned. He wasn't certain if this drive was making him feel younger or taking years off his life. Whichever it was, it was thrilling.

Signage indicated they were nearing Monaco. Mark moved the Arion into the right lane on the highway. The Lamborghini did the same. When Mark took an unmarked exit at full speed and without signalling, the Lamborghini continued past. Its driver reduced speed and took the next exit. A short time later, an older model red Ferrari took the same exit as the Arion.

Kent was still wide-eyed, his heart racing, as Mark continued along the exit, following it beneath the highway, then curving back over it, rapidly gaining altitude. Soon they passed a sign reading: *Privée Entrée Interdit*. Mark reduced their speed and came to a full stop at a padlocked gate, beside which there was a single utility pole. There were no homes nearby. The landscape was rugged and dotted with numerous rocky outcroppings. The vegetation appeared dry, and even the few ancient olive trees were struggling to survive.

"Here's the gate key." He tossed it to Kent.

Kent unlocked the gate and swung it open, allowing Mark to drive through. Then he swung the gate closed, replaced the lock and secured it from the inside. Returning to the Arion, he returned the gate key to Mark, all the while wearing a "what's next?" expression on his face.

Mark drove them a little further, then parked to explain. "The Arion is my toy, but there's little in the way of places where I can play with it. I bought this property to permit me that. It used to be an airport landing strip apparently—some involvement with the war effort in North Africa during WWII, as I understand. This straightaway ends on a sea stack just beyond the promontory, to which it was likely attached at some point in the past. Now it's connected by a short, but very necessary, bridge. I had a second gate installed here to distinguish between the track and the straightaway out to the tip."

Kent was stunned. "Great view from up here."

"There's nothing directly below the cliffs here, just a sheer drop to the Med. The geologist I used to evaluate the stability of the property told me that the connecting piece, out there, at the other end of this short bridge, probably separated as a result of seismic activity at some point in the past. Just to the west of us is Eze-sur-Mer, and I think you can see St. Jean beyond. The cape off to the east is part of Monaco," Mark said, pointing toward the various landmarks.

They stood awhile, admiring the view, the haze building with the heat and melding the sea with the sky off in the distance toward Africa, somewhere beyond the horizon.

"I had this place resurfaced for a track, so I could run the Arion at near-full speed. The paved surface is the shape of a lower-case letter d, and the oval portion is just a bit banked. O spent hours with me out here doing training. On that utility pole," he said, pointing to the pole by the entrance gate, "there's a video camera which feeds into the security office back on board the *Theia*. Why don't we give O a little wave?" As they returned to the Arion, Mark added, "I thought you and I might take a few turns, and if you're up for it, you can even give it a try—if you want. No pressure, just an offer."

Kent gulped. "Do you have any water, Mark? My mouth seems awfully dry."

Mark drove the Arion around the track a number of times in what he considered warm-up or practise rounds, then stopped to trade places with Kent.

Visibly nervous—and well aware of the steep cliff at one end of the track—Kent took the steering wheel in hand and started the Arion, slowly accelerating, trying to develop a feel for the powerful vehicle now under his control. Mark had cautioned him that he could attain 60 miles per hour in a mere 2.3 seconds. That was nearly one-hundred kilometres per hour—in 2.3 seconds! His first circle of the track was turtle slow by comparison with what Mark had been doing. It wasn't just the presence of the cliff. He was also driving a multi-million-dollar vehicle! Following Mark's instructions, he managed to climb into the range of the fourth of the seven speeds available. They were flying, but the Arion provided a sense of grounding and security. The sensation was exhilarating, though Kent couldn't achieve the level of confidence necessary to go any faster. He would never know all that the Arion had to offer.

Once again, they traded places, and Mark demonstrated a bit more of what the Arion could do. He was having fun, and Kent was more relaxed than he had been initially, though his stomach had moved to fill the void left by his heart, which seemed to have entered his head—he could hear it beating loudly in his ears. It was evident that Mark knew what he was doing. He and the car were one, even at 350 kilometres per hour.

"The speed we're going now is 220 miles per hour—the max that's attainable by that Lamborghini you saw behind us on the highway. On the other hand, we could hit 273 miles per hour—that's 440 kilometres per hour to you—but it looks like you've had enough."

Mark was right. Kent was starting to turn green, and it wasn't with envy. "I think you had me praying, Mark," Kent said, trying to convey some humour with a smile while simultaneously trying to calm his quivering insides.

When they came to a full stop, Mark made a quick telephone call while Kent walked to take one final look at the view. Although he fully intended to divest himself of his business commitments and live a quieter life with Lucy, years of habit made him assess the potential the site might have for future development. He recognized several avenues that might be pursued, if Mark were interested, and logically assumed that this might have been an additional reason for Mark to have brought him to see it.

Soon he was joined at the cliffside by Mark. "Some view, eh?" Mark said, taking a broad stance, a hand on either hip, deeply breathing in the sea air, which seemed somewhat cooler at this increased elevation. "I find it mesmerizing . . . just draws you in." He proceeded to climb over the low gate, which marked the entranceway to the little bridge, then crossed the bridge, making his way to the sea stack on the other side.

Somewhat reluctantly, Kent followed. "I'm not as comfortable out here as you seem to be, Mark," Kent observed, eager to return to the safe side of the barrier. "Wow, you've even had them resurface this area. Reminds me of the stories about the ironworkers who were comfortable working on the Empire State Building. The breeze is a bit stronger out here, isn't it?"

Mark smiled, then turned to return to the Arion.

When Mark had pulled the Arion back to the gate, Kent was once again given the key to unlock the padlock. Mark drove through, and Kent closed the gate behind the car, this time applying the padlock to face outward.

The roadway they followed in departure was connected to other roughly surfaced paths and eventually led to one that provided return access to the highway, going westbound. Traffic was heavier, and Mark seemed less inclined to speed, his need for it satisfied for the time being.

A red Ferrari pulled in behind them and maintained a safe distance from the Arion.

Mark voice-activated the Arion's audio system and commanded it to play Gershwin's "Rhapsody in Blue." "This was a favourite of my Theia. I'm discovering that I like it more and more. Interesting that," he mused. He pulled the Arion into the passing lane to accommodate a much slower vehicle, and then returned to the right lane. The driver of the Ferrari did the same.

"So, I've chewed your ear about all the changes in my life since Theia's passing. What's brought about yours?" Mark asked.

"Well, 2015 was our pivotal year, between the Monroth project and the Aureus project. Actually, the property on which the Aureus project sits was part of it all," Kent offered as preface to the tale he was about to share.

"So, this change came about as a result of your business involvements?" Mark asked.

"No, not at all. It's actually more Lucy's story to tell, but since I ended up kidnapped, tazed, drugged, and confined in the trunk of a car, I guess it's mine as well. Unbeknownst to her, she had a crazed and vindictive relative of sorts who started to stalk us. The guy, Julius Roman— or Giulio Roman, according to Interpol—had actually been a mob hitman when he was younger and ended up a drunk, mad at the world, or at least the part of his world that contained Lucy and me."

"Sociopath? Psychopath?"

"Yeah, I guess—one or both of those. He actually killed Lucy's grandaunt. The sweet woman was about ninety-six years old, and he killed the old dear. Apparently, that happened while I was in the trunk of his car. Turns out that over the years he'd wiped out many of the people Lucy had thought were her blood relatives."

"Thought?"

"Turns out her father had been adopted into this crazy family. She then had a whole other family story to sort through—that's where the old aunt came in. Anyway, this crazy mob guy appears to have also killed Lucy's father."

Mark kept his eyes on the road, but his mouth was agape as he listened to the whole sordid tale, or at least as much of it as Kent was willing to share without Lucy's input. Eventually, the story wound to its conclusion and silence settled in for a long moment as Mark digested it all in wonder.

"Well," he said eventually, shaking his head, "She's one strong woman to have dealt with all of that. But now that you've told me, I certainly won't ask Lucy about it."

"Ask her anyway if you want. She was far more actively involved than I was, so she will have more to say about it. It's so true that 2015 was one hell of a year for us, especially March to September. She's adjusted well. It took some time, but I think she's come out of it much stronger."

"That sort of thing—and I'm not referring to the 'what' of the thing, but to the impact it has upon you—can change you profoundly, can't it? You end up evaluating things much differently, and it takes a while to reset your course in life."

In near unison, they sighed, breathing deeply, their lips pursed as they looked straight ahead. Traffic had thinned. Mark moved into the passing lane and gunned it. The Ferrari followed suit.

CHAPTER 27

Lucy and Kent were outside, on the upper deck of the *Theia,* when a highly animated Mark joined them. He appeared barely able to contain his excitement. A server brought their beverages on a tray and placed them on the low table in front of the seating area: Kir Royales for Lucy and Kent, a Crown Royal on-the-rocks for Mark.

When the server departed, Kent inquired, "Mark, what's up? Closed a big deal?"

"No, no. Nothing so mundane. I wanted to do something special for you two and was rather hoping this opportunity would arise—and it has. We've been invited to a party, a grand affair to be held on one of the yachts expected to arrive in Antibes within a few weeks. I prefer the quiet life for myself these days, but a flashy bash every once in a while can be fun—I just wouldn't want it here."

"Sounds like fun, Mark. Whose yacht? Would I recognize the name of the owner or the yacht?" Kent queried. Lucy remained silent, already concerned about wardrobe considerations.

"Have you ever heard of the Russian oligarch, Grigori Orlov? His yacht, the *Croesus,* just recently completed an eight-month refit. The *Croesus* will be moored offshore for the party, and guests will be ferried there and back in tenders. You've got to understand: the *Croesus* dwarfs the *Theia*." His body language clearly communicated to both Kent and Lucy that this was to be a major social event.

"Croesus, in Greek mythology, was a wealthy king and the origin of the phrase 'rich as Croesus,' right?" Kent offered.

"You're nearly spot-on. Croesus was, as legend tells us, the King of Lydia in the sixth century BC and supposedly the richest man on earth at that time. I know this only because my wife, Theia, and I attended a party on board the *Croesus* the summer she died, and she was a fount of knowledge about such things. It should be fun to see how they've redone her. Not that they needed to. She was only four years old!"

Kent could sense Lucy's discomfort. "How did you come to be acquainted with him?" he asked. "I don't want to pry, but I am curious."

"Don't worry about that, Kent. Grisha made his fortune in metals, as have I. We just went about it a bit differently. I hear he was in the KGB, whereas I wasn't, not the CIA either for that matter," Mark said, chuckling at the absurdity of the idea of him being involved with any of the alphabet agencies. "We bumped into one another at a yacht party while we were in Sint Maarten one year and found we had something in common. The only thing either of us was interested in talking about then was business, so we were a match—but not so much as to be actual competitors."

"Exactly what do the women wear to such affairs, Mark? I'm a rather casual-dress person, and I don't think I've brought anything with me that would be suitable—assuming I even knew what was suitable. I wouldn't know what to shop for," Lucy interjected, her voice revealing some stress about the matter.

"No worries, Lucy dear. Let me take you down to Theia's stateroom. It's pretty much as she left it. Take a look at her clothes and jewellery. You can use anything you find there. If you like something and it fits, wear it. If it needs altering, go ahead and have that done. At the very least, you might get an idea of what Theia thought appropriate for such events. I think I have some photos taken at previous events as well. Would you like to do that now? We can just leave Kent up here—I think I saw some bikini-clad guests lounging on the yacht berthed next to us. Not that I usually notice such things, mind you." Mark winked at Lucy, and the two of them headed inside, leaving Kent to enjoy the view by himself.

Theia's stateroom was located adjacent to Mark's. He unlocked the door, and Lucy noticed him pause and take a deep breath before turning the handle to enter.

Lucy couldn't help but gasp as she entered what had been Theia's private space. In the centre of the dressing alcove, on a plain white plinth, Lucy saw a sculpture that stunned her. "Camille Claudel's *La Valse,"* she whispered.

"Yes, it was my gift to Theia on our twenty-fifth wedding anniversary. She liked the lapis lazuli wave of this one, and I liked that she liked it. I loved her."

"Oh, Mark, I'm so sorry for your loss. Are you sure you're prepared to have me to go through Theia's things?"

"Yes, definitely. Ignore me—just a silly old man. Theia has no use for them, and I know she would have enjoyed spending time with you, Lucy. She would most likely have acquired an Awen to add to her collection."

"It's a magnificent collection, Mark, and I would have been honoured to have been a part of it." Their eyes met in understanding, and when Mark's moistened, they turned from each other.

"I'll unlock the safe for you. See what's there that you might use. You can remove them to your safe so you can live with them for a while before making your final decision. Please secure the safe before you leave. Any clothing that interests you, just take to your own stateroom, okay? I'm going to see if I can dig up those photos for you."

"Thanks, Mark."

When Mark had left the room, Lucy found herself standing in front of *La Valse*. She was enraptured by it. The Art Nouveau sculpture was about half a metre in height. The figures, a man and a woman—both naked—were positioned as if in a waltz, entwined with their heads tilted on the verge of a kiss. While the figures themselves were bronze, the bottom portion of the sculpture was Mediterranean blue lapis lazuli and formed a wave, echoing the movement of the dance and suggesting the graceful skirting of a gown. There were other versions created by the same artist, some in plaster and some entirely in bronze, but Lucy thought this version with the lapis wave was the most beautiful she had ever seen. She had been unaware of its existence, and now she found she could think of little else. To her, *La Valse* represented a century of passion, love, and dedication.

CHAPTER 28

It was Sunday, and Lucy awoke to a very different view through her window. They were no longer in port. At some time during the night, the *Theia* had exited her berth at Port Vauban and left Antibes. They were at sea. Then it occurred to her: today was Bastille Day, July 14th, the third anniversary of Theia's death in Nice.

While France would celebrate *La Fête Nationale* with a variety of festivities and much fine food, there would be no celebration on board the *Theia*. Three years was insufficient time for Mark to have put Theia's death in the terrorist attack out of his mind. No time was sufficient for that. Lucy wondered how he would cope. And she wondered where they were going.

She dressed for breakfast and entered Kent's bedroom through the adjoining door, just as he was approaching from the other side. *Great minds.*

"I *see* we're at *sea*. This comes as a surprise, but not a bad one. Did you know?" she asked Kent as they made their way to an indoor dining area.

"I was in the process of telling you a while ago actually. I remember asking you what you had planned for the coming days, and you said, 'more painting, relaxing, and whatever,' if I remember correctly. So, surprise! This is 'whatever.' Somewhere along the line, the subject must have changed, and I didn't actually get around to telling you. Sorry."

"No problem at all. It's actually a rather pleasant surprise for me. And I'd much rather this than a crowded festival. Fine to watch, but I don't like participating. I'm still essentially an introvert."

"That's what I figured. You realize the significance of this day for Mark, right?"

"Totally. This is not a day he'd be partial to fireworks, champagne, and whatever else goes on. I'm curious, how old was she?"

"Theia was sixty-nine when she was killed, so Mark was seventy-one when she was taken from him." Kent squeezed Lucy's hand, a pained expression on his face. "I can't begin to imagine . . ."

Their conversation quieted and then ceased as they approached the dining area. Usually open to the air, today, the curved glass sliding doors were closed due to their travel. Mark was lounging nearby with a glass of juice in hand.

"I hope that you're not bothered by the movement of the yacht, because Chef De la Cour assures me he has prepared a lovely breakfast feast for us. His take on the traditional American breakfast."

Lucy hoped that her groan had not been audible. She always looked forward to the traditional French breakfast. Did this now mean bacon, fried eggs, and pancakes? Possibly grits and sausage and biscuits with gravy?

She need not have been concerned. Chef De la Cour had taken great liberties with his interpretation. In conversation over the course of their stay, he had learned what each considered their ideal breakfast, and that is what he now served. Lucy breathed a sigh of relief.

Lucy's Perigord strawberries were now out of season, so the Chef had assembled an array of complementary berries, including gooseberries, raspberries, blackberries, and blueberries with an available variety of strawberry for her enjoyment. His attention to detail was impressive. There were butter croissants with rose-petal jam, as well as almond croissants, which were Kent's favourite, and chocolate brioche for both Kent and Mark. Kent enjoyed an omelette with Gruyère while Mark had his crispy bacon, over-easy eggs, and pancakes with maple syrup and freshly-churned butter. As Mark and Kent enjoyed their Americanos, Lucy sipped her latte. She considered that feeding the guests on board the *Theia* must be similar to catering to the taste preferences of the members of a large family with no two wanting to eat the same thing. Clearly, Chef De la Cour was up to the challenge.

"Where are we off to, Mark?" Lucy inquired.

"I thought we might go toward Italy, visit Capri, then continue toward Greece and visit some of the small islands—perhaps Turkey as well. Have you been to Cyprus? What do you say?"

What could she say? She was already on a yacht headed to Greece and had no reason not to.

"Sounds like a plan, Mark."

Kent reached for another almond croissant.

The hours passed pleasantly. Lucy did some work on her paintings but spent much of her time slathered in a 60 SPF lotion and covered head-to-foot in a caftan, enjoying the sun and breeze, and nodding off on a lounger near the swim spa.

Kent and Mark joined her at lunchtime, after which Mark disappeared. Later in the afternoon, Kent went to the gym for a workout while Lucy asked if O would join her for a beverage so they could talk, and she could work on her German.

If there were a gene for learning other languages, it appeared that Lucy had inherited hers from Gianni Sarto, her grandfather. English, French, Swedish, German—she thought that she might consider Italian next. After a lengthy conversation with O, she left for a workout in the gym, and he returned to his office, which was just off his stateroom, near Mark's quarters.

Mark had commissioned the bespoke box for Theia. It was eighteen-centimetres in length, twelve-centimetres in width, and ten-centimetres in depth. The fittings were gold; the box itself was lapis lazuli. The key he wore around his neck fit the lock on the box. For nearly three years, the box had been sitting on the credenza behind his desk, close by so he could talk to her. She never answered. She never would. He felt alone. He ached.

He grabbed a tumbler, added a couple of ice cubes, and poured a generous amount of Crown Royal Cask No.16. The Canadian whisky delivered a smooth burn.

He removed the box from the credenza and placed it in front of himself on his desk. He turned on his computer, and when the screen came to life, he logged in and entered his photo files, searching for the old photos—the ones he'd scanned and downloaded from the hard-copy originals. Finally, he activated the music, gently filling the room with the old favourites they had enjoyed together and a few others he'd found meaningful more recently.

He talked to her, telling her just how much he missed her and how sorry he was that they'd not been together that night in Nice. They'd planned to enjoy the holiday festivities together and walk the crowded Promenade des Anglais hand in hand. That was how it was supposed to have been.

He'd not done it on purpose—he wanted her to know that, to know just how much he loved her. *No, How much I still do.* He'd promised to have a life with her once the kids could be relied upon to take care of the business. Of course, they could; that had been true even years earlier. Ultimately, Titan didn't matter, Theia—his special Titan—did.

He felt that he'd failed her. After all his successes, the loss of Theia was his most profound failure. He'd promised to have everything set up so that, when she left her position at Stanford at the age of sixty-five, they would spend the rest of their lives together. He had failed. When she died four years later, she died alone but for the company of strangers. He should have been there and not at a Titan shareholders meeting. How empty and meaningless that sounded. His greatest vow had been made to her, not them.

He'd turned over Titan to his sons then, but it was too late. No matter how he explained things to Theia, she never answered. She never said she forgave him. She had always been such a forgiving person. Why couldn't she forgive him just this once more? Oh yes. Of course. She'd been dead these past three years. She might have died anyway and left him all alone, but at least they would have had those four years together, just the two of them, experiencing the world together on board the *Theia*. He'd just taken it for granted and thrown it away as if it were inconsequential. Now he knew better. Now it was too late.

The air filled with the sounds of Frank Sinatra singing an old Irving Berlin song, "When I Lost You." Over a hundred years earlier, Irving had understood and would have shared his pain. He threw back another drink, failing to detect—let alone enjoy—the flavours, and only sensing its smooth heat.

When O entered Mark's office to check on him later that day, he found him much as he had the previous year and the year before that—slumped at his desk with Theia while the computer ran through a slideshow of photos of Theia through the years. And beside him, a half-empty bottle of Crown Royal. O overrode the voice command and silenced the music. He helped Mark get into bed and left a bottle of water at his bedside. It pained him to think that he wouldn't be there to help him next time.

CHAPTER 29

During breakfast late the following morning, Mark announced that he had mapped out in general their tour of the eastern Mediterranean for the next two weeks. Captain Fisker would chart the course and make whatever adjustments seemed prudent given specific conditions they might encounter. They would try to restrict travel to the nighttime, so as to provide plenty of opportunity to enjoy the sights during the day—whatever appealed to them at the time.

"I say 'two weeks,' but it might be longer. Who knows?" he exclaimed. "It's certainly doable in that length of time, but we might just find ourselves so enthralled by certain places that we stay longer. We'll play it by ear. I assure you, however, I'll have you back in Antibes for the party on the *Croesus*. Can't have you miss that!"

Their first stop was just south of Naples, near Sorrento and the Isle of Capri. Mark had insisted they visit Pompeii at the foot of Mount Vesuvius. His desire for them to see and do everything caught them off guard, but he was their host and to decline seemed somewhat rude and actually quite absurd. By the end of the day, they were nearly too exhausted to eat—a product of too much sight-seeing and sunshine. But that too became part of Mark's plan, so after a nap, they enjoyed a late supper, eager to see what Chef De la Court would offer. Although the *Theia* could secure and store sufficient food for over a month, Chef had sourced fresh local seafood, fruit, and vegetables. He was prepared for most anything they might desire.

Lucy enjoyed nibbling a variety of seafood appetizers and then moved on to a main course of *orecchiette con cime di rape*, a pasta with broccoli rabe. Kent couldn't decide between *spaghetti alle vongole* and *risotto alla pescatora,* so Chef provided a half portion of the pasta with clams and a half portion of the risotto with fish for him to enjoy. Mark requested the *spaghetti alla puttanesca* or "whore's spaghetti," in part to commemorate Lucy and Kent's misunderstanding of his conversation with Rayan during the meeting about O. The scent of garlic, anchovy, and hot chilli pepper accompanied the dish, and Lucy was relieved they were dining *al fresco.*

Lucy overslept the following morning and awoke with a pounding headache. She had scheduled a conversation with Yoichi for seven in the morning, Toronto time. Dehydrated and in need of fluids, she contacted the kitchen to request a large smoothie of juice and yoghurt. Today she would enjoy breakfast as her lunch.

Today would be an unusual day in other ways as well. They had stayed anchored during last night's feast, travelling toward Sicily only after she had gone to bed. They would be cruising during most of the day. That made it unusual. She wondered why they were breaking from what had become their usual pattern, then decided that it was Mark's prerogative to change his mind. She readied herself to receive breakfast and looked forward to her chat with Yoichi.

Lucy's liquid breakfast was immediately healing, and she arranged for a cappuccino to be brought to her room. More liquid—and caffeine.

"Buongiorno, Yoichi," she said, greeting her sleepy agent in Toronto.

"Uh-huh . . . Where are you?"

"North of Sicily, heading for Greece last I was told. How are things?"

"Same ol' thing. 'No news is good news' and all that. I'm still trying to wake up," Yoichi said while exaggerating her pained expression. "Oh, I've got the shipper lined up for the Theia Witherspoon art collection, but nothing has been signed yet. They take care of everything. 'Martin and Mansfield.' You won't have heard their name, but it's *the* firm used by the major galleries when they have collections touring."

"You're kidding me, 'M'n'M?' Swee-et!" Lucy said.

"It's too early for that amount of corn."

"You can't have expected me to pass up that one." Lucy sipped her cappuccino, savouring the deep, rich Italian coffee and the silky froth of steamed milk.

"What's going on? Doing any painting?"

"Oh my, yes, Yoichi. I had to get more supplies! I've got tons of photos and ideas, some sketches and a bunch of paintings started, as well as the finished ones I've accumulated and need to ship off to you. I'm just waiting to have more done, so I don't need to go through the rigamarole of arranging for shipping too often."

"Okay, that sounds good." Yoichi paused, then started anew, "I'm sorry, I'm really dragging today. I need to cut this short for now and will contact you when I have all the forms from Martin and Mansfield. It's pouring rain here right now, and a grey day plus the way I feel is not a good combination. Say 'hi' to Kent for me. Sorry."

"Okay, I understand. Hope you feel better soon. Say 'hi' to Donald for me."

Hmm, thought Lucy, after she'd disconnected from the call. *My greatest problem right now is having indulged in too much food and drink last night. I hope there's not more to Yoichi's gloom.*

The day passed uneventfully. Kent spent much of it in quiet contemplation. Of what, Lucy couldn't say—and Kent wouldn't. Lucy lounged, took a swim, and drank a lot of fluids, *sans alcool.* O agreed to do some self-defence training with her in the gym. She wasn't certain which O he was, but she was no longer bothered by the need to figure everything out. She left the matter in his capable hands.

She also managed to continue work on her paintings. She was struck by how different they were from those upon which she had built her reputation. While she hoped that the buying public would gravitate to her new style, ultimately, that was not of concern to her. This was how she felt—light and optimistic—and if others didn't want to share in that feeling, well, that would be their loss. She had experienced her own darkness in the past and was well aware that darkness persisted around the world. She had seen enough of it for herself. She would, as the nuns had often said when she was in school, "light a candle," but whether that candle was immediately extinguished, ignited a fire, or became an eternal flame, she couldn't worry about it. She wouldn't let that consume her.

Mark had called Lucy and Kent to join him for drinks in the forward lounge. "There, in the distance, you can just begin to make it out," Mark said, pointing to a bright orange spot in the distance. "That's the 'Lighthouse of the Mediterranean,' the island of Stromboli. It marks the entrance to the Messina Strait between Italy and Sicily, through which we'll pass as we leave the Tyrrhenian Sea and enter the Ionian Sea. The strait's only three-kilometres wide. If you connect Mount Vesuvius with Stromboli and then go a bit further south, you'll locate Mount Etna—three volcanoes in a row. This whole region is rife with active volcanoes. If Stromboli blew, there'd be quite the tsunami here, I suspect. The current eruption began July 3rd, so we're seeing pretty much the tail end of it. Generally, she's content to spit and spatter and bubble away. Every so often, she belches lava, throwing boulder-sized quantities of the stuff around. I wouldn't want to be too close when that's happening. Both Etna and Stromboli are continuously active—and they're only about a hundred kilometres apart."

Kent frowned. "When you say 'continuously,' is that literally, or . . ."

"Well, I'm told that Stromboli has been active for the past twenty-five-hundred years, and while the degree of activity varies, something is always happening. It's never quiet. The island is about the size of Manhattan but only about five-hundred people live there.

"Some are predicting an eruption from Etna very soon. I really don't understand how people can live a contented life in such a geologically unstable region; nevertheless, the roots of civilization run very deep here. Perhaps that's why Theia loved the Med so very much." Mark sighed, then stood and exited the lounge, taking a seat on a lone chair situated on the deck, near the rail. He gazed ahead, toward Stromboli, but he didn't see Stromboli.

Lucy and Kent remained inside the lounge, not wanting to disturb Mark and his thoughts.

"You've been rather quiet all day, Kent, anything in particular on your mind?" Lucy asked, somewhat concerned.

"Just thinking. Years ago, when I was still a student at uni, I attended a small gathering to honour Benoit Mandelbrot, who had come to speak on campus about fractals."

"What's a fractal?" Lucy interjected.

"It's a form of patterning." Kent explained. "If you divide a fractal pattern into parts, you see that it is comprised of nearly identical but smaller copies of the whole. If you then look more closely at those smaller copies, you see that each is comprised of even smaller copies of the same—or similar—pattern, and so on. It's common in nature. As a mathematician, Mandelbrot created a formula that is used in special effects, among other things, to make scenes appear more natural. If you ask a set designer to design a seashore, it's likely to look like a seashore, but still also look a bit contrived and unreal. If you apply a fractal approach and modify the input, the resulting seashore looks—and feels—like the real thing. Although it may not actually look like any specific place on earth, it will look natural, as if it could exist here—or perhaps, on some distant planet."

"Okay, I'm not certain that I'm with you, but I guess I have some greater understanding of the concept. It sounds like, ultimately, it's a mathematical formula that makes things seem more natural."

"By George, I think she's got it!" Kent declared, sounding a bit like Henry Higgins.

"And this is what you've been so very deep in thought about while we've been cruising the Med today?"

"Well, actually, I've been wondering how I might combine that with the design of multi-residential structures. If anything constructed by humans were in need of being more natural, more in tune to nature and appealing to us as being part of nature, surely it's our homes. Instead, we tend to build boxes and layer them atop one another, perhaps placing them askew and adding boxes of greenery, but all the while, we're dealing with boxes. I think it confines and slowly suffocates our spirit. Not mine specifically, but humankind in general.

"This trip . . . this environment . . . it's such a breath of fresh air," Kent mused. "I'm not referring to the luxurious mode of travel either. It's very pleasurable, but I'd have had the same experience with far less, as long as we were travelling together. It's all so wonderful, isn't it? The variety in the shapes of the islands and their mountains and the naturally occurring vegetation. I love the manner in which the landscape is formed by the interaction of plants and weather with the earth, then modified over the years by those same forces and elements. To use a wine term: it's the *terroir* that moulds us. We need to interact with our environment, but in modern times, we have modified it so dramatically that I think we're having trouble relating to it. It's as if we're inflicting dramatic changes of the same magnitude as that wrought by seismic activity due to the volcanoes and earthquakes. We've got to get back to feeling the earth and interacting with nature in a different way.

"So, that's what's been on my mind. It's a project and I'm planning to work on it. Not to the detriment of our time together, but just as you and your art will always be one—no matter whether your work is in or out of fashion at any given time—the same with me and this idea. I think it'll feed my spirit. I haven't the slightest idea if anything will ever come of it, but I'd like to try. I feel I must. Perhaps someday you'll find me in my office with a rendering I've completed in my sleep."

Noticing that Mark had vacated the lone chair and moved elsewhere, they rose to join him on the deck. Lucy put her arm around Kent and leaned in close. She breathed him in deeply; he smelled wonderful. He turned and gave her a kiss.

By the time they went to bed, Mount Etna lay behind them, holding her secrets and revealing little of what was in her immediate plans. A fine tracery of orange lava marked the southern slope. Stromboli in the distance glowed red and belched.

The next day, Mark again appeared to have something up his sleeve. Lucy and Kent had enjoyed the morning, visiting various coves along the western coast of Greece, in some cases taking a sports tender into water too shallow for the *Theia.* The sky was clear and blue, the sun relentless, and the cool water welcoming. The water was as clear as the sky, and the morning had been spent snorkelling in the company of a pod of bottlenose dolphins. Lucy and Kent had returned to the *Theia* in need of a light lunch and refreshment.

"How was the snorkelling?" Mark asked during lunch.

"Great! I looked at the book you have on board the tender, so I know that I saw a parrotfish and a painted comber," Lucy bubbled enthusiastically. "And the one that looks like a large caterpillar, because of the bright blue dots it has. We even saw a loggerhead turtle. But I also saw some killer whales, so that rather dimmed my enthusiasm."

"They weren't killer whales, Lucy. They were false killer whales. They were black and grey, rather than black and white, right? Whereas the black and white ones feed on seals and might possibly mistake a human for a seal, these feed on much smaller fish, or so I'm told."

"Oh. Okay. We also saw a basking shark, but I'd already read about them, so I knew it was harmless unless you're a krill. Huge mouth! Exhilarating."

"And I needed to stop her from touching a red scorpionfish she found hiding in the rocks," Kent stated, exasperated.

"I have difficulty not touching pretty things, I guess."

"Well, that pretty thing would have inflicted quite a sting. They're venomous," Mark informed her. "No seals, I guess." Kent shook his head, confirming Mark's assumption. "There are monk seals, though they're not common," Mark explained. "They frequent this area but generally earlier in the season."

Shortly after lunch was concluded, Mark invited them to the gym. One section of wall in the gym was an LED array similar to the one in the gym Lucy and Kent had back home.

"Once Kent mentioned this LED installation to me, I was convinced it was a great idea, but there's one feature that I really haven't bothered to use much over the years," Mark said.

"I think we're now somewhere appropriate for its use. Then he initiated the voice command system, saying, "Outside."

The LED wall suddenly filled with a view of the sea beneath the waves. Just then, O appeared in the picture and began to feed the fish, thereby attracting even more. Then he waved goodbye and swam away, leaving the small audience in the gym to the piscine entertainment. It wasn't long before O joined them in the gym. He was slightly damp, and wore swim trunks and a smile.

"I've set the cameras in several different directions," he explained. "One is outward, another downward, also fore and aft—that's bow and stern. And there's one that looks straight out across the water. When you say 'outside,' the first selection is random. If you want a specific camera, you then use the commands: out, down, front, back, above. I thought that might be easiest for you to remember. At night, with the underwater lights, you'll attract all sorts of fish. And, of course, tonight is special."

"Special?" Kent asked.

"Yes," Mark went on to explain. "We're going to spend some time over Calypso Deep, which is the deepest part of the Hellenic Trench, and hopefully do some whale-watching. The sperm whales calve in these waters. The whales are able to dive into the Deep, so we might be able to see one coming up—or going down. The sperm whales act a bit like moose, you might say, being Canadian. That's you, I mean, not the whales. The males spar for dominance of a harem of females and then interact with the young. I don't foresee Captain Fisker becoming another Captain Ahab though, since we're going to mind our own business and just quietly observe. No guarantees though. Could be a bust."

"That sounds very exciting, Mark. I look forward to tonight. And I guess that we can turn on the cameras anytime we're in here for a workout, right?" Kent asked.

"That's right. There are so many islands we'll be visiting; you can exercise a bit here and still enjoy the sea view without having to spend your entire day in the water getting all wrinkle-fingered and soggy."

"By the way," added O, "you can also see the feed from these cameras displayed on the video screens in your staterooms. Combine that with some music, and you will sleep very well indeed."

"The *Croesus* offers something a bit different. I hear they've got a viewing room with glass about twenty centimetres thick—that's eight inches. In addition, there's some sort of hole through all the layers, straight through the hull, with a glass lining protruding from the hull and an elevator providing access. We must look for it when we visit," Mark suggested.

The weather remained as perfect as one might wish, yet the seas suggested a storm. There were swells, which increased in magnitude as they neared Calypso Deep. Finally, Captain Fisker announced that they had arrived at their destination: 36° 34'N 21° 8'E. Lucy was happy to be in the massive yacht; she suspected that a small vessel might have had problems dealing with the swells.

When Captain Fisker joined them, Lucy seized the opportunity. "The sea isn't as calm here. Has there been a storm or an earthquake in the region? I mean, Etna was expected to enter a very active phase, wasn't it?"

"That's a reasonable supposition, but while Etna is becoming increasingly active, and this area has certainly seen its fair share of earthquakes, that's not the whole reason for these swells. It's actually the usual state of the seas in this region and appears to be related in some manner to the depths of the Hellenic Trench.

"If we exclude the effects due to salinity, water is most dense at a temperature of four degrees Celsius," he explained. "Therefore, at great depths—four kilometres on average in the Hellenic Trench—we should expect the dense water to be four degrees Celsius. Calypso Deep is nearly 5267 metres in depth—that's 17,280 feet. Surprisingly, the deep-water temperature of the Hellenic Trench is measurably higher than expected. I suspect that this is related to the things you've already noted and that the variable seismic activity results in a warming of the waters at the greatest depths. That would cause a mixing, as the warmer water, being less dense, rises. It is that mixing which is likely expressed as the surface swells we are experiencing.

"I wish you good luck in your whale watching. We'll remain above Calypso Deep during the night, unless there is reason to move into calmer waters. The underwater lights and hydrophones have been deployed. We are in whale-watching mode."

"Do you think there are any down there, Captain?" Kent asked.

"Oh, they're down there alright," Captain Fisker assured him. "They've been detected on the sonar. Sound detection should pick up the sperm whales' clicks and pips and squeals and trumpets, so when they're close, you might get some audio warning. The trumpet sound can last several seconds, so that's enough to get your attention. Besides, they're very loud. It is most likely that, if you see a sperm whale, it will be either heading down into the trench to feed, or coming back up after having eaten. I don't think this is an area they'd just hang around to socialize."

"What do they eat?" inquired Lucy.

"As with the sperm whales in all the oceans, they eat large squid. However, there are no populations of giant squid in this area, as I understand. Any they've found have been located at the far western end of the Mediterranean, so I think those squid are more likely visitors from the Atlantic. Although the sperm whales can dive to depths in excess of two-thousand metres (in excess of seven-thousand feet), here they tend to feed on squid living between five-hundred and eight-hundred metres beneath the surface. They are smaller than the giant squid eaten elsewhere, meaning less than twelve-metres in total length."

"Now that's a long meal!" joked Lucy. "I hadn't thought to ask before: how big are the sperm whales?"

"They tend to max out at about twenty-metres, but more commonly at about sixteen-metres. That's a sixty-tonne whale." When there were no further questions, Captain Fisker returned to the bridge.

The gym where they would view the underwater scene was unlike the usual, more utilitarian gyms. The gym on board the *Theia* was beautiful and largely open to the air, though given the increased movement of the vessel, most of the open areas had been closed for the day. There was a conversation pit with abundant seating in front of the LED screen. Chef De la Cour had arranged for the evening meal to be served on the large coffee table in the conversation pit. The evening was spent in pleasant conversation, with members of the executive crew joining them periodically to listen for the clicks that would indicate the presence of a sperm whale, all the while keeping an eye glued to the LED screen. They saw a lone basking shark, a single ocean sunfish, several swordfish and schools of bluefin tuna, bonito, and flying fish, but no leviathan. Eventually, they called it a night and returned to their staterooms with plans to continue monitoring the scene on the screen in their room. As the last member of the group exited the area, a dark shadow was drawn across the LED screen, accompanied by a series of loud clicks.

Lucy returned to her stateroom and immediately adjusted her video screen for both sound and visual. If there was a sperm whale out there, she was determined to see it. As she readied herself for bed, she tried to keep an eye on her video screen, on the lookout for a whale. As she finished brushing her teeth, she thought she heard an odd and eerie sound. She rushed from the bathroom just in time to see a large fluke clear the screen as a sperm whale rose out of the depths to take a breath at the surface. *Ah, timing is everything!*

She planned to continue monitoring the screen. *I can sleep tomorrow.* Unfortunately, her body had other ideas, and she quickly fell asleep, not stirring until morning light announced the arrival of a new day.

CHAPTER 30

"Where are you going, Carmine? Come, sit down and have something to eat," Gina implored. "Talk to me!"

Carmine was pacing in his mother's kitchen in his parents' house in Ventimiglia. And he was ranting. "He said it would be mine! But now the police have seized control!"

"You can't do anything about this. Patience. You must wait; that is the only way. Later, maybe much later, you will have Pomodoro del Sole, like your Uncle Vincenzo promised."

Carmine's inheritance was being held up by the police investigation into the activities of his deceased uncle, Vincenzo Rizzo. As Vincenzo's favourite nephew, he had inherited the restaurant in Naples, and though he'd never been involved in the restaurant business, he was eager to become a businessman like Vincenzo, his hero.

"You should not have quit your job with border security. That was a good job, Carmine. You should talk to someone and recover your job."

"I'm going to go to Naples. I'll stay there and pressure the authorities to give me access to the restaurant."

"What kind of pressure? And who do you plan to pressure? At this time, there is nothing you can do. Talk to someone, and reclaim your job at border security, Carmine."

"I'll go home to Stromboli."

"You have never been to Stromboli! And with the eruptions now, they won't let you on the island. Here . . . sit. Have another cup of coffee and a cannoli." Gina was running out of patience with her youngest son; there was nothing she could say to sway him from his reckless behaviours.

"I'll hike Etna then. I've done that before with Uncle Vincenzo. He said it's in our blood. We must make this pilgrimage to the volcano to reaffirm who we are and to draw strength," Carmine explained.

Gina bobbled her head back and forth, considering Carmine's words. It was true; for generations her family had taken its strength from the volcanoes. Even when the family moved from Stromboli to Messina, the volcanoes remained a part of them. But Carmine's father was Genovese, and Carmine had only ever lived in this region, having rarely visited Sicily, and then only in the company of his uncle. Instead, she would pray for Carmine, and make a novena.

"Why do you do this to me, Carmine? At least stay for another nine days; give me time to complete the novena, then decide. Do this for me, Carmine," Gina implored him. Reluctantly, Carmine agreed, but a mother knows when her child isn't fully committed to a course of action.

Despite having promised his mother that he would remain in Ventimiglia, Carmine couldn't resist travelling to Naples to check on *his* restaurant. And once in Naples, he found himself merely a day's bus ride from Messina and Etna. He had delayed his trip for a few days, but he had tired of receiving advice from people. His late uncle had told him that a person needed only one good friend. Uncle Vincenzo had advised him to maintain his independence. Carmine had no such friend, and he found no one to travel with him to Sicily, so he concentrated on exerting his independence. Promptly, he left Naples to head for Messina. Ninety minutes after arriving in Messina, Carmine was in Catania, eager to begin his ascent of Etna, which loomed above the city.

In the morning, Carmine caught a ride with one of the Catanesi, who dropped him off as far up the mountain as was possible. He emerged from the vehicle and into a moonscape. The terrain was rugged, rocky, and devoid of plant and animal life. Carmine wasn't accustomed to hiking, but he was motivated to seek the summit and take strength from the volcano. He trudged onward and upward, well away from the few other hikers he had seen earlier on, who were accompanied by guides. As the climb took him ever higher, Carmine was struck by how chilly the air was, even though it was well into the summer. In some spots, the path was narrow and the wind threatened to send him toppling over the edge. He took extra care and concentrated on the careful placement of each step.

The cold air mixed with the moist air gathered from the Mediterranean, creating patches of thick fog, which resulted in a penetrating chill throughout his body. He dug in his pack for the small bottle of *grappa* he had brought to toast his success and his Uncle Vincenzo, and took a quick gulp to warm himself. The moist air held the scent of sulphur, but over time, he became accustomed to it, and it no longer bothered him. Besides, there was little choice in the matter; sulphurous air was all that was available to him if he wanted to breathe. He continued trudging upward along the slope, step by step by step . . .

Carmine traced old lava flows upward toward the summit. He noticed that while his body was chilled and his jacket was damp, his feet remained comfortably warm in his hiking shoes. With each step, Carmine left behind a footprint—the black imprint of his sole. He had been advised to purchase different hiking boots, but in his eagerness to begin the trek, he had not wanted to waste time shopping. Behind him, a small lava tube cracked open, and its bright-orange contents oozed out.

Suddenly, there was an explosive sound as Etna belched. The air was redolent of sulphur, and ash rained down upon him. For Carmine, this was a form of baptism, and it gave him strength. He was nearly at the three-thousand metre elevation mark. Step by step . . .

Carmine remained ignorant of what was occurring beneath his feet and within Etna's cone, until lava in the cone mixed with steam and resulted in a massive explosion that knocked him to the ground. As he tried to regain his footing, he was pelted with hot rocks and steam that had been propelled from within the cone. His damp jacket sizzled as it was struck by the small, hot projectiles. Carmine winced in pain with each impact, sheltering his head with his arms in an effort to avoid more serious injury.

When he stood, he surveyed the scene which surrounded him. Details of the mountain's terrain had changed; things were now very different than he remembered from earlier in the trek. Small fissures had opened, and orange tendrils of lava decorated the slope both in front of him and behind him. His feet were becoming uncomfortably hot, and he saw that his soles were becoming disengaged from the uppers of his hiking shoes. *Cazzo!*

Carmine saw no other person nearby, and no cars were visible in the parking lot at the highest elevation. He was alone with Etna. Another explosion sent him tumbling down until he hit a large boulder that had been thrown from Etna during a previous explosion. The impact stunned him, delivering a sharp pain to his shoulder and arm, and he heard something snap. As he looked upward while attempting to regain his footing, he saw the slow encroachment of an orange layer, looking like icing upon a cake. As quickly as he could, he moved from the path of the lava. His broken arm made it difficult to maintain balance. He tried to run down the slope, but the path was so narrow that he was afraid he would fall again and be at the mercy of gravity. Walking off the trail was out of the question: the rocky surface was unstable and shifting. Increasingly, he saw lava tubes of ever greater size form and crack open, spilling their contents. *Cazzo!*

Carmine gasped for air. It was hot, sulphurous, and laden with ash. He tried for a second breath and scorched his lungs in the process. The searing pain drove Carmine to utter a child's prayer. He had no time for fear. Soon the soles of his hiking shoes separated from the uppers, and Carmine repeated his prayer. He had already suffered minor head injuries, burns, cuts, and bruises, as well as a broken arm, and now he would experience injury to his feet. Step . . .

CHAPTER 31

"Hej," Alice called out as she arrived in Lucy's studio on board the *Theia*.

"Hej. Good morning, Alice. I so look forward to enjoying *fika* with you," Lucy said, chatting away while she cleaned then put aside her brushes, and Alice set the coffee and pastries on the small table on the terrace. "I appreciate the opportunity to work on my Swedish. My friend, Eve, will be so impressed when I return."

"May I see what it is you're working on?"

She hesitated. "Generally, I don't like to show a painting before it's completed, but yes, if you'd like to see, just come around here. It's far from being complete, so you really should see it again once it's done."

"It's a very large canvas, isn't it?" Alice observed as she approached.

"Yes, but the sea is also very large."

"Oy! I wasn't expecting anything quite so dramatic," Alice exclaimed when she saw the product of Lucy's efforts. "I find that I am drawn into it! As if I could actually enter it!"

"Then it must be going well, because that's the sense I want to impart."

"If I were trying to paint something like this, I'd probably just paint all the water blue, because water is blue, but the result would be so far from what you've achieved that it would be laughable. Somehow, though you've used very little of that same blue, yours looks . . . or maybe feels . . . more like how I *feel* it might *look*. Does that even make sense?"

"Well, if I merely wanted to convey what it looks like, then I'd first need to make certain that I've actually seen every subject I paint. That means I'd probably need to take photos of absolutely everything in order to refer to them as I paint. However, that's not what I'm trying to do."

Back at the table, Alice poured the coffee, and Lucy selected her pastry, a small éclair.

"You said that conveying what it looks like is not your intention," Alice observed. "What is your intention then?"

"I do convey what it looks like, but my intention is to convey the feeling or mood that I associate with that place or thing. It's lovely when others can identify that feeling or mood, or even if they detect one that I didn't actually intend. For me, what's important is that emotional connection."

"Well, I don't know how accurately you've painted the scene, since it's not one I've ever seen—"

"Me neither."

"—but it feels real. It's as if I might have been in a submarine yacht and that's what we saw on our travels. The whales, the rough terrain beneath us, the way your eyesight can't pierce the water at a distance, so fish seem to appear so suddenly, or you come upon something suddenly . . . all those things make it feel real."

"I appreciate your insight, Alice. Thank you."

They continued to chat in Swedish until *fika* was over; then Alice cleared the table and departed with the service cart. Lucy stood in front of the painting awhile, giving the composition additional consideration, but she found that inspiration had left her, so she abandoned her painting and placed a quick call to O. Then Lucy left the studio and headed to the gym for instruction in self-defence and German.

It should have been a quiet night, but a storm had quickly developed and was approaching from the west. Some believed it was the expression of a micro-weather system formed due to the increased volcanic activity in Sicily. Mount Etna had entered a very active phase, announced by a cataclysmic seismic event, which rained superheated boulders and ash as far as the Strait of Messina and was followed by an active lava flow that persisted days later.

O was checking the security cameras late in his shift when he spied something rather unusual. Lucy had just entered her studio. Although she had not worked so late previously, what had drawn his attention was the fact that she was wearing only her nightgown. The satin sheath was unlikely to be her normal painting attire. He left a message for his brother, then abandoned the security office and headed out to locate Lucy.

Lucy entered the studio and immediately approached the painting that Alice had found so interesting. Had Alice been present, she would have seen a much different painting from the one that Lucy saw when she looked at the same canvas. Lucy selected the colours she would require and applied daubs of the chosen hues to her palette; then she selected her brush and palette knife.

She approached the canvas with blind confidence and began applying, then scraping away, the pigment and gel media she had set out on her palette.

Outside the door, O listened and then retreated from the location, exiting onto the terrace directly from the main corridor. He moved carefully while keeping his eye out for Lucy. The swells increased, and the wind picked up as he positioned himself on the portside terrace outside Lucy's studio.

O recorded his observations for the security log, then remained in position, uncertain of the most appropriate course of action. He couldn't see the painting that held Lucy in its thrall. She gave no indication that she saw him, even though she was facing in his direction. Finally, she stopped painting and stood awhile, transfixed in front of the easel.

He watched as Lucy opened the terrace doors on the far side of the studio. She returned to the easel and took the painting into her hands, turned, and began to walk toward the open doors. He quickly returned to the main corridor and exited onto that same terrace. Lucy was already on the starboard side of the forward terrace, clutching the painting, which was being buffeted by the wind while she struggled to hold it securely. Although O was well within her sightline, it was apparent that she had taken no notice of him. There was no change in her body language or her facial expression, and she made no eye contact. Lucy's mind appeared to be elsewhere and not on board the *Theia*.

A sudden gust of wind took hold of the canvas and ripped it from Lucy's grasp. She remained calm and proceeded to make preparations to fetch it from its landing spot on a lower deck where it had become wedged among the loungers stacked and secured there. Lucy climbed over some chairs stacked on her terrace, bent far forward, and reached for the canvas, which remained far beyond her grasp. When she failed to retrieve her prize, she calmly began to hike up her nightgown in order to climb from the terrace to the deck below. She appeared undeterred by the sudden gusts of wind.

Before Lucy could execute a leap onto the lower terrace, O was upon her, securing her within a massive bearhug. She didn't cry out in shock or struggle to return to her task; instead, she seemed to take comfort in the embrace. She was still asleep. He guided her back to her stateroom and helped her settle back into bed.

Upon returning to the security office, Oko updated the security log and noticed that Ebo had also made an entry. Apparently, after reading the first entry by Oko, he had taken position to watch Lucy as well, though from a different location. He had retrieved the painting and had placed it back on the easel in the studio.

The storm that hit during the night wasn't quite over when Lucy awoke from her slumber. She felt she hadn't slept well, but couldn't specify any restlessness or sleep disturbance as the cause. She noticed that there was a message for her from O, requesting an immediate meeting.

"How immediate?" she wrote.

"As soon as you feel comfortable to meet. Definitely before you get a start to your day."

"Thirty minutes. The studio. I've got coffee!"

"OK," came his reply.

Lucy quickly tended to her morning routine of freshening up and dressing, then she left her stateroom and made her way to the studio. O was waiting for her at the door to the studio, a covered basket in hand.

"Guten morgen, Frau Gillespie," O greeted her.

"Guten morgen, O," Lucy responded. "So, what's up?" She entered and moved toward the Nespresso machine. "Café? Type?"

"Cappuccino, *bitte*. I've brought pastries." O inhaled deeply and began his explanation while Lucy made the coffee and brought it to the small table.

"You had a very eventful night last night, though it appears that you do not remember. Have you examined the painting on the easel this morning?" O asked gently.

"No, I haven't. Tell me, was I sleepwalking?" Lucy sat and let out a deep sigh.

"Yes, I believe so." O outlined what he had observed the previous night and showed her the video from the security cameras.

"This isn't the first time, O. Something similar has happened twice before, but that was four years ago, and I was under considerable stress back then. That's not the case here. It looks like I owe you my life, Oko." She rose, took his hand in hers, and kissed his cheek. "Thank you. I guess I should take a look at the infamous painting then, shouldn't I?"

The painting had been rather dramatically modified. While it remained an underwater scene with whales and other sea life, the technique used might be best described as deconstructive impressionism, and it didn't reflect the style Lucy was currently employing. The currents and eddies of the water at that depth were suggested. Although the brush and knife work required study and contemplation, Lucy could interpret much of what she saw on the canvas. In the distance, a pod of sperm whales slept just under the surface, and a large sperm whale was rising from the trench with a massive squid captured in its maw, but certain other applications of colour seemed to lack a specific purpose. Lucy wondered what there might be that she wasn't seeing. Perhaps, in time, more might be discovered in the painting.

"Can we please keep this entire matter between us, O?" Lucy asked, trying to refrain from pleading.

"I am sorry, but that will not be possible. It is our duty to provide full reports to Monsieur Witherspoon. I do not know what he will do once he's informed. I think that he will most likely discuss the matter with you and probably your husband. He will want to keep you safe."

"I just don't want anyone to fuss or worry about me. This is the third time I've wandered, but nothing bad has ever happened to me, even though this time it sounds like something might have had you not been present, O. I haven't the slightest idea what triggered this. Actually, I don't even know *what* has been triggered. Why this painting?"

"I am sorry that I can't be of help in that regard, Madame. But, at least, you can speak with your husband before Monsieur Witherspoon does and frame this as you wish. I fully understand your desire not to be contained or limited as a result of your somnambulism, but I do think it's best if certain key people are brought up to date on these events."

Lucy agreed with O's assessment of the situation. "Will you accept this painting as a gift, O? With my thanks. Just let me sign it, and let the signature dry before you remove it to your stateroom."

Graciously, O accepted Lucy's token of appreciation and remained with her in the studio while she sent a message for Kent to join her there. After having made himself available to answer Kent's questions regarding the previous night, O then departed to report to Mark while Lucy and Kent discussed the significance of her nocturnal wandering.

Kent's concern was substantial. "I don't know how to help you, Lucy. If you know, please tell me!"

"Kent, I wouldn't have realized that anything unusual happened last night had O not told me. I found it hard to believe, even after he showed me the video. As far as I'm concerned, I had a reasonable night. It was perhaps not the best sleep but certainly okay. I don't know what's triggered this. No idea at all. Weird. I fell asleep with the outside view on my video screen, listening to the audio. The painting was one I was already working on, the sleep-painting episode merely resulted in a few changes. Significant ones, sure, but it's not as if the whole painting is new, not like the first two were years ago."

"Okay, I won't dwell on what could have happened, because nothing significant did happen. But I am going to worry about you nevertheless, you know. Perhaps you're communicating with the whales; we know you've got good language skills," Kent suggested in an attempt to inject some humour into all this. "Maybe it's time we got you back on land, or at least closer to it."

CHAPTER 32

Yoichi and Lucy had scheduled a call. Lucy arranged to be served a salad for lunch in the studio, so she could join Yoichi while the agent in Toronto enjoyed her breakfast.

"Good morning!" Lucy greeted her.

"What? Not in the language of the region you're visiting? I'm shocked," she said playfully.

"We've been all over the eastern Med, and I'm not even sure where we are now," Lucy said. "It's been a wonderful trip, and now we're returning to Antibes. Then there's this big party in a few days. Yikes!"

"Ah yes, you and parties . . ." Yoichi said, knowingly. "Remember to get your nails done. And don't you dare roll your eyes at me!" She admonished her friend. "Promise me you'll take the time to get all gussied up; I want a photo of the end product."

"Gussied up? This is nearly 2020, not 1930."

Yoichi responded by changing the subject. "Where have you visited since last we spoke?"

"We visited several interesting places in Turkey—I've used some of them in paintings— and then we went to Cyprus and visited the various archeological sites you mentioned from your trip all those years ago, kind of like following in your footsteps—and Nate's."

"Speaking of Nathan Bellamy, I hear that Interpol has taken him into their custody. Someone said he has a partner in his criminal enterprise. Word is that it's a woman. I don't know what she's supposed to have done in this endeavour. Perhaps he figures that, if he flips on her, his own sentence will be reduced. But they'll need to hear her side of the story first, I assume. They haven't even located her."

"I'm relieved that his activities were curtailed before he got his claws into Mark. I mean, he already had a copy of Mark's Gentileschi, so probably would have tried to substitute it and steal the real thing, just as he attempted with Serge in Paris. It would have been tragic for Mark to have lost Theia's art collection on top of the tragedy of having already lost her. The whole thing was just serendipitous, wasn't it?"

"Definitely," Yoichi said. "Well, now that all the paperwork is in order for the shipping of the artwork, yours included, give me a call when you get back to Antibes, and we'll set a date for the movers to go aboard and pack the collection and your paintings as well. Theia's will be in secure storage; I don't want to take possession of them. They'll be photographed as they go in . . . you know the drill. By the way, what are you eating?"

"Not much," Lucy said, not actually answering the question. "We're having bouillabaisse tonight to celebrate a return to French waters, so I'm trying to keep it extra light during the day. Any excuse for a celebration, but I'm not knocking it. Celebrating even minor things is quite delightful, so I've discovered."

Lucy slept in late the next day, as she had planned, having spent part of the previous day being pampered in the spa on board the *Theia*, enjoying a massage and a variety of beauty treatments in preparation for the big party on board the *Croesus* the following night. *Yoichi would be so pleased.* Today would be spent out of the sun, relaxing, just as she had been advised by the aesthetician.

Lucy lacked real makeup skill, which comes only with practise. At home in Toronto, Yoichi would always arrive early before any big event and help with it. But Yoichi wasn't going to be able to do her makeup for this big party, as she was six-thousand kilometres away. Fortunately, Alice promised to arrange for the best makeup artist available. Lucy was relieved.

All this fuss for a friggin' party! she thought. *I didn't do all this when Kent and I got married!*

Lucy was a bit of an introvert and large parties made her nervous, especially when she was unfamiliar with the venue and knew few people in attendance. When she had asked, Mark told her there would probably be a few hundred people or so, but he wasn't privy to those details, so he couldn't be certain. *Great, I'll know three people—four if I look in a mirror.*

She had gotten a lot better with crowds over the years since the challenges of 2015 though. She knew she was strong and that her confidence had grown enormously since then.

Kent entered her room just as she finished readying herself to meet the day. "The *Croesus* has arrived in the bay, just outside the harbour. For the best view, just go to the top level. Wait until you see this behemoth. I've spilled juice on my trousers, so I'll join you as soon as I've changed." And then he was gone.

Lucy topped her head with a large, floppy sun hat and, following Kent's suggestion, made her way to the uppermost deck.

The bay was dotted with the usual sailboats and motor yachts, entering and exiting the harbour, and she noticed a cruise ship but couldn't see the *Croesus*. Then it hit her.

"Oh, my goodness!" she exclaimed.

"What do you think of the *Croesus,* Lucy?" Mark asked. "Was this worth returning from our Aegean adventure?"

Kent arrived before she could answer. "What are we looking at, Mark?"

"I thought that was a cruise ship!" Lucy admitted.

"Well, I've looked at similar-sized cruise ships, and they tend to carry seventeen hundred passengers. I actually found one that was one hundred and fifty feet shorter and carried two thousand passengers, so your reaction was completely reasonable, Lucy.

Mark grinned. "From what I've learned, there's a regular crew in excess of one hundred taking care of the *Croesus* and about forty to fifty invited guests, so there's probably twenty to twenty-five staterooms. I figure we might have an additional three-hundred and fifty joining the party tomorrow night, bringing the number of guests to four hundred. Then again, I could be wrong. Unless someone tells me, we won't be able to tell how large the group is though, since they'll be scattered through various areas of the vessel. The *Croesus* could easily accommodate a greater number for such a party, but I think Grisha wants to keep this rather select. Intimate."

"Intimate?" Lucy blurted. "I can't think of even ten people as being 'intimate'."

"Well, he does seat ninety people in the dining room. Remember that the *Croesus* is over 230 metres in length, so that's over 755 feet."

"And that's what? A superyacht? Mega? Giga?" Kent inquired.

"Those terms are pretty fluid. I'd say that *super* applies to the smaller of the large yachts; something in the range of thirty to fifty metres. *Mega* initially referred to the cost of the vessel, but they'd all be *mega* at today's prices, so it's now assumed to refer to vessels above fifty metres in length. And *giga* is a new term and not generally used, but probably refers to those above seventy metres in length, though there are already so many they might want to narrow that down further and make it a minimum of ninety, or perhaps, one hundred metres. If you want to use the correct term, Kent, and if we take my interpretation as accurate, then the *Croesus* is a *mega* yacht several times over. Does that put its size into context for you? The *Theia's* merely a half-pint by comparison. The *Croesus* is double her length, and there's the additional deck and the wider beam to consider.

"The Russian oligarchs are driving the market with their one-upmanship. Some years ago, a chap took possession of his new yacht and had the biggest new vessel until, a brief time later, another launched his, which was a mere hundred and fifty *centimetres* longer. Apparently, the second chap had some insider information about the construction of the first chap's, so he had the yacht he was having constructed made just a bit longer than originally planned, which came as quite the shock to the first chap. He was so disappointed, you'd have thought his world had come to and end. And then, as with the *Croesus*, every four years or so they do a complete refit, getting upgrades and new toys. Of course, such a refit takes nearly a year, so they arrange to have another yacht while their primary vessel is in the shop. It's all rather adolescent, isn't it?

"The *Croesus* will have it all—and more. Sets a new standard in 'mine is bigger and flashier than yours.' That's another thing about these vessels: with all the cutting-edge tech, once launched, you can bet that someone will have some newer and better tech than yours just about the very next day. It's like greyhounds chasing the rabbit at the track."

"So, how many decks am I looking at there?" Lucy asked.

"Eight, compared with the *Theia's* seven. And while we've got one helipad, the *Croesus* has two. There's a conference room, games room, dance floor, sushi bar, full spa, a full gym—two actually, since there's a separate one for crew members—indoor and outdoor pools, Jacuzzis kept at variety of temperatures . . . and much more."

"I guess, more and bigger tenders too." Kent commented.

"You've got it! Some of the tenders are elaborate yachts unto themselves and will look like little versions of the *Croesus*. Mama with her babies." Mark looked at Lucy and Kent, who were at a loss for words. "During the world wars, the largest ships were accompanied by smaller supply vessels. That's what some owners are doing with their yachts. They are accompanied by a smaller vessel that provides storage and supplies, as well as accommodation for some crew members. I refer to such vessels as a Renfield, like in 'Dracula,' but the term isn't catching on, darn it.

"Oh, the other thing is that, based on what the *Croesus* had before the refit, I'd say you can expect that there's a functional missile-defence system as well as a bullet-proof owner's suite. There's also a technology available now—and I presume the *Croesus* will have had it applied, or installed, or however they do it—that makes it impossible for people at a distance to sneak photos, like the paparazzi tend to, given the people who frequent such vessels."

"How would that work, Mark?" Kent inquired.

"I really don't understand it, Kent. I probably wasn't paying attention when it was described to me. As I understand it, when a photo is taken, the technology causes a flare, and the photo appears over-exposed and unusable. But like I said, I don't know the details, and I've not shopped around to install such a system myself, so I can't tell you any more than that."

"Actually, I think I read about items of clothing that do the same thing," Lucy said, "not that it's the kind of thing I need worry about. Thanks for preparing us a bit for what we can expect tomorrow. However, it sounds as if there could still be loads of surprises on board."

"Undoubtedly," Mark agreed. "Oh, and one final comment, given the recent refit, you're now looking at the first one-billion-dollar private yacht, though likely not the last."

CHAPTER 33

Lucy spent a second quiet day. At the appointed hour, she started to prepare herself for the party on the *Croesus*. She began by laying out her apparel, evening bag, and accessories, including her cellphone, on her bed. She wasn't planning to phone anyone, but selfies might be possible, especially if she posed with members of the younger set and took a few photos that just happened to feature aspects of the *Croesus*. She knew Yoichi would like to see. *Yes, this was more Yoichi's scene.*

The gown she had selected from Theia's wardrobe had never been worn. She was unaware of the event for which Theia might have purchased it but felt uncomfortable asking Mark about that. The dress was a fine fabric called mulberry silk. It had a form-fitting bodice, which extended asymmetrically beyond the hips. Layers of bias-cut skirting reached upward to her hip on the left side and about mid-thigh on the right side. The back dipped low, and the front displayed a halter neckline.

The hues were variations of blue with just a touch of green—this was, after all, Theia's dress—with the darker at the bottom giving way to nearly pure white near the top of the neckline. It wasn't an ombre effect but done in swirls and waves intertwined with one another and evoking the various shades apparent in the seas.

Silk-thread embroidery had been used to produce the pattern of colours and resulted in a garment that was soft, comfortable, and remarkably shimmery. Only the asymmetric skirt was accentuated with a small quantity of crystals. Lucy assumed they were crystals and not diamonds, but with her recent experiences of excess, she was uncertain. No matter. The effect was magical.

When Fabrice arrived to do her hair and makeup, Lucy was ready in her dressing gown. For much of the time, she let him work without comment. She wanted to look like herself, just more polished. From what she had seen in her travels, that was the popular approach to makeup in the region anyway, so she was trusting of Fab's efforts. She knew that he kiddingly referred to himself as "Fab the Fabulous," and she hoped it wasn't an overstatement. Periodically, he would cross to the bed and take another look at the gown, taking inspiration from its pattern and colours.

"Fini!" he declared triumphantly, and Lucy opened her eyes and smiled.

"Merci, Fab. Ç'est parfait," Lucy replied, pleased with what she saw in her mirror.

When Fab was gone with his cart of cosmetics and implements, Lucy gathered the jewellery she had selected earlier from Theia's safe. The dress didn't require the necklace, so she returned it to her own safe for the moment. She had considered the emeralds and even the deep-blue sapphires, but instead used only a pairing of pavé-set diamond-pendant earrings and a two-inch wide pavé-set diamond-cuff bracelet, both in platinum. While most of the diamonds were white, there were also many that were blue, though they varied widely in value from light to medium blue. *Of course, Theia and her love of blue.* The shades were clustered and graduated rather than randomly scattered. Lucy was very pleased with the result. Against the backdrop of her auburn hair, somewhat lightened by the sun, the diamonds appeared to drip white hot from her earlobes and set her wrist ablaze with sparkle. Like her dress, the effect was one of fluidity. *Not bad. Not bad at all.*

She made a quick telephone call to Kent and discovered that he and Mark were ready and waiting in the main lounge. She grabbed her evening bag and left her stateroom to join them.

The men rose from their seats as she entered the room. Mark smiled from ear to ear with his approval. "Beautiful!" he exclaimed, smiling and clasping his hands together.

Kent crossed over to her and whispered in her ear, "Sweetheart, you look fantastic."

She knew that she did.

Then he continued, aloud, "I thought you were going to get all dressed up tonight, but I see no change here." He winked.

Lucy playfully punched him in the arm. After a few photos were taken, they made their way to the tender, a luxurious, enclosed passenger-transport vessel with ample comfortable seating for sixteen passengers. They were four: Lucy, Kent, Mark, O.

They sat opposite one another in the transport vessel. Lucy looked across at Kent and thought that he looked very handsome, perhaps becoming even more so as he aged. He had maintained his youthful vitality into his forties. There was the odd strand of grey beginning to pepper his thick, dark hair, though most of the grey was at his temples. A confirmed clothes horse, Kent knew how to select well-tailored suits and he put his look together with ease. His tuxedo was well-constructed from a fine fabric and fit impeccably. *Gillespie, Kent Gillespie,* she chuckled to herself, thinking how he might deliver the line. It would be done with panache.

In short order, their vessel pulled alongside the designated docking area of the *Croesus*. O exited first, followed by Mark.

When their party was checked off the guest list, Kent exited, then put his arm out to Lucy, steadying her in opposition to the movement of the tender vessel against the *Croesus*. In that touch, he could feel the trust she held in him, and she the concern and care he felt for her.

It was as if they were entering through the VIP entrance of a luxury hotel, perhaps the George V in Paris or Burj Al Arab in Dubai.

The level into which they had entered featured the beach club. All the related toys were displayed, including shiny new jet skis and surf boards with kites and sails. The tender garage was open, and Lucy noticed Kent and O were transfixed by something within. They were looking at a motorcycle with a futuristic angular chassis, apparently new, even to O, and most definitely new to her and Kent. Mark joined them, and with him was a younger man who Mark introduced as Alexei, the youngest son of their host, Gregori Orlov, owner of the *Croesus*. Alexei appeared pleased that they were admiring his motorcycle.

"When they produce this, they are required to limit the speed to under three-hundred kilometres per hour. I had them remove the limitation, and now we can go more than three-hundred-fifty kilometres per hour. Here, I will make an opportunity—Antibes to Monaco in under fifteen minutes. When I do this . . . zoom!" Alexei said, looking at Lucy, expecting that she would now be in even greater awe of him. He would have been disappointed had he realised the truth. Alexei brought the three of them to greet his father and then left in search of a more adoring audience.

Grigori Orlov was physically similar to Mark and approximately the same age. His personality made him appear larger than his measurements would indicate. He virtually filled the *Croesus*. When introduced to Lucy, he took her hand and engulfed it within both of his, then gently kissed it, his eyes smiling playfully. “Rufina, welcome. Enjoy . . . eat, drink, dance until morning if you like.”

“Rufina?” Lucy decided to correct this apparent misunderstanding. “I’m sorry, I don’t understand. My name is Lucy.”

“Ah,” Grigori said, apparently amused that she was setting out to correct him. “‘Rufina’ means ‘woman with red hair,’ and I think you are the only one tonight, or at least the only one I have noticed.”

“Ah,” Lucy said, copying Grigori’s tone.

“Mark tells me that you are an artist of considerable renown, but I have not seen your paintings, unfortunately.” The last word was said with an exaggerated mock sadness.

“Actually, my work is signed ‘Awen’,” Lucy said. A slender man standing very near Grigori appeared to take note of that on his e-tablet.

“Please, call me Grisha. Now, Mark insists I get to know Kent, but later we shall find one another, and I shall take you away—” he smiled, his eyes twinkling playfully, “to meet my lovely wife, Agafya.”

The conversation with Kent followed a similar pattern but without the flirtation. When their conversation was concluded, Grisha continued to greet other newly-arrived guests, and Mark ushered Lucy and Kent away for a tour of the *Croesus*.

Mark noticed that Grisha had taken a parting glance in Lucy’s direction, and he chuckled to himself. Kent noticed it too and chortled.

“Grisha loved that sparring, Lucy,” Mark said.

Lucy thought there would be no way possible for her to convey the beauty, grandeur, opulence, and perfection of the *Croesus* to Yoichi. Whatever Yoichi might imagine, she would tell her to make it more so—and more so, yet again. Champagne flowed freely and was often accompanied by a reminder that Cristal was created in 1876 for Alexander II, Tsar of Russia.

Mark knew his way around the *Croesus*, having been a frequent visitor prior to the recent refit, and was able to point out the changes that had been made. "The climbing wall is new. That's probably for the kids. I can't imagine Grisha taking up scrambling, let alone mountain climbing. And I see there is an additional medical clinic; there's probably one for guests and one for crew. You know, that's not your usual medical clinic; these are both completely functional ICUs."

They had taken an elevator down to the level of the beach club and the tenders once again, and Lucy was approaching her fill. She wanted to engage in normal party activities. Kent, however, was interested in examining the rotating columns on either side of the "beach," which resulted in the expansion of the surface available at the water's edge at the stern of the vessel. It wasn't apparent when the yacht was berthed, with its stern near the dock, but out on the bay, this portion extended outward and increased in width as well, opening somewhat like a fan, or the tail of a peacock.

"Grisha's got that Sikorsky, so I thought he might have tried for a third helipad while he was at it. That might have negatively impacted the look. Instead, they've installed a system similar to that on aircraft carriers—the helicopter is taken below by way of an elevator platform, moved aside, and then the platform returns empty. Interesting approach. What did you think of the submarine?" Mark asked.

Kent answered, "I don't get it, Mark. Why?"

"If you need to ask 'why,' Kent, then there is no way you could understand. Instead, the question asked is 'why not?' The default position is to do it, have it, control it. In another four years, the *Croesus* will undergo another refit, or be replaced by something bigger and better."

"Let's find the partiers," Lucy urged, interrupting the men.

"Why not?" they answered in unison.

Soon thereafter, Mark left them and headed in Grisha's direction, leaving Lucy and Kent to check out the various lounges, bars, games rooms, and other social areas. They discovered a large room with a stage area, on which a popular band Lucy recognized was playing live while people danced on a lighted floor. In another room, designated as a disco, a rave was going on. They could see Alexei acting much like one of the characters Lucy and Kent had only seen in films. He and his entourage of adoring female companions and male friends were crowded into a semicircular booth in the corner, drinking champagne, wasting caviar, and sharing a powdered white substance that, on land, might have made them the focus of the police. The young women, provocatively dressed, were each making it clear to Alexei that they were readily available and loved him very much.

"O translated for me something he overheard being said in Russian concerning our young friend," Kent said, "It's a Russian saying: 'Intelligent thoughts have always followed him, but he was faster'." They left Alexei to his fun.

Wherever they wandered, Lucy and Kent were offered assistance, food, and drink. While they were standing on deck, looking out over the water, yet another attendant approached them. Kent was preparing to indicate that they required nothing at that time when the attendant offered information about an unusual audio experience available in certain areas.

"You wear the earbuds and use the control card or your phone to select the type of music you would like. You will both hear the music playing at the same point of the song, so you can dance or perhaps even sing to the music," the attendant explained, "while others listen to their own preferred choices. May I suggest the Ebony Saloon? It will offer the opportunity for you to dance, inside or outside."

The attendant offered to escort them to the Ebony Saloon, but Kent requested directions, hoping to get lost along the way. He and Lucy made their way through the main corridors, eschewing use of the elevator. Just as they reached the bottom of a flight of stairs, they saw Grisha and O enter a doorway, through which Mark had said Grisha's stateroom and private office were housed in a bullet-proof shell.

"I wonder what's up. I saw Grisha and O enter that same door earlier tonight." Then she whispered into Kent's ear. "Different O."

CHAPTER 34

There was an attendant at the door of the Ebony Saloon, holding a tray of earbuds and control cards. After a peek into the dark interior, Kent suggested they get the earbuds positioned and operating prior to entering.

"What sort of music were you thinking?" Kent asked.

"You pick first, and if I think it needs a change, I'll select something after thirty minutes, okay?"

"How about we start with a pop selection from the 1970s—to match the decade of that Dom Perignon you liked—then move forward. I don't think I'm capable of any of the ballroom selections like waltz or rhumba or cha-cha," he said, swaying his hips as if to Latin rhythms. Lucy giggled and was still giggling as the attendant opened the door for them.

The room's shiny, black interior created the sensation of limitless space. Infinity. As her eyes adjusted to the dark, Lucy realized that there was sufficient light provided by the myriad pin-point light sources on the ceiling to navigate the space easily. The dance floor was lit from beneath, and the effect was that of stars in a nighttime sky, making the dancers appear to be floating in space. There was movement in the stars, triggered by the presence of the dancers, times when a sudden dazzling brightness would sweep across the floor in an arch, just for a moment—a visual swoosh.

Lucy giggled again when she took a look at the dancers, moving contrary to the seventies pop to which she was listening. *If I weren't already at my limit, I'd have more champagne or something before going on that dance floor.*

What she was going to say was lost, as Kent, a big smile across his face, swept her into his arms upon hearing the early bars of a favourite song, the Pointer Sisters' "Fire." In that moment—in the arms of the man she loved, dancing to a song they both really liked—nothing else mattered. The song built in intensity, leaving them both spent by its final notes.

They left the dance floor and chose a table. In honour of their host, they requested vodka. To their surprise, a bottle of Jewel of Russia Ultra Black Label vodka was brought to their table as one might be brought a bottle of champagne in a fine restaurant. The bottle was cold, having come from the freezer, and it was placed upon the table, contained within a sleek, angular wine cooler. Kent thought it had an architectural aesthetic. It was engraved: *Croesus*. Everything onboard seemed to be monogrammed with the name of the yacht.

The attendant poured their drinks into two frozen shot glasses, before returning the bottle to the cooler. Subsequently, a selection of appetizers appeared front of them. Kent requested an explanation of the items.

"The black caviar is Beluga. The eggs are large and delicate. The lighter-coloured caviar is Osetra. You will find it has a unique flavour. This, the third caviar, is a special gift to you from Monsieur Orlov. It is an Iranian caviar called Almas. It is white in colour, because Almas is produced from the eggs of a very rare albino sturgeon between sixty and one-hundred-years old." Lucy thought she detected a note of sadness in the server's voice.

The serving dish also contained blini and dark bread with butter, chopped onion, pickled tomatoes, quail eggs, sour cream, and tiny boiled potatoes flavoured with dill—items intended to cut the saltiness of the caviar.

"I'm going to taste the vodka before I start the caviar," Lucy said. She took a sip and declared to Kent, "This is quite different from what I remember about vodka. This actually has quite an interesting flavour—peppery. It also reminds me a bit of non-carbonated mineral water. But it's really smooth. Potent, but smooth."

"You're starting to sound like the vodka version of a wine snob."

Cautiously, they began to taste the various types of caviar, selecting among all the accompaniments, except for the chopped onion.

"The vodka really goes well with the caviar, doesn't it? I guess there's a logical reason behind this Russian tradition. The second one, the Osetra, is a bit firmer than the Beluga and tastes rather nutty," Kent said.

"I'm feeling a bit bad about eating the Almas caviar, but I guess we should, since Grisha made a point of sharing it with us. I feel guilty eating eggs from a rare creature who managed to attain such an advanced age." Lucy explained.

"I know that they no longer need to kill the sturgeon to get the eggs, so we can hope that these eggs were collected by these newer methods."

"What are the odds?" Lucy countered.

After their caviar and vodka break, she noticed Mark enter the saloon. He spoke to the crew member tending bar, who then consulted one of the attendants, the one who had served their table. Lucy watched as the attendant and Mark turned and nodded in their direction. Mark was still approaching their table when Grisha's personal assistant, the slender man, arrived at Kent's elbow, inviting him to join in a discussion with Grisha in his private office. Kent was less concerned leaving Lucy for a while, given Mark's timely arrival. Kent excused himself, though it was clear to Lucy that he would have preferred to remain with her.

As there were only two chairs at the table they had selected, Mark took Kent's vacated seat. "Kent shouldn't be long. Are you enjoying yourselves?" he asked.

"Yes, very much, thank you. I couldn't begin to describe this experience to anyone. They'd not believe a word of it," she sighed. "The lighting in this room produces quite a magical effect, doesn't it? And the wireless earbuds are great. We visited the other areas, but this was perfect for us."

"Let's see, I haven't taken a close look at mine. Hmm-m . . . cutting-edge brand, as expected, and probably an early release. What style music have you and Kent selected?"

"We've started with the Pop 1970s selection."

The attendant returned, and Mark requested vodka. "And I'd like the Kamchatka crab, please," he said. "But no abalone or lobster," he added.

"Caviar?" the attendant asked.

"Almas."

"As a surprise, Grisha provided the Almas to us as well," Lucy informed him.

"I think he sent it over for Rufina," Mark said, smiling, "and Kent just happened to be here. It's the most expensive food in the world, you know. Almas runs in the neighbourhood of thirty thousand American dollars per kilo."

"Is that why people select it?"

"Me? I happen to like caviar, and Almas is lower in salt. It's just a habit. Theia got me to avoid extra salt whenever I could, and now it's just something I do. Not to the extreme, mind you. I don't really worry about the salt, especially when only the Beluga or Osetra are available."

"I feel sorry for the sturgeon."

"Look at it this way, Lucy. If you abstain from the caviar, you will merely be depriving yourself of enjoyment. The sturgeon won't benefit at all. The eggs have already been taken and purchased by Grisha, and containers have been opened and their contents will either be used or eventually discarded. Whatever you choose to do will not cause Grisha to exclude it from the next party he holds."

The server brought Mark's appetizer. It was an artfully arranged presentation of the crab, with a dusting of herbs and a sprinkling of black Beluga caviar. The Almas followed later, with condiments and more vodka.

"Looks like a lovely night, as usual. It's nice to have the invisible doors for a function like this, the same idea as with the casinos in Vegas," Mark observed, changing the topic.

"I really can't tell how many people are at this party. You said it would be difficult, and you were right. They're all so spread out. The social areas aren't empty, but they certainly aren't crowded either."

When Kent returned, he kissed Lucy, whispering into her ear, "I'll tell you when we're in private." Then he pulled up a third chair to the table and made a few comments to Mark, who responded briefly. For a short time, there was friendly banter among the three of them, then Mark excused himself.

"Dance?" Kent asked. Lucy nodded in agreement. But first she separated a piece of bias-cut fabric from the skirt of her dress. The extra piece of fabric provided additional fullness to the skirt when it was attached, but was also available to use as a wrap. There were two slits for her arms, so the wrap wouldn't slip off but remain properly positioned.

For a short time, they danced on the starlit dance floor, then decided to continue on the deck. The song was emotional, nearly mournful. It was seductive and undoubtedly romantic. They held one another as if creating a synergy and sharing their life force. Their bodies swayed to the music, and the rest of the world disappeared for them. Had they been aware, they might have noticed that the other dancers had stopped and cleared from the floor. Lucy and Kent were alone in their dance.

Mark returned, and finding the table empty but for Lucy's evening bag, located them dancing outside on the broad terrace. He stood, leaning against the wall. As he watched, his earbuds tuned to the Pop 1970s selection Lucy and Kent were hearing, his gaze softened, and his mind drifted.

The scene reminded Mark of something quite lovely, but he couldn't put his finger on it. The song was "Do You Want to Dance," sung by Bette Midler. Kent held Lucy in a loving embrace. He bent his head in close to hers. Her dress swirled and shimmered around their feet, the darker blue becoming lighter as it reached upward toward her hips. In the gentle sea breeze, her wrap periodically billowed a bit near her head, appearing to engulf it. And amid all the shimmer and subdued sparkle of the skirt and wrap, there would appear a sudden flash of brilliance from the diamonds in Lucy's earrings and bracelet, Theia's earrings and bracelet.

It occurred to Mark that the scene before him embodied the romance of *La Valse*. Even as the song ended, the couple remained entwined. Then Kent bent down and kissed Lucy on the lips. Her eyes closed as she savoured the moment.

CHAPTER 35

Lucy's call to Yoichi was scheduled for two days after the party. It was only seven in the morning in Toronto yet already one in the afternoon in Antibes.

"You're eating light again, I see," Yoichi said, noticing Lucy's lunch selection.

"Yeah, two days since the party, and I'm still suffering from too much of everything."

"Tell me," Yoichi urged. "Start with the food."

Lucy ran through all the dishes she'd noticed on offer. It took a while for her to even begin running out of details. "Let's see, what else. Um . . . there was Wagyu beef tartare, made using rare brandy and truffles, then these little pies called piroshki with all sorts of fillings. Oh, and in the cinema, they offered hot dogs but they were made with Wagyu beef and cognac."

"You bothered to watch a film?"

"Gosh, no. We just popped in to see what the cinema looked like. I didn't even bother to see what the film was. Apparently, the chairs move to enhance the action on the screen, but I didn't try it out. I guess the cinema would come in handy if the weather became bad and your location didn't provide other options."

"Get to dessert," Yoichi urged.

"They had the best cake I ever tasted, called *medovik*, a Russian honey cake. There must have been fifteen or more layers. It was soft, sticky, creamy, and dreamy, and decorated with elaborate spun-sugar creations and flakes of twenty-four-carat edible gold leaf. Everything was decorated beautifully, lots of edible flowers and macaron towers. You name it, and if it might be considered special for some reason, I'm confident it was there."

"What was his wife like? Twenty-something and svelte?"

"No, she's neither. Her name is Agafya, and she's actually quite grandmotherly. I sense she indulges her sons; they have three, and grandsons as well. I get the impression that she's protecting her territory from her daughters-in-law."

"Does she have daughters? Or granddaughters?"

"I'm not clear on that, but I don't think daughters, perhaps granddaughters. I don't know. We chatted awhile, but she was periodically interrupted by other guests, so conversation was a bit difficult."

Lucy leaned in a bit closer to her screen. "Apparently, I look like Mark's late wife, Theia. Perhaps that's why he's been so sweet toward me. Agafya's husband called me 'Rufina,' which means 'red-haired woman,' and she says that Theia was also called 'Rufina' by him. I sense he's quite the lady's man. It must be tiresome for her, watching him flirt and these young things all hanging around, ready to pounce."

"Little ones?"

"No, at their youngest, the grandkids are teens. There was a room just for them near the cinema with the hot dogs. The room had a window containing really thick glass, so you can see what's in the water. It was set up with a DJ, just like one of the New York or Miami clubs might be, but for younger ones. The youngest son, Alexei, had another room set up with techno music for an older crowd, and it seemed to have all the trappings of a stereotypical rave."

"So, a real party boat?"

"Well, yeah, but there are so many social rooms that there was something for everyone. You know, one of the venues contains a stage that can accommodate a fifty-piece orchestra? The night of the party, there was just a dance band in that location. I knew them but can't recall their name right now. I think many of the more staid or older crowd were in the main lounge, which had more conversation pit seating, and live music that was just pleasant and melodious. There was a string quartet at one point, then a pianist and a flutist with what I was told is called a *quena*. That's the traditional cane or wood flute of the Andes. Quite a lovely sound, rather ethereal."

"Anything else?"

"Ah . . . fireworks at midnight?"

"Okay, the next time you come to one of my parties, I'm just going to give up trying to impress and serve a block of processed cheese slices with soda crackers. Maybe a few celery sticks as an extra treat."

"We'd still have a great time!"

"We would," agreed Yoichi.

"What has been arranged from your end regarding the transport of the artwork from the *Theia?* My understanding is that everything has been arranged, but we're awaiting confirmation for a day and time. I'd like to know, so I can plan around it. I'd like to be present that day."

"You understand correctly," Yoichi said, nodding. "They're expected to arrive—that's three men and a truck from Martin and Mansfield—day after tomorrow, unless that's a problem for you. They'll have all their own equipment and supplies."

"No, that sounds good. I'll confirm that with Mark, but assume it's okay. He's been asking on a regular basis."

"There's not much left of August. Have you decided where you're going next?"

"I don't know. I think we have both enjoyed everything, but perhaps need to recharge in that special way you can do only at home. This has worked well, because we've kept busy, me with my art and Kent with his French lessons and just soaking up the ambience. He said that it's given him a much-needed new perspective. As far as a purely relaxing vacation though, perhaps this is too long for us. I'm not ready to run off to a tropical island like Gauguin, but perhaps short trips, anywhere from two weeks to two months, might suit us better. We'll just have to see. Kent said that Mark offered his house in Bali to us. Apparently, it's quite a secluded hideaway. I'm thinking perhaps Ireland would be nice in September. And Kent has mentioned London as a final stop."

"So, you don't know. Well, sounds as if Bali might provide some inspiration as well. Let me know how the move goes, okay? Gotta run now. Take care!" With that, Yoichi signed off.

Packing went smoothly. Security was heightened while the items were prepared for transport, and the crates containing Theia's collection were loaded into Martin and Mansfield's vehicle. The truck looked like a longer version of a bank security truck. Another large crate held the canvases completed by Lucy in Antibes. The crates were checked and re-checked to ensure that they were secured and could be transported safely for successful delivery to the proper addresses. Theia's collection would be delivered into humidity-controlled secure storage while Lucy's would be delivered to Yoichi at the Song

Gallery. Oko watched the proceedings from the security room on board the *Theia*.

Ebo stood beside Lucy on the deck. "I just wanted to take this opportunity to wish you all the best," he said. "You might not see me around much for the balance of the month. O is moving into a new job situation beginning the first of September, perhaps sooner if necessary. We plan to display your painting in our new stateroom. It has been my pleasure to converse with you in German and help you train in self-defence. It appears that you and Monsieur Gillespie make use of your training, perhaps too much, from what he says."

"You might be right about that," Lucy answered. "Would your move have anything to do with the meetings O took with Grigori Orlov the night of the party?" she asked.

"Well, you know I cannot comment on such a thing," he said with a wink. They spoke awhile longer, then each went about their day.

Without the artwork, the yacht's walls looked empty and devoid of personality. It was a sad look, and Lucy was concerned for Mark in such an environment.

However, Mark seemed cheery, and as the month wore on, even his posture seemed to improve. She was pleased for him. To compensate for the lack of artwork, Mark had the number of flower arrangements on display increased, concentrating primarily on white roses, orchids, and blue-white lisianthus.

CHAPTER 36

It was September. Lucy, Kent, and many of the tourists were gone from the Côte d'Azur, Lucy and Kent electing to fly north to visit the United Kingdom and the Republic of Ireland rather than accepting Mark's kind offer of his house in Bali. The season was still bustling with locals enjoying themselves on the beaches and in the water. The winds had increased, so too had the number of kite surfers. The seaside paths remained open and would remain so until the mistrals picked up and brought strong waves crashing against the rocks, leaving a slippery surface behind as the water receded. The mega and giga yachts would soon begin to prepare for the long voyage westward toward the Caribbean for the coming winter. The smaller ones would likely follow the coastline of Europe northward toward Britain and Ireland before heading south again down the coast of Canada and the US to arrive at their destinations.

Such preparation was not occurring on board the *Theia*. She would remain safe in Antibes, a deep and sheltered harbour.

Mark awakened gently from his deep and restful slumber. He showered and shaved, applied his cologne judiciously, and dressed in his favourite suit. His shoes were new, as was his silk tie with a pattern in shades of blue. He had purchased the items at a shop in nearby Cannes during his last outing there. He took hold of the small florist box, that he'd arranged to be delivered the previous evening, removed the boutonnière—a large, perfect white rose—and affixed it to his lapel. Once again, he ran a comb through his thick grey hair. He looked at himself in his mirror. The barber had given him an excellent cut, perhaps because he'd said this was to be an extra-special day.

He unlocked a desk drawer and removed a small stack of letters, already in their envelopes, some bearing addresses and others merely a name. He placed them at the centre of the desktop, together with a note he'd written and signed more recently—though they all bore today's date. Then he turned to the credenza behind his desk, took the lapis lazuli box carefully into his hands, and left the *Theia,* nodding in acknowledgement to the crewman who had been left on duty to provide security.

Taking the key from his pocket, he unlocked the Arion's garage, situated on the wharf, leaving the lock and the key in place. Then he manoeuvred himself and the box into the Arion and the Arion out of its garage. He was careful and, not wanting to disturb the neighbours in the yachts berthed alongside, made little noise. He didn't bother to take a look backward toward the *Theia.* As he exited through the security gate at a low rate of speed, he gave a small wave of acknowledgement to the attendant on duty. *Poor guy, up all night and now at the end of his shift. Must be tired,* he thought.

O would always follow behind at a distance in the red Ferrari, but O was no longer head of security on board the *Theia.* Mark had dismissed his bodyguards. No longer was the heightened security necessary, not since Theia's art collection had been transported elsewhere.

There was little traffic. It would pick up later, when people began their commute—though most commuters probably used the trains instead. Mark kept to the speed limit, not wanting to upset any of the traffic police. They too would likely be coming to the end of their workday, eager to return home to their families. Soon he had passed Nice, then Villefranche-sur-Mer. In no time at all, Cap Ferrat lay behind him, and he was nearing Eze-sur-Mer. Beyond lay Monaco, but he wasn't going to Monaco. Soon, he signalled right and exited from the main highway, first travelling under then over the main highway as it snaked upward some four hundred metres above the sea. He had new tires on the Arion and noticed that the ride was a bit firmer than usual.

Having reached his destination, Mark unlocked the padlock on the gate and swung it open. He returned to the Arion and drove through the opening, returning by foot to lock the gate once again. Back in the Arion, he drove ahead to the second gate, the one marking the edge of the track beyond which lay the sea stack. This gate had never before been opened, not since being installed. He unlocked it and swung it back, securing it in the open position by looping the chain around the low guardrail that edged the main track on either side of the gate. He secured the chain with the padlock and left the key in the lock. He took the time to walk the length of the short bridge to the outermost edge of the stack. There, he bent over and looked out at the water below. It was too late in the day for fishers and too early for tourists; there were no boats nearby.

Out of habit, Mark gave a wave in the direction of the security camera located on the utility pole by the entrance gate. With O now gone, he wasn't certain to whom he might be waving. Finally, he returned to the Arion.

Mark checked his hair in the mirror and ran a comb through it one last time. He needed to look good for Theia. This was their fiftieth wedding anniversary. He removed the gold chain from around his neck and used the gold key that had dangled from it these past three years to open her Mediterranean blue lapis lazuli box. He removed two gold rings from his pocket—an engagement ring with a modest-sized diamond, and a simple gold band that was a match to the one he wore. He opened the box, and as he had done many years before, kissed the rings and gave them to Theia. They were now back where they belonged.

He activated the ignition of the Arion and commanded the voice-operated system to play Gershwin's "Rhapsody in Blue," in a continuous loop. Then he began to drive, following the curve of the banked track to the left. Constantly accelerating, his velocity increased rapidly. Mark's face bore a hopeful smile of anticipation. He had succeeded in getting the electronic key for the release of the Arion's governor. In the absence of a functioning speed limiter, he was no longer confined to an upper limit of 440 kilometres per hour.

Around and around the track he flew. "Rhapsody in Blue" filled the air and his heart. Theia was with him, and soon he would be with her. Theia, the Titan of precious gems, she who imbued them with their value, their desirability—without Theia, nothing held value.

On the final lap, having reached the highest speed he had ever been able to attain in the Arion, he left the banked track and followed the pavement through the open gate, across the short bridge, and beyond the end of the sea stack. The Arion flew. The air was filled with music, Theia's music. Mark could hear her voice calling him. The pitch was lower than he remembered, but it had been over three years since he'd last heard her voice.

Flying in an arc, the Arion broke free of the earth and then the sky as it eagerly sought the welcoming waters of the Mediterranean, enticed by Arion's father, Poseidon, god of the sea, of earthquakes, and of horses. It pierced the sparkling surface, sinking slowly into the azure waters' understanding embrace. There, in the depths, as if called by the Titans themselves, the Arion found a deep crevasse, created in a previous seismic event, and continued to sink ever deeper, beyond azure and toward indigo. As he sank, with Theia in her lapis lazuli box and both of them together at last in the Arion, the low pitch sound was repeated. The earth itself uttered its approval and blessed the happy couple. The crevasse jolted to a close over them, and seismic activity brought the entire sea stack tumbling down upon them, sealing their tomb. They would spend eternity together, as he had promised.

CHAPTER 37

Kent took her hand in his. "We'll do this again, I promise, but I think it was a good idea to return home now. What's that word that Eve uses? *Frisk?* We are merely *frisk*; we are not truly well. Once we've had some time at home, I'm sure that all the good times will come flooding back to us. It's just that right now, like you, I feel like a deflated balloon."

It was late September, and Lucy and Kent had cut short their travels and flown into Toronto's Pearson International Airport on a British Airway's flight out of Terminal 5 at Heathrow.

Lucy nodded. "Eve would probably remind us to embrace *lagom,* the recognition that we've had enough after all the excess we've experienced over these past months, especially our summer on the Côte d'Azur. Now we're back to aiming for just the right amount, everything in moderation, balance. But speaking of excess . . . You know, you never got around to telling me about your conversation with Grisha during the *Croesus* party."

"Oh, just business. It seemed so much more important at the time. I think that Mark tried to arrange for all sorts of positions or opportunities for people he felt close to. It turns out that Grisha and some of his friends will quite possibly do business with me at some point, somewhere in the world. Especially now that I'm not selling the company to Espie. Remember how Mark connected O with Grisha? It seems he took similar steps for many of his key employees. He provided each with a financial gift and a job opportunity with one of his friends. Apparently, despite letters he left detailing his plans and even a couple of videos—one being of the event itself—there were still legal hurdles to address before the authorities were prepared to declare him dead."

"How are you privy to all this information?"

"Some from Roman but mostly Grisha. I think they're finding it difficult to make sense of Mark's actions. I feel that I do understand, but I haven't been successful in conveying that to either of them."

"So, no one actually saw it happen?" Lucy asked.

"Actually, Papa was viewing the feed from the security camera at that time. Poor woman, it must have been terrible for her. I understand that O was the first person she called, so that's how Grisha became involved so quickly.

"You know," he continued, "you were included as well, in Mark's planning, I mean. Whether or not you realize it, you are now Grisha's new art guru. He doesn't ask; he tells. You are always free to decline, should he ever get around to making a request of you, however."

"He's Russian. Shouldn't I be the 'art tsar'?" Lucy asked. "Besides, I understood from his wife, Agafya, that he already had a woman acting in that capacity."

"Ah, but you are Rufina! Grisha referred to the other woman as Chernyye Volosy. I'm told that just means 'black hair.' Then he got off on a tangent and said some other words, which I was later told meant blue and grey. But I dunno . . . the way he used those words sounded more like cursing or pejoratives. There's likely more to the story. Anyway, he said that Agafya was also pleased with the departure of this Chernyye Volosy. Rufina, my dear, when you were speaking with Agafya, you were being interviewed."

The limousine made the left turn through the open gate of the Gillespie estate and followed the tear-shaped driveway to the portico. Lucy and Kent smiled at the little welcoming committee waiting to greet them. Elinor and Helen, Yoichi, Eve, and Albin were all present. While their luggage was being transferred from the limousine to the house, Lucy shared hugs and kisses with all her friends. A year had been a very long time to be away, yet already it was as if they'd never left. Good friends are like that.

"Is Donald okay?" Lucy asked Yoichi, noticing his absence.

"Yes, but you'll never guess where he is: Paris! He'll be home within the week."

"And who is this sweetie?" Lucy asked, addressing Eve and stroking her golden retriever's head.

"This is Cookie," a smiling Eve announced, with a nod toward Albin. "She picked her own name. We called her every other name, but Cookie was the one she really responded to."

As they moved into the house and the limousine pulled away, Albin pointed out the obvious crowding in the foyer.

"What's all this?" asked Kent. One item was a crate just over one metre in height and approximately one-half metre in length and width. Another was considerably smaller, about the size of a boot box. The final one was what Kent described as being a "suit box."

"These all arrived just a few days ago," Albin explained, handing over an envelope containing instructions for opening the items. Then he left to obtain the necessary tools.

While they dealt with the crates in the foyer, their luggage was taken to their bedrooms, joining those items that had been shipped from their earlier destinations. "This is going to take a very long time, getting organized and settled again. I don't remember what I put in some of those containers that we shipped from New Zealand and Australia," Lucy declared. "That was simply ages ago!"

Albin and Kent carefully began to deconstruct the crates. Lucy identified them as originating with Martin and Mansfield, the art shippers Yoichi had arranged for the Theia Witherspoon collection. Her heart leapt when all that remained was a velvet cloth draped over Camille Claudel's *La Valse*, the same bronze with the lapis lazuli wave she had admired on board the *Theia*. She already had an inkling of what she would find in the suit box: the dress she had worn for the party on board the *Croesus*. She draped it carefully across the dining-room table, treating it like the work of art it was. She hesitated to open the smallest of the boxes.

"Oh, for heaven's sake already!" Yoichi exclaimed, as she and Eve tried to encourage Lucy to move more swiftly to satisfy their curiosity. The reveal elicited an audible gasp from everyone. Mark had sent her the jewellery she had worn that night on the *Theia*, as well as the other items she had tentatively selected but had decided against wearing that night. And as lovely as it all was—and it was that—she would have returned it all quite happily if it meant that Mark might again be among the living.

Although it had been weeks, she could still feel the pain that had ripped through her when they'd first heard the news. O had reached them by phone shortly after they'd arrived in Dublin, telling them of a letter he'd received from Mark, in which their friend had explained what he was planning to do and why. O hadn't wanted to believe it, but after exhaustive investigation, on board the *Theia* and at Mark's track near Eze, he'd had no choice but to accept its veracity. Mark was gone.

"There's a letter for you," Kent said, snapping her back from the memory. "It's from Mark."

Lucy thought it best to wait for a more private moment to read the letter, planning to share it with Kent after the others had left for the night. They cleared the dining table and transferred the artwork, clothing, and jewellery to Lucy's suite, along with Mark's letter.

Helen and Elinor set the table and served the meal, which they had prepared for the homecoming celebration, the menu having been devised by Elinor. "I selected among foods considered to be very Canadian, so we've got Bloody Caesars, mini lobster rolls as appetizers, moose stew with Yukon Gold potatoes—my uncle provided the moose—and a choice of mini butter tarts or Nanaimo bars, with ice cream, for dessert," she proudly announced. They toasted their friendships, shared stories, and enjoyed the unusual yet distinctly Canadian menu.

"Oh, I nearly forgot; there's a delivery for you as well, Kent," Albin said as he left the table to retrieve a large envelope and cardboard shipping tube.

"I know what this is. It's the documentation, including the blueprints, for the house Bert was building. I've been retained by Elsa to complete the project, to make it salable as soon as possible. Anyone want to accompany me on a walk and quick look-see after coffee?"

"How will you get in?" asked Lucy.

"There's supposed to be one of those key lock boxes affixed to it, the coded type that real-estate agents use. I understand that the lawyer took care of that when she came to do the identification. The house still has a temporary door. Fortunately, the final front door and lock are often postponed right to the end of construction, so that the trades can gain access using the key lock box and there's less chance of damage or security breaches. It might have become rather destructive if this were a finished coded lock and Bert had yet to record the code and share it appropriately."

Everyone expressed curiosity, and they set out promptly after the meal. Cookie acted as if she thought it was the greatest thing to have so many people accompany her on one of her walks, giving each of her human friends a moment of special attention. It didn't take long before they stood in front of the new house.

"Ugh! Typical Bert," declared Kent. "It's going to take some work before I'm prepared to associate my name with this monstrosity."

"Smaken är som baken, delad," Eve declared.

Lucy laughed and translated: "Taste is like your butt, divided."

"You have been working on your Swedish!" Eve happily observed.

As soon as the front door was open, Cookie pushed her way inside, pulling her leash from Eve's grasp. While the others looked around the space, Cookie focused her attention on a curved section of wall. She was agitated and pawing the blue granite inlays.

"Vad flan! Cookie!" cursed Eve, somewhat embarrassed by her canine's behaviour. "She's never acted like this, Kent. Really!" Nothing could shake Cookie's interest in the curved wall with its blue granite inlays. Cookie became increasingly agitated. She barked and continued to paw at it.

"What is it that you find so interesting?" Kent examined the blueprint, which was a copy of the one Bert had filed with the city. "Ah, I see. Cookie wants into the wine cellar. Something interesting in there? Perhaps a bottle of Romanée-Conti 1945, eh? How do we open this? Any ideas, Albin?"

"Cookie is pawing those inlays. Any chance one is a button?" he suggested.

They began to depress the inlays in a methodical fashion. When they finally hit the right one, the curved door slid open.

Eve grabbed hold of Cookie before she could enter the room. The wretched miasma emanating from inside made it obvious that there was a dead body within. Elinor ran from the house to escape the gut-roiling stench and found a private spot in the yard to wait for her stomach to settle. When they managed to get past the fetid smell of human decay, they saw its source: the body of a woman, with black hair and blue-grey skin.

Helen had already placed a call to 9-1-1. By the end of her conversation with the police, it was decided that Detective Inspector Brennan would be leading the response team. The rest of the group didn't need to be told. They had already decided to leave and wait outside for the arrival of the police.

Eve busied herself with Cookie. "You are such a smart Cookie," Eve said as she scratched around the golden's ears. "You know things that people don't, don't you? There is no cow on the ice now. *Ingen ko på isen.* Everything is okay. Isn't it, Cookie?" Cookie moved in close as if sensing Eve's upset, and they snuggled.

"Her hair and size . . ." pondered Albin. "I think that's the woman who was at the house when Espie was shot some five months ago. You think she's been in there all this time?"

"But who is she?" asked Yoichi.

"I don't know," Kent said, shaking his head. "This is not how I envisioned the end of this decade. I think I already need a holiday," Kent said, then heaved a sigh. Everyone agreed. "Well, clearly the worst is over. We're home and safe. This will certainly delay things for Elsa Carlsson, but it's a matter for the police and doesn't directly concern any of us. Within a few months, we'll be into 2020 and much better times. I'm confident of that.

"The timing may seem inappropriate, I know," Kent continued, "but I've got to concentrate on something positive. How about we plan a New Year's Eve Party to welcome 2020? Or maybe the bunch of us can take off to a secluded Caribbean island in the dead of winter. I'm open to all ideas. There's a whole world out there to explore!"

Lucy shrugged, and sighed wistfully. "Well, as Mark would've said, 'Why not?'"

CHAPTER 38

Leo drove Elsa and Juji to Elsa's new weekly activity. The facility was pristine and secure. It was well-staffed and offered fine attention to its residents, all of whom were patients with advanced dementia. No sooner had the trio entered through the front doors of the facility than Juji saw Lars Andersson on the approach.

"Lars, I don't think this is the time—"

"No, it is. I just need to have a brief conversation with Dr. Carlsson. Please." Lars' tone was different. Genuine. It took Juji by surprise.

"That will be fine, Juji," Elsa rejoined. "Sorry if we appeared rude, Lars. I guess we must have our minds on too many things today. My apologies. What can I do for you?"

"Dr. Carlsson, I've heard mention that there might soon be human trials for a drug to treat Alzheimer's, or perhaps, there already are?"

"Perhaps."

"I would like you to meet someone, please." Lars led Elsa down a corridor to one of the suites. Leo and Juji followed behind, uncertain of his intentions. *"Hej, Mamma . . ."* he bent down and gently kissed the forehead of a frail elderly woman, clearly suffering the wasting associated with dementia. "Since I first heard mention that Nanovo might have something, I have tried to contact you in order to get my mother into the trials. Truly, she has nothing left to lose."

"I'm so sorry, Lars. I didn't know. Believe me, I do understand. We hadn't been ready before, so you've not missed out. We are just now beginning the trials, and while I don't know whether your mother would qualify to be a part of the official test pool, I think we can probably place her in a special pool, with my own parents. Just give your personal contact information to Juji, and we'll get back to you. I promise." With that, Elsa grasped Lars' hands in both of hers and looked him in the eye, seeing for the first time the man behind the radio personality.

Elsa no longer worked at Nanovo; she was no longer engaged in neuropharmacology at all. There was much of her past that she had lost to the chloral hydrate interference with the Mnimi treatment of her dementia, but she was otherwise intact. She had her music, her friends, and her children, and they had her. Elsa returned to the lobby and sat at the piano as she did each week. She played her chromatic scales and arpeggios, and entertained with sonatas and nocturnes. She was deeply content to be merely a small part of a greater whole.

She belonged.

EPILOGUE

Each day, Ebo and Oko looked at the Awen painting Lucy had given to Oko. After learning that Alice, who had also transferred to the *Croesus*, had seen the painting prior to its completion, Oko invited her to view the final product. Bringing a fresh pair of eyes to the scene, Alice was able to interpret an area that had been a persistent puzzle to O.

"I can see it quite clearly, but I don't know how to help you see it, without spelling it out, and I don't think I should. Concentrate on this area," Alice said, pointing to the region of the painting that appeared to have scrape marks and a few flashes of blue, black, and silver-grey. These were the applications of colour that had confounded Lucy as well.

Oko's jaw dropped. "Now I can see it." Initially he couldn't believe what was before his own eyes. Then he grabbed his phone. "I'll try to take a photo. I want to share this with Madame Gillespie." After a few tries, he finally got one he was satisfied with. "This one should work." He turned it toward Alice, "What do you think?"

It was early in the afternoon, and Lucy was in her dressing room, continuing to sort through those things she'd shipped home from various places throughout the past year of travel. The telephone call from O took her by surprise.

"Hello O! How are you?" Lucy asked.

"Well, Madame, we are well. You and Monsieur?"

"We are both well, thank you. To what do I owe the pleasure of this call?"

"Alice and I have noticed something in the painting you gave to me. Remember that area that confused you because you couldn't figure out why there was colour there? We have seen what the colour signifies, and I have sent you a photograph, which I think reveals it sufficiently."

"Let me take a look at the photo first, O. Yes, I have it—oh my! How?"

"That was how we reacted as well. We can only surmise that you had an empathetic connection with Monsieur Witherspoon, picked up on his words and body language, and then your subconscious put it all together. You do have insight. Remember how you knew we were Ebo and Oko?"

"Yes, but that's different, isn't it?"

"I don't know. Is it?"

"I don't know either, O. I just don't know," Lucy muttered, as she continued to stare at the photo displayed on her phone. The screen revealed the photo enlargement of a background section of her painting. A figure that had been previously identified as a diving sperm whale when seen at a distance, was revealed to be a much smaller object, a car—an Arion—emerging from a large cluster of bubbles and sinking nose first into the trench.

September 3, 2019

My dear Lucy,

Please indulge me this one last time and accept these small tokens in the spirit in which they are given.

There is no one, no couple, more deserving of La Valse. Your passion, love, and dedication exceed that rendered in bronze and lapis by Camille Claudel.

As I watched the two of you dance that night on board the Croesus, you seemed the embodiment of La Valse. I could also think of no more appropriate recipient of Theia's gown and jewels. You brought them to life for me, and for that, I am grateful.

If you are tempted, and I fear you will be, to shed tears for me, please don't. I had a great love in my life, but I didn't appreciate it sufficiently at the time. That was my mistake alone. While I was alone in that error, I shall be united in its resolution. Theia awaits.

I have made some opportunities available to you and Kent. Only you two can determine whether any of them will fit into your lives. If you do pursue some of them, have fun! If you choose not to, the advice is the same, have fun! I just want to give you the key to the doors, not push you through.

Look fondly upon your travels of this past year. Those you encountered look fondly upon you. There is no tragedy here. I think it was Norman Cousins who said, "The tragedy of life is in what dies inside a man while he lives." I have been dead now for too many years.

In all sincerity, and with love,
Yours,

Mark W.

"The song has ended but the melody lingers on."

~ Irving Berlin

THE END

GLOSSARY

al fresco Italian; *in the open air*

Arion Fictional model of car; in Greek mythology, Arion is an immortal winged horse, the son of Poseidon and Demeter, known for his great speed

arrondissement French; similar to *borough,* Paris has twenty

bof-bof French; *so-so,* replaces an older French idiom: *comme si, comme ça*

bon après-midi French; *good afternoon*

bonjour, monsieur French; *hello sir*

bon matin French; *good morning*

bonsoir French; *good evening*

boulangerie French; *bakery;* frequently also carry mains and side dishes in the manner of a delicatessen

buongiorno Italian; *good morning*

café	French; *coffee*
Catanesi	Italian; residents of the city of Catania in Sicily
cazzo	Italian; a vulgar interjection that is the equivalent of *damn, shit,* or *fuck* in English.
ç'est moi	French; *it's me*
ç'est parfait	French; *it's perfect*
Corsini	Fictional car company, derived from 'corsa,' which is the Italian word for *race*
Cow on the Ice	A calque; a metaphrase or literal translation of a Swedish idiom which means *there is danger* or *reason for concern.*
crepi il lupo	Italian; translates as '*may the wolf die.*' This is the response to the shoutout 'in bocca al lupo,' which translates as *in the mouth of the wolf* and means *good luck.* The idiom is equivalent to *break a leg.*
Croesus	King of Lydia who reigned for fourteen years: from 560 BC; attributes ascribed to the fictional yacht *Croesus* regarding size, features, and finishes are a composite of those found on existing (2019) motor yachts.

danse de la rue	French; refers to early stages in the development savate, describing the rough and tumble of street fighting in Paris
derrière	French; *behind*
en plein air	French; *outside*
entrée	French; *entrance* or *first course of a meal*
entrez	French; *enter* or *come in*
excusez-moi	French; *excuse me*
fika	Swedish; *coffee or coffee break;* both a noun and verb
fini	French; *finished*
frisk	Swedish; healthy in the sense of "without illness", but not necessarily in good spirit or feeling great
gelateria	Italian; *ice-cream shop*
hallå	Swedish; *hello*
hallongrotta	Swedish; butter-cookie with raspberry jam centre

Haussmann — A reference to Baron Haussmann who carried out the extensive reconstruction of Paris, developed the wide boulevards, installed new water and sewer pipes. The new apartment buildings were constructed with adherence to strict guidelines and thereby achieved a high degree of uniformity. They are generally referred to as Haussmann buildings.

HMP Birmingham — Her Majesty's Prison in Birmingham, England

hors d'oeuvres — French; *appetizers or snacks*

in bocca al lupo — Italian shoutout translates as '*in the mouth of the wolf*' and means '*good luck.*' The response is 'crepi il lupo,' which translates as '*may the wolf die.*' The idiom is equivalent to *break a leg.*

ingen ko på isen — Swedish idiom; literal translation is '*no cow on the ice,*' but the idiom means *there is no danger,* no *reason for concern.*

ko på isen — Swedish idiom; literal translation is '*cow on the ice.*' but the idiom means *there is danger* or *reason for concern.*

lettre de cachet — French; a letter bearing an official seal and usually authorizing imprisonment without trial of the person named in the letter.

La Valse	There are many versions of Camille Claudel's sculpture by this name; however, the one depicted in this story is a fiction.
Le vrai savate	French; *the real savate*
Lute Parisien	French; street-wrestling in Paris which began after street-fighting was banned by Napoleon
Merci, Fab	French; *Thanks, Fab*
metric conversion	One metre is equivalent to 3.28 feet. One foot is equivalent to 0.3048 metres. One hundred kilometres per hour is in excess of sixty-two miles per hour. One hundred miles per hour is nearly one-hundred-sixty-one kilometres per hour.
mes amis	French; *my friends*
minette	French; term of endearment; *little kitten,* diminutive for *kitten*
Mnimi	Fictional drug; Greek word for *memory*
mon bébé	French; term of endearment *my baby,* only used in reference to males
mon nounours	French; term of endearment *my teddy bear*
monsieur	French; *mister*

mon trésor	French; term of endearment *my treasure*
moules et frites	French; *mussels and fries/chips*
Nanovo Group	Fictional company
Nôtre Dame de Paris	French; specifically referring to the Notre Dame Cathedral in Paris given the popularity of that name for churches across France
Oldham	English town and part of Greater Manchester
oui	French; *yes*
pâtisserie	French; *pastry or cake shop*
pH	Chemical measure; specifically, the negative log to the base ten of the concentration of hydrogen ions; ranges from 0–14 where a pH less than 7 is acidic and a pH greater than 7 is basic.
Portnoy, Dzhon	Fictional artist
pour moi un espresso double	French; *for me a double espresso*
Proulx-Allard	Fictional architecture/interior design firm
puis-je avoir	French; *can I have*
sans alcool	French; *alcohol-free*

s'il vous plaît French; *please*

stumm German; *mute, quiet*

Sverige Swedish; *Sweden*

syncope Also referred to as "fainting" or "passing out"; a temporary loss of consciousness usually related to insufficient blood flow to the brain.

terroir French; wine term referring to the complete environment in which a wine is produced: soil, climate, topography, as this is seen to be reflected in the characteristics of the grape and ultimately the wine.

Titan In Greek mythology, the twelve Titans are the children of Uranus (Heaven) and Gaea (Earth); there are many vessels and businesses with this name, but none of them was an inspiration for the vessel and business in this novel

traiteur French; *caterer*

un espresso pour madame French; *an espresso for madam*

vad flan Swedish; swearing; equivalent to *what the devil*

Author, artist, and DIY enthusiast, J. A. Gibbens holds degrees in science and education from the University of Waterloo and Queen's University. After twelve years of teaching at the secondary school level, and more as a business owner, J. A. Gibbens began her writing career with her debut novel, ***L'Orté Point—The Awen Chronicles–Book 1***, released in 2021.

She currently resides in Guelph, Ontario, with her husband, Greg, and a woodchuck that lives under their deck.

Look for the exciting third instalment of ***The Awen Chronicles—Epitaph: Full Circle*** (expected release 2023).